D1104513

FIFTY-THREE WEEKS

WEEKS

DALE STOHRE

Copyright © 2022 Dale Stohre

All rights reserved. No part of this publication may be reproduced, distributed, or transmitted in any form or by any means, including photocopying, recording, or other electronic or mechanical methods, without the prior written permission of the publisher, except in the case of brief quotations embodied in critical reviews and certain other noncommercial uses permitted by copyright law. For more information or for permission requests, please contact dalestohre@gmail.com.

ISBN: 979-8-9869530-0-7 (Paperback)
ISBN: 979-8-9869530-1-4 (Hardcover)
ISBN: 979-8-9869530-2-1 (eBook)

Book interior & cover design by Taylor Ahlstrom, photos by Dale Stohre

Printed by Amazon Publishing in the United States of America.
First printing edition 2022.

Cover photos: Church interior: the Central Pori Church, Pori, Finland
Sculpture: The Old Stone Church, Cleveland, Ohio

To Beth, the love of my life.
To our children:
Stephanie, Stacey, Michael, Chris, Anna, Sara,
and our magnificent grandchildren:
Olivia, Bryant, Gavin, Zoe, and Emma.

You bring me so much joy.

TABLE OF CONTENTS

Prologue 1

New Year's Day 4

The Call 7

A Widow in Her Distress 9

Let There Be Light 14

Decision Time 16

Deadlines 23

Ten Million Dollars 28

Stale Donuts 32

The Ambush 36

Home 42

Nightmares 47

Questions, Questions 49

Ashes 52

Unscheduled Guests 57

Good News . . . Bad News 60

A Thorn in the Side 65

The Inevitable 72

This is My Witness Now 76

Crying for Carl 80

Hand in the Cookie Jar 86

The Insurrection 89

Bad News 92

A Day the Lord Has Made 94

Holy Week 98

The Towel and Basin 104

Ultimatum 107

Seeking Sabbath 110

Easter 114

Paid in Full... 120

Outrageous 122

Home, and Homeless... 126

Research.. 128

Rough-Hewn Grace 132

Saint Paul.. 138

House Rules 143

Homecoming 148

Finding the Perfect Place 153

Making the Case.. 157

Liturgically Challenged.. 163

Interlude 167

The Request... 171

Preachers, Prophets, and Fools 175

Point of Order 177

A Dream Larger than Me... 182

Welcome to the family 187

Advent One 190

Seven Figures to the Left 193

Holy Moment 197

Bittersweet 200

Watermark 204

To Walk Again on Jesse's Land................................ 209

Acknowledgements 215

PROLOGUE

C arl, a man I do not know, is facing a death sentence. He has AIDS, and it is well on its way to destroying him. Once proud, trim, and fit, Carl often heard that his body was his gift. No one says that now. The clothing in which he took such pride—bold colors, perfectly matched, designed not just to flatter but to proclaim his presence—now hangs sorrowfully, stained and torn fabric much too big for Carl's shrinking frame. What once drew admiration mocks him now. The colors seem out of place; they shout summer, but this is December.

There are treatments for AIDS—potentially lifesaving treatments. But Carl refused them and won't tell you why. Perhaps, some assumed, he was depressed or addicted. Mere speculation by those who never bothered to offer compassion instead of judgment. In any case, Carl used what little freedom he had to reject the burden of fighting for his life. In an already hard existence, one more battle seemed to Carl a bridge too far.

At the same time on the same cold winter day on the same street, a woman and her daughter have used up their allotment of time in a shelter for women and children. Their car, a very tired Escort wagon, is now the closest thing they have to a home.

I do not know the women in the Escort either. But I will, and they too will haunt me.

Carl's release from Cook County Hospital is not good news because he has no place to go. As a patient he had food, clothing, and shelter, all of it clean and safe. All of it warm. With his immune system all but gone and his body wasted, the wind is not simply annoying; it is lethal. The winter has a long way to go, and the odds are against him. Carl entertains no fantasies about the warmth of spring; it will take every strength he can muster to survive the night. He will settle for a place to sleep, and if he awakens in the morning, and that is not certain, it will be Christmas Day.

On Christmas Day, I am awakened by a kiss.

"G'morning." Not very original, but I'm not fully awake and won't be without a healthy dose of caffeine.

"The correct response, dear husband, is 'Merry Christmas.'"

Rolling toward the middle of the bed, I'm greeted by a sight that will out-class anything I will see this Christmas Day, or any day.

The world's retailers, both physical and online, are fretting over the numbers they amassed before the "Christmas season" ended last night. For people like me who work on Sunday mornings before the gathered faithful, the "season" that just ended was Advent; Christmas actually begins today. That's a distinction without a difference in one sense: along with the world's retailers and shippers, I'm exhausted, awakening to what I hope will be the first of a few stress-free days, followed by a year with more respite than the last.

With matted hair scurrying in all directions, Trish (Dr. Patricia Garraty to you) fills my field of vision gloriously. Her just-awake smile is one of God's finest works.

The moment is interrupted—or is it enhanced?—by the other smile in my life. "Coffee's ready . . . gifts are waiting, and by the way, why are my parents still in bed?" Meet Melissa, whom we have spent the last almost seventeen years trying very hard to please. Trish rolls her head towards the door, smile still intact. "We'll be down eventually, Melissa. Just be patient. And no peeking."

Melissa knows that on Christmas she can step over the line a bit and get away with it. "Christmas officially starts now, people. Do I have to come in there and get you?"

"Well, husband? Do we stand our ground?"

"I suggest an unconditional surrender. Melissa's gift-o-meter is running. I'll shave, you shower first?" She nods; our feet meet the floor.

Fifteen minutes later, my hair's still wet, and we're in the family room sipping coffee and enjoying the smell of cinnamon rolls in the oven. A fire is already blazing; there's a tree with seven hundred white lights overlooking a small mountain of gifts, beautifully wrapped for about five minutes more.

Some of the gifts are for me, but I don't need them. In the two women who surround me on this Christmas morning, I am blessed above all living things.

It is ironic that many live without the security of a home, family, or hope, while we gather amidst loved ones and remember in song and tradition the birth of One who became flesh under conditions more like that dreary Chicago street.

CHAPTER ONE
NEW YEAR'S DAY

Allow me to introduce myself. My parents, Martha and Samuel Garraty, named me Noel. As a child, I wondered why my parents gave me a name associated with Christmas, since my September birthday is three months before the holiday. But when I realized it's nine months *after* Christmas, I asked as tactfully as I could if something wonderful happened between Martha and Samuel on a certain Christmas. They didn't answer, but I did notice a smile and a wink . . .

It will be helpful for you to know—but don't hold this against me—that I'm a minister, as was my father. My vocation has fallen in the eyes of some, but before you return this book for a refund, let me prove that whatever stereotype you may have of such people, I'm not one of *them*. I eat, sleep, bathe, ache, and worry just like you do. I've had all the necessary shots; I have a mortgage; I cheer for the home team and lean toward one political party (no, I won't tell you which one). I indulge in nutritionally questionable foods, and I'm prone to occasional (perhaps frequent) grumbling. I will be telling you about that in some detail. Meanwhile, I am watching a parade.

"Happy New Year, dear husband." Trish bears a gift of toast and refills my coffee. "You're watching a parade."

"Just like last year."

She grins. "And, once again, it fails to impress you."

"How can you tell?"

She chuckles. "For one thing, it's on mute."

Ours is the classic college sweetheart story, except that we both were in love with someone else. Patricia Morris (hereafter known simply as Trish) was born in Indianapolis to a truck driver father and a mother whose full-time job, besides raising two daughters, was volunteering. Mom served on the school board, led a Girl Scout troop, chaired the PTA, was on the Governor's Advisory Committee for the Arts, and wishes she'd joined the Peace Corps. Trish came from good genes, and was blessed with abundant compassion.

I would tell you that she was drawn to my many charms. She may counter that while I was tolerable, it was my stubborn persistence that tipped the scales. I might suggest that my promising financial track must have looked pretty sweet too, but none of that is the whole story, one I'll tell in time.

The first day of January (Happy New Year, by the way) is a day with which I have a love-hate relationship. Some years, minus the love. The Rose Parade fills the time before the football games, when I will un-mute the TV. Winter days can be dreary, and the snow has lost its charm, but as the Reverend Noel Garraty, I need to jumpstart First Community Church of River Glen, Illinois, fifty miles and a world away from Chicago. Other executives can energize their staff by reminding them how nice it would be to keep getting a paycheck. I'm also an executive, but I don't pay my "employees." They pay me. My task: to motivate volunteers who don't need to arouse from their holiday slumber until they want to.

So this morning, I make an executive decision I make every January First: the holiday season is officially still on. I'll jumpstart the world tomorrow.

Trish is a therapist by trade with degrees in child psychology (distressingly useful in understanding her husband). She reads my mood, and since it's just the two of us in the room, she'll try to change it.

"I think we both had a good year, Noel. I like the prospects for this one."

"I guess."

"No—really. You led well last year despite being short-staffed—not to mention also being a good husband and father."

"Thanks."

Her hand finds mine. She's patient; she has more to say, and I know it. But I keep staring at what is now a silent five-minute commercial marathon. Two minutes and four commercials in, she breaks the silence.

"The review really stung, didn't it?"

"It did. I guess this is a church with high expectations."

There's a drivenness that bleeds into the life of First Community Church. I share that same drive. What stung was my annual performance review, inflicted on me three days after Christmas. The Personnel Committee threw the numbers at me: income up about 5 percent against expenses up about 5.5

percent; attendance showed a modest increase while membership, thanks to an influx of young couples, recorded a net increase of twelve. Better than the average in my denomination, which is trending downward. But I'd promised *ten* percent growth across the board last year. So what went wrong? Did you make enough hospital visits? Your sermons are too long/short/abstract/ personal/ dry/humorous. You spend too much time in the office instead of cultivating potential members, but whenever we call the office you're not there. And by the way: you've left a lot of unused vacation time on the table, but you seem to be gone a lot.

"I should have expected it," I confess. "I'm not impressed with the numbers either. I'm discovering that I have some critics" (you'll meet a few) "and they're restless. They see my job in part as putting Old First on the religious map, like that megachurch down the street with two gyms, a bookstore, food court—"

"Careful, dear husband. You're flirting with jealousy."

"As I said, two gyms, a bookstore, plus traffic control on Sundays, *and* a yearly retreat on a cruise ship. How do you 'retreat' on a cruise ship? But I'm not jealous, Trish."

"But some of your flock are, aren't they?"

"Yeah. Five years ago that megachurch didn't even exist, and today? It's twice our size. Plus, we lost a handful of members to them, and I think that stung the most."

Trish lowers the temperature in the room. She's good at that. "Numbers matter to these folk, don't they?"

"Really. But frankly, I like our more traditional Sunday morning style."

"You don't want to preach in front of a rock band?"

I smile. "I'm almost forty-five—I'm too old for that."

"You'll never be too old for me, Noel."

"Thank you." Trish presses her forehead against mine in one of those wordless messages meant to encourage. A squeeze of her hand, and with footsteps on the stairs announcing our daughter's entry into New Year's Day, Trish leaves me to my parade.

I should note that I'm fairly self-confident, with some decent accomplishments on my resume, accompanied by a bit of pride which you may find off-putting. But at least I admit it.

Finally: a football game. End of the first quarter; scoreless, But maybe the offense will awaken. Maybe there's an offensive thriller just around the corner.

CHAPTER TWO
THE CALL

On fourth down and five yards to go, Notre Dame's quarterback runs straight ahead and gets four yards while a receiver stands in the end zone, begging for the pass that never comes.

The monotony of the game gives me time to revisit my conversation with Trish. Why *aren't* we growing? Truth be told, we're a shrinking slice of the American pie, and no one has easy answers. But I ask myself—who said that our first objective is to grow?

Finally, some points on the board. A safety. The other quarterback plays it safe: on third-and-one, he hands the ball to his running back, who drops it three yards in the backfield where the defense recovers. I may be the only person still watching. The commentators try to keep a few million viewers, barely awake after last night's festivities, from checking out. Halftime brings a break for fresh coffee and some Danish warmed in the microwave. Score: 2–0. *C'mon, people. This spectator does not want a defensive stalemate.*

Fourth quarter: score is 9–3. Neither quarterback can find a receiver, and the only touchdown was a defensive pick six.

The house phone rings. Trish answers, but after a few seconds gets a dial tone. I look her way; she shrugs. Wrong number, maybe. I continue paying occasional attention to the TV.

"I still don't understand your fascination with football." Melissa announces her presence just over my right shoulder, challenging her father's fascination with a game too inelegant for her taste.

"So why are you watching it with me?"

"I am walking through the room on my way out the door, Dad. Carrie's invited me over for a day of anything but football. Besides, ten seconds of seeing grown men pushing and shoving does not constitute watching." She loves to declare her love for her dad by challenging his most dubious habits. It is my fatherly duty to defend myself, in a debate neither of us has any desire to resolve—this is too much fun.

"You still don't see the poetry, the grace, the sheer beauty of the forward pass, do you?" She pats me on the head.

"No. But if it helps you recover from the burden of adulting . . ." I'm smiling. I know full well, so is she. "Carrie's here, bye!" The door closes. I can hear them already talking before she reaches the car, and she's off, rescued from football for another day.

This time, my cell phone rings. The game's almost over, and this drive will seal the game one way or the other. Reluctantly, I pick up just before voicemail does.

"Happy New Year. This is Pastor Garraty."

Silence.

CHAPTER THREE
A WIDOW IN HER DISTRESS

I f this is a crank call, I'll hang up—but there's vaguely familiar background noise. "Good afternoon. Can I help you?" More silence, except for some erratic breathing, and . . . is someone crying? That background noise . . . this isn't a crank call. That "noise" is the white noise typical to a hospital. I stay on the line, and say calmly, "You're at the hospital, aren't you?"

With that the dam breaks, and a voice, female and elderly, releases a flood of emotions in a series of sobs. I give her the time she needs to pull herself together. She finally is able to speak.

"Pastor Garraty? It's Margaret." That's all I need to hear. It's Margaret Kaskey, wife of Edward, whom I'm guessing has either passed away, or is at the brink. This moment has been coming for some time. "Margaret; shall I come?"

"Please . . ." is all she can say.

"I'll be there in fifteen minutes."

"Thank you."

The game comes down a first-and-goal at two minutes and ten seconds left, and I head to the bedroom. I'll need my clerical collar, not a sweatshirt. I tell Trish where I'm headed, trying to suppress my mild irritation at another interrupted day off while sounding like a pastor, but she's not buying it.

"Noel—I hope by the time you get there, you'll be in a better place for them." She's right. The last thing Margaret and Edward need is a pastor hinting that their crisis is an intrusion. It's not, really. I will be in a better place. But Trish gets some credit for that. Thank you, God, for a wife with an excellent BS detector. You'll get to know more about Trish. Just not now. Trust me: it will be worth the wait.

Right now, Margaret's husband may have died. He's been dying for a while. The process can be slow, but today it may end for Edward M. Kaskey, and Margaret needs me with her, if he survives as much as if he's already gone. Barely a month ago their children, grown and rooted in faraway places, gathered for what they sensed was their last Thanksgiving with Dad. They've returned home to both coasts, and Margaret's alone.

This will be a hard day for her and for her pastor, present with a frightened woman and a once brilliant and powerful man. New Year's isn't always happy.

I arrive at the hospital and head directly for the ICU—I've been there a dozen times in the past year—where I find Margaret standing near one of the small rooms that surround the nurse's station. She's talking to a doctor. When she sees me, she sighs in relief and introduces me to the cardiologist. At her request, he gives me a ten second update. He hasn't had another heart attack. I look toward Edward's bed and find his head bandaged, his left eye swollen shut, his left arm wrapped in elastic bandages. While I'm seeing this, the doctor describes his injuries as the result of an auto accident.

"Edward was driving to a convenience store," Margaret interjects. "Just to get some donuts and juice for this morning."

He was broadsided, the doctor said, by someone apparently under the influence.

"I asked him to go. We always like watching the Rose Parade. But if I hadn't . . ."

The doctor rescues her: "The injuries aren't life threatening in themselves."

What he doesn't need to say is that Edward's so weakened from his years-long battle with heart failure that his injuries *are* in fact life-threatening. "We've made him comfortable. The downside is that given the sedation, he may not know you're here."

I thank the doctor and take Margaret's arm. We walk into the cubicle marked "G" and stand on either side of Edward's bed. It's like the ICU sets on television. Lots of machinery, tubes, an oxygen mask, buzzes and beeps, a monitor showing heart rate, oxygenation, respiration, blood pressure, and more. I leave interpreting them to professionals, but I know that a flat line is a bad sign; I've seen a few flatten out in my short career. Mr. Kaskey's heart continues to beat.

I always assume that a patient can hear more than they may be able to acknowledge. I never assume they're beyond reach of my voice—and certainly not beyond the reach of God's. Assuming that my parishioner hears, I speak to him.

"Edward, it's Pastor Noel. I'm here with Margaret. You're not alone; we're here, and the God you have loved for so many years is with you now. You know and we know that your future is in the hands of our wise and faithful God. So while you may not be able to respond, I want to pray with you, Edward—

My prayer calls on God's comfort and strength for Edward and Margaret. I also give thanks. At times like this, I remind us of the gifts of grace, peace and the presence of God, no matter the circumstances. I end as I always do, acknowledging our common bond in Christ.

I open my eyes and see Margaret openly weeping. I used to think that I'd said something horrible when people cried after the "amen," but I'm pleased to see her emotion. Like many of her generation, she places a premium on outward strength. *It's time, Margaret, to give your emotions a much-needed release.* I walk around the end of the bed and silently stand, my hand around her shoulder, making no attempt to quench the tears.

A male nurse steps into the cubicle. Instead of checking the instruments or IVs, he whispers that he'd like to talk to me. I step outside with him, expecting some dire news about Edward that he wants me to help him break to Margaret. Instead, he's from triage. "Reverend, we have a patient who could use a cler-gyperson. Being New Year's, it would save us calling our Chaplain in."

I check with the nurse attending to Mr. Kaskey. According to her, Edward is stable, and I can step away. I reassure Margaret and follow the nurse. I ask whom I'm seeing. "Don't know his name. Came in about the same time as the Kaskey case. Car accident."

I stop. He stops. He smiles sheepishly. "Yes, Reverend, he's the driver of the other car."

"The guy who ran into my parishioner."

"Is that a problem for you, Reverend?" Actually, it's kind of awkward, but "it's OK. I'll see him." He probably feels terrible about what he did.

"How badly was he hurt?"

"Hardly at all. Just cuts and bruises."

"So why did they bring him in?"

"Combative and irrational."

"Drunk?"

"High on something. Kinda goofy."

"OK—how?"

The nurse grinned. "You'll see. Take it from me, he's entertaining."

The nurse leads me to an ER cubicle. He pulls the curtain back and disappears.

I notice a patrolwoman in the hall. I suspect she's there to make sure this patient won't walk away without an escort. The patient looks a bit . . . untidy: a black eye, stitches on his forehead, matted, shiny hair and an unkempt beard. His eyes wildly scan around the room, arms and feet in constant motion. He's not one of my parishioners, though he may have just killed one of them. I introduce myself. He's not impressed.

"Who are you? You a cop? I won't talk to no cops."

"No, sir, I'm a minister."

"You don't look like a preacher." Yeah, I wear this clerical collar because it's trending. "You're lyin' to me. You're here to take me to jail. I'm not sayin' nothin.'"

"I'm just here to help, OK? Look, you were in an accident. You're hurt, and the person you ran into is hurt—"

"I didn't see that white car. Came out of nowhere." Then I remember: the Kaskey's drive a white Buick. "Got in my way. Old fool."

I think that if there's a fool in this tragedy, I'm talking to him. Fortunately, he speaks before I utter words I wish I could say. "I don't wanna talk about it." I guess he decides I'm not on his side because he turns his face toward the wall.

"Sir, I *am* a pastor, and I'd like to pray for you." I pause for some kind of acknowledgement. Nothing. I begin praying. "Loving God, I pray for this your son. Grant him peace, a clear mind, and a gentle spirit. Be with him in the difficult days ahead. Even in this tragedy, draw him to yourself. Be gracious and merciful. In Jesus' name, Amen." A pretty generic prayer, but it's my day off, and he ran into one of my favorite parishioners.

Still, no response. I turn to leave. While he doesn't think I'm a minister, I am, and he is just as much a child of God as Edward, or me, or anyone else. I step away.

Back at Edward's room, not ten minutes have passed, but it's full of very busy people and equipment. Mrs. Kaskey is nowhere to be found. While I was gone, Edward took a turn for the worse. I stand in the hallway as they attend to my aged parishioner. The monitor over his bed shows essentially flat lines, its warning tone grim and steady. Margaret was almost certainly there when he and his wife, perhaps now his widow, needed me, and I was missing.

The commotion stops. The people in scrubs look in silence at each other, then begin disconnecting their equipment. I know what I need to know. I find the new widow in a private room outside of ICU, created for just such a time. She is sitting with a nurse, eyes red and tears spilling down a face which now looks even older and more fragile than her eighty-four years. Her hands are folded on her lap, trembling. The nurse stands to her side, slowly rubbing Margaret's back. I catch the nurse's eye and shake my head slowly; she knows what I mean. By now, any irritation at being called in on a holiday is gone. Margaret needs her pastor to be what the word literally means: a caring shepherd. I sit next to her on the couch.

"Margaret? I'm so sorry. Edward just passed away."

Margaret dissolves, leaning over until her head is on my shoulder; the sobs are unrestrained now. I put my right arm around her, and my left hand grasps hers. And for the next three minutes, saying nothing, not moving, I perform the most important act of pastoral care I may perform all this coming year.

There are rules about physical contact, and risks to almost any physical touch. In our litigious society, the fear of lawsuits inhibits spontaneity. I understand that. I believe in risk management and insist on stringent policies to keep our staff out of trouble. But on this New Year's Day, this forty-something minister doesn't care. With my arm around the shoulders of an eighty-four-year-old member of my flock, my role is not to avoid worrying the church's legal counsel. It is to be Christ to those who need love and grace. In those minutes (and hopefully in the weeks ahead), I chose to be precisely that to what the Epistle of James would call "a widow in her distress." The truest expression of "pure religion," James called it.

CHAPTER FOUR
LET THERE BE LIGHT

"How's your mom holding up?"

Gail, online journalist and Margaret's younger daughter, is at the back of the chapel preparing to Livestream her father's service for out-of-town family.

"Mom still amazes me. She's calm, a little fragile—especially when people start reminiscing about Dad. But her mind is clear. Oh, my brother isn't giving the eulogy. Says he'll fall apart, and I believe him. Allen wrote something. I'll read it."

"Will it be any easier for you, Gail?" She needs a few seconds but takes a deep breath before answering. "I think so."

While she grew up at Old First, I've only known her as an adult coming back to visit her parents. I heard enough from them to know that she's fully capable of giving witness to her father's legacy. And capable of expressing her own grief without shame.

"Pastor, I'm glad you were with Mom when Dad died."

"So am I."

The memorial service for Edward Kaskey is a tribute to his stature in the community, but I believe more to his character as a human being—one who without pretense loved his neighbors. His daughter read her brother's eulogy, and then in her own words spoke as one who loved and was loved by her father. I don't think her mother was surprised when she said that she prays for the man whose alcohol-impaired driving took her father from her. Edward and Margaret were generous, funding a host of charities and their church. But mostly, people trusted him. Whether on the school board, city council, or a host of committees, he leaves a hole in a community that turned out in force to celebrate his life.

"It is fitting," I say, "that the sun shines on us as we stand around the mortal remains of Edward Kaskey. It is a brilliant winter day, as it should be, for he was a light to those around him." My text is Psalm 15, and I remind us all that in public and in private, Edward was an honorable man who lived that text. He "spoke the truth from his heart," and "kept his word, even to his hurt." To that I add my own witness to Edward's character.

"I mourn with you the passing of not just a fellow human being, but the rarest kind. It's how we should hope to be remembered. John Donne was right. When we lose our Edward Kaskeys, the bell tolls for all of us."

I ride to the cemetery with the funeral director. After the mourners drive away, the cemetery staff releases the brake on the cradle holding the casket, which slowly disappears into the earth. It is strange to watch, knowing that the coffin and its contents will never be seen again. *You too are mortal*, it says, as clock and calendar relentlessly mark the countdown to our own life's end.

CHAPTER FIVE
DECISION TIME

"**S**tand clear of the closing doors."

It takes about ten seconds for the doors to open and a dozen or so commuters to step across the yellow line from the train to the platform. About nine others step aboard before the unseen conductor announces the next stop and warns us not to be half-in-half-out when the doors slide shut. Not much time, but New Yorkers know the drill. Except this time, someone steps aboard slowly enough to keep the doors from closing. The conductor reminds us to stand clear, tries again, and this frail, fifty-ish man is aboard—barely.

On my first trip to New York City, I assumed this was an anomaly. But this time around, representing Old First in an interview with a prospective new colleague, I sense that this is New York Normal.

Once the doors close and the train picks up speed, no one seems to notice the old man. The forty or so passengers are face-down, staring intently at paperbacks or screens. The unsteady gentleman begins to speak. "May I have your attention, please? On this day that the Lord has made, do you have it in your hearts to be compassionate for an old man? I am homeless and poor and I need . . ."

No one flinches. Well, I start to. He could use even some change, he assures us—no gift is too small. I could give him a dollar. It's in my shirt pocket. The seasoned New Yorkers ignore him as if he's not there. He's right in front of me, and out of the corner of my eye I sense he's looking at this tourist from Illinois within arm's reach. I could help him. Or could I? I don't know. My instinct is to give him money. My theology reminds me that "freely have you received; freely give." My fingers find that bill in my shirt pocket. I look as discretely as I can; I hope it's a single, but it's a ten. Conventional wisdom: giving them money enables their dysfunction, because no one is homeless unless they somehow made a mess of their lives. My heart wants to give; my head tells me it's irrational—besides, I'd be the only one doing that, and I might look gullible. I should follow the lead of my four dozen neighbors in the car. If I give, I'll feel unsatisfied that nothing I do will really make a difference, and I'll be haunted by seeing a brother in need and turning away. I finger the bill . . . he moves along.

My time with our potential new hire, Brad Davis, is all I could hope for. Bright, mature, strongly endorsed by his references, he lives up to the hype without trying to. He's at ease in himself and gives off no I-need-a-job nervousness. I open our conversation by dispensing with titles, since I like to think I'm approachable:

"By the way, Brad—no need for formalities here, just call me Noel."

"If it's all the same to you, I'd prefer to call you 'Pastor Garraty.'" I'm a little surprised, but that's his call.

"OK. Whatever seems appropriate to you. 'Pastor Noel' also works—if you want to."

"If you wish."

I learn that Brad's father is an investment guy. Born in poverty, worked full time while getting his B.A. in business and got an entry-level job in a major brokerage. Brad's father climbed the corporate ladder. He focused on retirement and estate planning, a career that pays for Brad's seminary education.

"Your dad has quite a story, Brad. You must be proud of him."

He smiles. "I am. No better man, husband, father, than my dad."

"Love to meet him."

"He'd like you too, Pastor."

I decide to wax philosophical. "Your father is a living witness to what can happen with hard work. He's reaping the rewards; I'd guess he loves his job."

Brad looks past me, thinking before he replies . . . cautiously.

"Yes, I guess he likes what he does."

His phone rings. He excuses himself to take the call and leaves me wondering: What's in that void between "loving" his job and merely "liking" it?

When he returns, I ask. "You said that he liked his job—"

"He does."

"After I said I'd guess that he *loved* it." If he wants this to continue, great, but it's none of my business if he wants to change the subject. At first, a long silence seems to confirm that he won't follow this path. But then he leans forward, and there's pain in his voice.

"Pastor, the longer he works, the more his heart breaks. He's in the wealth business—managing people's wealth, growing people's wealth, often making rich people richer. He does it well."

"But . . ."

"But that's not what drew him into finance. He wanted to make a difference in the lives of people like me. People of color. And most people of color can't make use of his services, because they all too often have no wealth to manage."

This seems like a good time to tell you that I haven't always been a pastor. After earning my degree (a lot of my textbooks had "money" in the title), I managed other people's wealth—and I was good at it. I had the BMW, nice house, a picture-perfect family. I had everything except contentment.

My solution: try harder, which changed me from charming to cranky, rude, and intolerant. God wanted me to do what I'm doing now. He and I were still wrestling when the Great Recession pushed me to the edge. I weathered the recession quite well. So did some of my clients. But a few who trusted me with their retirement nest egg . . . lost their dream.

I rationalized it as the risks of our free market and the American way. But credit default swaps, irresponsible mortgages, underwater homeowners, and a Ponzi scheme or two revealed a greed-driven, pride-fueled myth that led a lot of people into a cul-de-sac.

Jonah became fish food before coming to his senses. I had to confront the fact that my "gift" for reading economic tea leaves was a house of cards. Like Jonah, I finally quit running.

I sold my firm to pay for seminary while Trish supported us, and then I used my white-collar resume to talk my way into the kind of church I aspired to: upper middle class, white collar. First Community Church in River Glen fit perfectly. I was with my peers again, though some of them wondered if they could trust someone who gave up the good life for one in a culturally de-valued profession. I serve a church where many people have the big houses and golden parachutes that I gave up willingly. But truth be known, I miss my BMW.

Hearing Brad talk about his father, I have no reason to doubt him. This isn't new information, just not information with which I've concerned myself. I never had a client who wasn't white.

"My dad works for the long term. Set aside a little every month, let it grow, reap the harvest someday. Invest your *inherited* wealth, let *it* grow, or sell your home, invest the equity, let *it* grow. Great ideas, right? But most black people in this country have no wealth to leave to their kids. They're usually renters; they've got no equity. 'Set aside a little for tomorrow?' Pastor, when you're poor, you don't know how you'll get through today."

More silence. Then, "Over thirty years, my dad has had nine Black clients. That's what's breaking Dad's heart."

I know enough to know that it's not their fault. Our otherwise prosperous economy isn't structured to bring everyone along. I can think of nothing worthwhile to say. So I shift gears. I review what we'd sent him about the role he'd fill. He's read it in detail and has plenty of questions for me. I have questions about his vision, his long-term plans. He's honest: River Glen's appealing in part because he'd be within fifty miles of his parents, who are getting up in years. He lights up when talking about Chicago. It's a hard place to be African American. But when he talks about the Windy City, his eyes sparkle. Are we a halfway stop on his way back to Chicago? Wouldn't be surprised.

I like this man. He looks like a good fit. Great with kids, his references say, and that's a bonus. But I have one more conversation scheduled, two time zones west of New York. I thank Mr. Davis, and head to La Guardia and another flight, this time toward tomorrow's interview.

At LaGuardia, I'm impatiently waiting for my delayed flight, when my phone rings. I know, it's rude when people say, "I need to take this call." Sounds self-important. But . . . I need to take *this* call.

"Good morning, Pastor."

"Good morning, Mary." Meet my office manager/administrative assistant, a fine human and keystone of the team that makes Old First a joyful place to work.

"Sorry to bother you—I'm sure you're already busy deciding who is going to join the staff and add to my workload." She's also got a biting wit.

"Actually, I'm still watching it rain."

"OK, good. Just an FYI—you'll notice when you get back that you don't have a printer because Ellen needs it. Her ancient printer finally decided to retire."

Mary works "full-time" (four days, thirty-two hours), though it often leaks into an extra hour or two which, she insists, is her gift to God and her employer. I catch her "cheating" by working a few more hours around the holidays, tell her to go home, and am promptly ignored in a friendly tug-of-war that she calls our "dance." Besides working full time here, she has a side gig writing a travel blog.

Ellen, who now has my printer, keeps track of our finances as one of our part-time staff, along with Rob, who keeps our hundred-year-old building from falling down.

"Thanks for the heads up, Mary. And please don't let anyone borrow my desk, OK?"

"I'll do my best. And did you re-schedule Friday's dental appointment?" Mary knows my calendar and has saved my showing-up-on-time reputation frighteningly often.

Work-from-home may have blossomed during the pandemic; we were already there. With the exception of Mary (and Frank, whom you'll meet), one or two half days a week in the office is sufficient for these people I've learned to trust.

Since I'm introducing my staff, meet Frank, our custodian. I confess a horrible bias I once had, based on one such person that gave my preacher-dad fits: churches should fire custodians after five years, because by that time, they're getting territorial: *The building is mine.* I was wrong. Turns out, church custodians often consider it their ministry to those who worship, work, walk the halls, or cook in the kitchen. Actually, no one is more pompous than a narcissistic, overly confident preacher. Custodians should not be fired after five years; they should get bonuses for lasting that long. A five-year expiration date for preachers? One could build a case . . .

Last but definitely not least (none of them are "least"), meet Tony, our music director/organist. Tony's protective of our larger-than-average pipe organ—just ask him if you can play around on it (I've tried). He's rare, in that good organists are hard to find, and he's capable of using every one of its 900-plus pipes. He's a treasure, and no, you can't have him.

For that matter, please don't take any of the them.

Flying west across the Great Plains, I noticed the crisp rectangular fields across Nebraska, Kansas, and eastern Colorado. These fields, from seven miles up, are mesmerizing. Perhaps because I like order. I strive toward organizational straight lines, neatly arranged, predictable, and safe. But as we speed west, foothill country and then mountains conquer all effort at order. In the West, creation itself disrupts the search for wealth in the soil.

I chafe at even little disruptions in my well-planned life. I'm a competent manager, and I like that. What I don't like and what haunts me now is being at the mercy of persons and things that can erase any straight line I draw. Like this back-to-back cross-country trip. Despite my plans, I am simply the passenger in seat 5A, an hour or so from Phoenix, and my meeting with Ms. Sophie Masters.

I meet Sophie outdoors in January—a treat in itself. She begins by honoring me with the truth.

"Rev. Garraty, before we go too far into our conversation . . . You flew all this way to talk about the role your church describes. It's tempting. But . . ." She puts her latte down, pauses, then: "If you called me and I accepted, I would pour all my energies into the work, and I'm confident that I'd be effective. But I don't think I'd still be there in a decade."

My questions are in danger of becoming irrelevant. I set them aside and put the ball back in her court. "So tell me about your dream job."

She thinks for a while, then responds. "My hope is eventually to be a solo pastor. Seminary taught me about how churches—existing churches, anyway—work. I get that. But my vision for 'church' . . . it's not very conventional. I came to faith from zero faith, kicking and screaming. I was and still am highly cynical about organized religion. Long story, bottom line: I want to surround myself with people like me who have little or no history with the church, or who've been burned by it. There are a *lot* of us."

I know. Many of those the church has hurt are still in the pews, often still suffering in silence. "So where will you find them?"

"Go where they go. My dream is to be the minority voice in as many conversations as I can find. Which makes me wonder: How would your church feel about a pastor who spends her evenings in bars and clubs? Looking for people with addictions? The homeless . . . that sort of congregation?"

She smiles a kind of mischievous smile. "Oh—also, I'm dressed a bit more, ah, tastefully today, so you can't see that I wear a lot of body art that might freak a few church folk out."

Sophie stops. We both know that our job description has more to do with those already among us. I've said that the church exists primarily for those who aren't in it. But my calendar is a betrayal of that claim, and this ex-Marine who saw combat as a medic dismantles a part of me that needs dismantling.

"Here's the thing: One reason I resisted the church was that it was all talk, but terrible at listening. I love people who are wondering and seeking, because I was one of them, and I get why they resist religion—especially ours." Another pause while she looks away at the people walking past our sunlit table. She nods toward the sea of humanity around us, and I see her face light up.

"Out there . . . among *them*? That's my happy place."

Flying home, something Sophie said stuck with me: "One of the reasons I resisted anything having to do with the churches I saw was that they were all talk, but terrible at listening." She's right. We think our opinions came straight from heaven, but once in a while we should just shut up, and truly hear what our world is dying to tell us.

By the time I land, I'm convinced that Old First is not her happy place. But the Church's future is in those like this woman with a call and a dream. She'll start her own church, in a setting that could only be served by one of the few, the proud, the truly fearless.

I get home and make a few calls. The last one is to Mr. Bradley Davis.

CHAPTER SIX
DEADLINES

I t's crunch time at Old First. Thursdays mean deadlines—very tight deadlines. Every week I promise that the bulletin will be ready by Thursday at noon. This time, I always say, I mean it: Thursday noon, not one minute later. I promise. Of course, things can always come up, and like clockwork, things come up. People get sick, and I need to go to the hospital. Husbands and wives need counseling. People die at inconvenient times. Which means I can't honor mere deadlines. Besides, a week ago I conducted Edward Kaskey's funeral. Yesterday, I came home from my New York-Phoenix marathon, and tomorrow I'll lead a rehearsal for Saturday's wedding. Why does anyone get married in January?

Just the same, in this second week of the year, I smell deadline victory. Ten a.m. and everything's done except picking the hymns. Hymns are a big deal. They have to resonate with what's before and after them, and most of all, I have to like them. So I'm thumbing through the hymnal, narrowing my choices . . . no interruptions for another fifteen minutes, and my secretary will see me walk in, hymn list in hand like Moses coming down the mountain with the Commandments. Almost there.

The intercom buzzes. It's Mary, "Mom" to two adorable kids, an outdoors type who'd be white-water rafting in Chile and blogging about it if she didn't need to keep the church running.

I make a huge mistake. I hit the "Talk" button. "Yes?"

"Pastor, we have an unscheduled guest." That's our code for: Someone's in the lobby, probably looking for a handout. But it's Thursday, and the clock is running.

I know what my true calling is—to be a servant-shepherd-guide-companion. That's what pastors do. Being the CEO doesn't fit clergy well, but as things edge closer to chaos—or when I'm simply tired—the CEO in me kicks in, and it isn't pretty. People are cut off mid-sentence—*I've made the decision*. I do not like that part of me. But I find it convenient to leave it unaddressed, hoping it doesn't come back to haunt me.

"I hate this." A familiar voice on the intercom replies. "Excuse me, Pastor?" Rats. The "Talk" button's still lit. "Nothing, Mary."

Do I hate these people? No—not really. I hate what they do to my schedule. Leadership calls for focus, staying on task, the ruthless protection of time. Thanks to a fistful of seminars, a $1,200 smartphone, and a good office manager, I know precisely what I'll do at this time on this date in 2029, subject of course to change.

I sigh and head for the lobby. There he is: looks sixty-something—though I've seen forty-somethings looking far older than they are—thin, bearded, shaggy salt-and-pepper hair, old charcoal trench coat (might be . . . yes—it's a Ralph Lauren, one that's seen better days) over a filthy sweater over a pink, button-down dress shirt, stained. Strangely, it all kind of works, as if echoing what may once have been a sophisticated sense of style. The look is marred by blue knit mittens and tan Timberline boots far past their prime. Grungy, loose-fitting navy slacks, and glasses, one bow taped in place. Hollow, haunting, empty eyes, devoid of expression. I feel sorry for this guy, though I'm also suspicious. What personal failing caused *this* life to melt down? He sees me, and with some effort stands erect, walking toward me with what's left of a cultured grace.

"Good morning, Father." I'm not a priest, but never mind. I give him my most indifferent smile.

"What can I do for you?"

"My name's Carl." Too soon to tell, of course, but maybe he's not going to tell me a well-rehearsed story. "I need to pick up a prescription," he says, "but my disability check won't come for a week. I really need that medicine. Can you help me?" His voice is flat, unexpressive, breathy. He sounds tired, and as he speaks I feel my own energy drain away. He looks me straight in the eye. Is he telling the truth, or is this just his standard handout pitch? I decide not to decide. Instead, I break eye contact and hide behind *my* standard pitch.

"Look—I have no money to give you. As a matter of policy, we never keep cash on the premises." I lie—not by much. We have some petty cash for office incidentals, so it's a lie nonetheless, and I feel the appropriate twinge of guilt. But I've learned to deliver this lie convincingly. "I can give you a grocery voucher, or one for cab fare to County Social Services. But that's all." I'm not smiling any more.

My assumptions have decayed; they are highly toxic now. I assume that if I give you money, you will thank me profusely and tell me how I just saved your life, and how you can't wait to get back on your meds—and you'll find the bottle shop and buy a different kind of medicine. I may be right. But what's different is that I now assume this. Carl my friend, you are guilty until proven innocent, and it's not likely you'll have the chance to prove anything.

I should not be judged for judging Carl. I'm just being prudent.

He takes the hint. A quick pleasantry delivered with a voice that reflects a sense that, *Yes, Reverend, once again I ask, once again I'm turned away, just as I've come to expect from you religious types,* and he goes away. I meet my deadline, but the satisfaction is tinged with unease over how I accomplish it.

Speaking of satisfaction: one of the highlights of my job is the annual Volunteer Appreciation Dinner. We do it right too. A caterer feeds the multitude, and a church member with a flair for the aesthetic decorates the room until it sparkles. We eat, laugh, give out a few awards, and I make a little speech telling them how much I personally appreciate them. I see in each of them gifts that God gave them that they give back by loving God's people. So this is their annual 'paycheck,' and they deserve it.

"This year, it's a double celebration in that we may soon welcome a new associate minister, completing our staff!" This is met with enthusiastic applause, plus vocal cheering from the youth.

People are in high spirits tonight. With Sophie Masters looking elsewhere, Bradley Davis is the candidate, and he looks like a home run. He brings impressive credentials, glowing letters of reference, and soon a diploma from a top-tier seminary. He's engaging, charismatic, and lights up the room.

The youth were given a voice in the search, and they challenged us to be open to minority, female, and LGBTQ+ candidates—which stirred some debate. We declare ourselves officially welcoming of our gender-nonconforming siblings, but frankly not everyone's at the same place there. Some of us are welcoming, some are merely tolerant, and there's a difference. Still, our Gospel calls us to extend an unconditional welcome, and as a church at least, we mean it. So do I. Not even six months in, he'll make my life much easier.

"I'm really excited about Mr. Davis, Pastor Garraty." I turn around. A seventy-something woman stands there, speaking softly enough for this to be a two-person conversation. She has that *You know what I mean* look in her eyes. Doctor Roberta Sanders, retired pediatrician known around here as "Aunt Roberta" for her love of children. She is one of Brad's cheerleaders. She lobbied among her peers for him, and this to her is a victory.

"I agree," I say. "I do wonder, however, if we're ready for him."

"It's uncharted territory for us, isn't it?"

"A little. I've heard some complimentary-but-awkward comments common to white folk talking about Black folk when they try to sound bias-free. And you won't quote me on that, will you?"

The good doctor chuckles. "My lips are sealed." A pause, before her smile is replaced with a look that calls me to attention. "Pastor Garraty, a lot of our future hinges on how receptive we are to a different face in our midst. I'm fully in Brad's corner. Still, there will be resistance."

"I know." But Doctor Sanders isn't finished.

"This could be transformative, yes. But frankly, we will need you to lead us into not just hiring this Black man but *embracing* him. And that means understanding and loving what he brings to us, most of which we don't know yet. That's a challenge for all of us."

Does his race matter? How the color of his skin plays out in an all-white church in a *very* white town remains to be seen. I think I'm reasonably "woke" despite the term's mixed reviews. I understand concepts like white privilege (we have an abundance), and I'm uneasy about how it leaks into our call to Brad. He fits a comfortable stereotype tailor-made for this place: he comes not just from a Black home, but a *successful* Black home, proof that anyone can succeed if they try, even hard-working African Americans. The past is past, racism no longer plagues us, there's equal and abundant opportunity in twenty-first century America, and by the way, we're colorblind.

When he arrives, we shall see where any blindness may lie. Martha's parting words will haunt me: "We don't yet know what we don't know."

Overall, most of the evening is fun.

The part that isn't happens during the social hour as I migrate from cluster to cluster, swapping small talk and catching up. One of those clusters includes my least-favorite parishioner, Mike Curillo, chair of the Personnel Committee.

Relationships matter. But I have yet to fully embrace the fact that I do not always play well with others. My competitive instincts get in the way; Good

Lord, deliver me. In the meantime, I'm still smarting from the inquisition that was my annual review, largely thanks to Mr. Curillo, so I'm not in a good frame of mind. Mike's a successful, self-assured financial guy. I know and he knows that based on the numbers I was as good at growing wealth as he is. In any case, there's a kind of competition between us. We have an ice-cold, just-civil-enough relationship that fools no one.

We often discover the truth about ourselves not only through our strengths but through our weaknesses—one of mine is about to spoil the conversation.

The state lottery comes up; big jackpot this weekend, someone says. A few what-I'd-do-with-the-money jokes, then someone puts me on the spot. "Pastor, do you buy lottery tickets?"

I step onto my soapbox. "Frankly I think lotteries are terrible public policy." I don't add how dumb I think people are to spend money on an almost certain loser like a lottery ticket.

Curillo calmly mentions that he often buys them.

Oops. But since I started this, I press it.

"Mike, I can't believe you do that. After all, you're a finance guy. How do you see that as a sound investment?" Which generates a titter—whatever that is—of nervous laughter.

My personnel chairman smiles smugly and says, "Well, half a dozen of us in my firm pool our foolishness and buy a batch of tickets. It's more for entertainment than any hopes of getting rich, but I think it's harmless. It's good for office morale to have the boss involved. Besides, Pastor—what if one of these days I win?"

I hope and pray he doesn't. I'd never hear the end of it.

CHAPTER SEVEN
TEN MILLION DOLLARS

I t's early Sunday morning in early February. With a service at nine a.m., I usually don't settle into the Sunday paper—the actual *paper* paper—until the afternoon. But coffee, toast, and the "A" section are on the table. The clock is running, and I can only taste what I will devour at my leisure in a few hours, but I catch a couple of paragraphs before suiting up for the day.

One headline catches me: lower right corner, page one: "Chicagoland Office Shares Winning Jackpot." I see the page number but stay on the front page for now. I chuckle. *Oh, Lord, please don't let it be Curillo.*

Sunday Worship is pretty normal in most respects, except that Mike Curillo's there. He's not quite a "CEO"—a Christmas and Easter Only attender—but he's not here a lot. I suspect he's got an agenda. Sure enough, during the "Sharing of Joys and Concerns" in the first service, he stands and gives thanks to God for how he and his family were blessed as one of six winners of yesterday's $60 million jackpot.

Not only is it audacious to think God had something to do with a lucky number, Mike's there to gloat as far as I'm concerned, and to rub it in. I think that during the first service. I'm convinced when he stays for the second service to make the same speech.

My hardest task this morning is shaking his hand and congratulating him. Mercifully, he doesn't say "I told you so."

On Tuesday morning, Mary informs me of a special Finance Committee meeting tonight. She doesn't know what it's about, so I call the chair, and find that it's in response to a request by the Big Winner. He wants me there. The financial secretary, treasurer, legal counsel, capital improvement chair, chair of the trustees, the entire missions committee, and chair of council are coming as well. Curillo doesn't reveal why, just that he has an announcement. No doubt he's going to announce a very generous gift to Old First. Everyone suspects that; his windfall has been all over the grapevine. His share: ten million dollars. A millionaire who buys lottery tickets. A big freebie to a guy who could earn that much the old-fashioned way in four or five years.

Whatever he's up to, he wants an audience. We meet at his country club over a nice dinner (on his tab; how generous). Everyone is wide-eyed at the elegant linens and crystal. He wants us to feel the full effect, and everyone is lapping it up.

Curillo walks in. The committee chairs and bean counters fall all over each other to congratulate him (and be first in line for whatever he doles out). He's soaking it up like a rock star with his adoring fans.

After the niceties, it's time for dinner. And after dinner, time to make The Big Announcement. Dishes have been cleared; coffee's been re-poured. The door is closed as if on cue. The room is silent. There's anticipation in the air.

"Pastor, friends, as you know, God has blessed Linda and me with an unexpected windfall. It's, ah, a little embarrassing"—everyone finds that hilarious. He turns serious. "But I believe this is a gift that needs to be shared. Therefore, my wife and I have prayed about it, and we want to tithe this gift to the church. I'd like to know your reactions, observations, ideas."

One million dollars to Old First (well, minus any taxes). There's a collective gasp, but I decided when I came to this well-choreographed performance that I would not respond in any visible way. There's a chorus of "Wow," "Wonderful," "Amazing," and one "Thank you, Jesus," with eyes and hands reaching for the ceiling.

There will be no shortage of ideas for spending Mr. Curillo's largesse.

"Maybe this is God's way of restoring the pipe organ."

"I think we need to seriously think about investing this in the endowment fund."

"I've always thought we should provide scholarships for our youth who want to go into some form of ministry. We could call it the 'Curillo Fund.'"

"Think of the outreach potential if we re-introduced the plans for a gymnasium!"

"I can't believe no one's suggested air conditioning the sanctuary." This suggestion wins a chorus of approving comments.

Finally, it comes around to me. I look right at him, and I am suddenly convinced that I can seize the initiative and demonstrate bold, imaginative leadership. I can also (though this is buried deep within, where my ego lurks) put my adversary on the defensive. Brilliant, Ego tells me. So I say what, at least at the moment, I truly believe is inspired. "Ten percent isn't enough."

Now *that* gets everyone's attention. The are-you-out-of-your-mind looks around the table could cut through titanium.

Curillo keeps his cool, smile frozen in place. He measures every word, but you can tell he's millimeters from blowing. "Well, Pastor, how much *should* we give?"

All eyes are back on me. "All of it." Silence.

I continue. "First of all, Mike, you don't need it. Secondly, since you never had it before, you wouldn't miss it. Third, you don't have to give it all to First Church. But I am suggesting that you think big about what this money could do. A tithe would be great—really, it would. But by giving it all, you could make a difference way beyond our church."

The finance committee chair is at the other end of the table. Good thing, because had he been next to me, his hands would be around my throat. "Pastor Garraty, it's not our place to tell Mike what he should do. That's between him and the Lord. Personally, I think a tithe is a damn—I mean, *very* generous proportion. And it's generous of him to allow us to share in deciding how it's used."

"Absolutely." This time, it's the endowment chair who'd love to add Curillo's dollars to his paltry resources. "Mike, whatever you want to give is wonderful. I think I speak for all of us at that point." He's looking right at me. "Or at least, most of us." If looks could kill . . .

I want to defend my point of view, but while saying what I said is debatable, I'm at least smart enough to know that I have zero chance of persuading this bunch. So I endure, as nearly everyone around the table tries to convince Mike Curillo that even thinking of a gift qualifies him for sainthood.

Mike endures too. He's being praised to the point of embarrassment, but it's not working because in what should be his moment of glory, his minister insults him. Mr. Curillo does not like to be insulted. And Mr. Curillo does not forget.

At the moment I said this, I believed it. By the time the meeting breaks up, I sense I am the only person in the room with a shred of commitment to my notion. As I walk to the parking lot hearing the tone of my lay leaders, I begin to wonder if maybe I'd been just a wee bit over the top and had let our rivalry influence my words. By the time I leave the long driveway of the club and get up to speed on Highway 37, I feel the first rush of panic. And as I turn onto Cherry Lane and home, I wonder what in heaven, or what on earth, or, speaking theologically, what in hell prompted me to be so stupid. By the time the garage door closes and I kill the ignition, I am near tears. As I slip into bed, I promise myself I'll update my profile tomorrow.

CHAPTER EIGHT
STALE DONUTS

Thank God for Caller ID. It's 8:15 a.m., and the phone rings while I read the newspaper and sip my morning coffee, postponing the inevitable drive to church. It's Wednesday, and this will be a long one. I'm stalling and don't feel one bit guilty about it. By the time I leave my office, I'll have put in fourteen hours, so I enjoy an easy breakfast in an empty house, with Melissa off to school and Trish already at work.

The cordless phone is sixteen inches away, but I make no attempt to pick it up. The little information screen tells me that this is someone I don't want to talk to.

Ministers are not supposed to lie. I take that seriously. I've told a few innocuous ones ("My, but this is delicious fruitcake"). But I've convinced myself that it's OK to let my answering machine tell someone that I'm not home when I am but don't want to talk to them. It feels, if not honest, at least acceptable—doesn't everyone screen their calls?

And this is one I *really* don't want to answer. It's Curillo, who's no doubt still smarting from the way I embarrassed him, my finance board, and myself last night. I'd love to do some damage control. It's just that I have no idea what I'll say.

Four rings. I either pick it up now or the machine takes things into its own hands. I sigh and pick it up.

"Hello."

"We need to talk."

"What do you suggest?"

"My office, one thirty."

"Ok, Mike, I'll be there."

He hangs up.

Last night, Mike Curillo fed me the best prime rib I'd ever had, in a room that spoke of one's high station in life. Today we meet in his company's break room, surrounded by paper napkins and Styrofoam cups. Our meal consists of day-old donuts, as if to say: Pastor, this is what I think of you now.

He begins without preliminaries. "What were you thinking last night?"

"Mike, I said what I was thinking at the moment. I didn't mean to embarrass you. But I did want to challenge you to think out of the box."

His eyes don't stray from mine, but they narrow. He leans ominously toward me.

"Out of the box? That was out of bounds. I'm not sure I can give anything after that. You took the joy right out of it. And if we feel that we simply can't give, you'll be responsible."

"Mike, look at it this way—"

"Now if you'll excuse me, I have work to do." He gets up, turns, and leaves the room while his employees watch him storm out, leaving me holding a stale donut. Or, since I suspect he'll use this against me, he's now left me holding the bag.

I can't let this stop here. I believe in honesty, I value transparency, and I believe in pursuing common ground, even with one's adversaries. The old adage: "Keep your friends close and your enemies closer," is one that I believe—even when, as with my brother/adversary Mike Curillo, I find it hard to reconcile.

In part, this comes from my belief in a God who pursues us. I'm not pursuing him like God does, however, because I blundered into this fracture through my own stupidity. Yes, you could call it sin.

The next day I call the Curillo's, and Linda answers the phone. "Hello?"

"Linda, it's Pastor Garraty."

No "Good morning" or "How are you?" follows. Linda knows what's going on. "I'm sure you want to talk to Mike." Mike comes on the phone.

"Yes?"

"Mike, I'm concerned about where we stand with each other." This time, I'll pick the place.

We meet at Friday's, out by the tollway. It's not as pricey as his club, a distance out of town, and noisier. All of which are good, because I can't afford his taste, privacy is paramount, and since this could get testy, I don't want to argue with my wealthiest parishioner where the locals can overhear us.

I'm already seated in a booth within sight of the front door. It's four thirty. Curillo arrives on time, which means he left his Arlington Heights office early for this. When he sees me, he's grim and unexpressive. He throws his coat on the seat and sits down. Then he looks at me, or should I say, right through me. I hope he's not packing heat.

"I hope you're about to apologize, Reverend Garraty, or this could be a short meeting."

"I do owe you an apology, Mike. I shouldn't have jumped on you like that. Especially in front of everyone. That was poor judgment on my part. I am sorry."

I don't think Mike was expecting that. He looks away, exhales, and actually seems to relax. But then his guard goes back up. "Why?"

Why what? I guess it's my problem to figure that out. "I spoke up in part because when I was in business, that's how I got things done. Leaders speak directly because they're expected to. I'm sure you do as well. But I forgot I was with volunteers, not people whose paychecks I signed."

"Yeah, sure. That's plausible. But the other part of my question is, why did you say I should give *all* the winnings away? Who gives you the right—"

"Mike, I know it sounded extreme. I just think it's a valid idea."

"Wait a minute. You really think I should give *all* that money away?"

I need to slow this down. I relax, put down my coffee, and pretend to ponder that for a moment before saying what I already knew I'd say to a question I knew he'd ask.

"I think . . . whatever you do with this could be your greatest legacy."

"*I* think you're out of your mind. Garraty, I'm only a simple lay person, not a theologian. But I know enough to know this: you're not God, and you have no right to lay that on me."

His anger grows by the minute. The ice beneath my feet is melting, fast. "I know, Mike."

Mike relaxes again. I continue. "Mike, I'm not God, and I have no right to tell you what to do. As far as I'm concerned, you can spend every penny of it on more lottery tickets, and I'm not in a position to pass judgment."

"Then back to my original question, Reverend: *why?* And while we're at it, why should Linda and I stay in a church where your little suggestion was all over the congregation within forty-eight hours? Do you know what it's like to have everyone staring at you when you just want to worship in peace?'"

Mike's anger morphs into something else: pain. The Curillo's are now the objects of unwanted attention. True, they'd won the lottery, and ten million dollars makes anyone a celebrity. And Mike announced it in the middle of worship. Twice.

But he and Linda are getting stares for other reasons now that the whole world knows—and he's right, everyone knows—how I put him on the spot. In the minds of some, any contribution less than ten million dollars will be a compromise. In Mike's mind, that's a no-win. He could give 99 percent, and it would be questioned by someone.

I want to believe I was challenging him to think and give boldly. What my arrogance accomplished was to destroy his ability to give *joyfully*. Not just because I suggested it, but because I did so publicly. I owe him that apology. Before he takes his family, and frankly their considerable talent and financial support somewhere else. Before all hope of reconciliation is lost.

"I hurt you and Linda, didn't I?"

"You have no idea."

"I'm sorry, Mike. I am so sorry."

This is a watershed moment in our relationship. Repentance and forgiveness. An opportunity for grace. A holy moment. I'm praying that it will be all of those things.

But it will not. The waitperson comes and asks what we want. Mike speaks first. "I don't want anything. Nothing at all." He tosses his napkin on the table and turns to me. "Thanks for nothing." He grabs his coat, gets up, and storms out.

I leave five dollars on the table, excuse myself and follow him toward the door, but I make no attempt to catch Mike. By the time I reach the parking lot, he's already fired up his AMG S-Class Mercedes, and he's on his way.

CHAPTER NINE
THE AMBUSH

After a lifetime in the church and firm belief in its sacred message, upholding the faith in (almost) every point, I have concluded that I am a heretic. I no longer hold to one of the church's cardinal tenets. I believe in God, although I still can't explain the Trinity to my confirmation class. I can recite the various creeds without having to cross my fingers *too* much. But there is one doctrine I have abandoned, and I'm not looking back. Although I know it puts my soul in peril, I have repudiated the most cherished doctrine of the Church, and I do so without apology.

I have renounced Robert's Rules of Order. I consider this revered, ancient, unquestioned, sacred text to be archaic, absurd, meaningless horse dung.

Some of you are young enough to have no idea what this is. I suggest you attend the annual meeting of any church at least as old as your parents, and watch restrained, orderly, violence at work.

Exhibit A: our annual meeting. Like every other clergyperson on the planet, I have learned that annual meetings can be the playground of demons. The arcane rules of Congress are child's play by comparison.

The fact is, no one understands Robert's Rules. I doubt Mr. Robert ever did. They can confuse and distract. They can force decisions with little reflection or discernment. They create winners and losers when people need consensus.

Jesus left as His last will and testament a passionate prayer that we would all be "one." But we are prone to parting ways: as individuals, families, or religious traditions, as if we had been granted an exemption from the bond Jesus built in suffering and blood. If you and I talk long enough and are honest enough, we will inevitably disagree. When we do, we often walk away indignantly, convinced of our superior vision of things. We excuse our divisions by blaming "them" for being not quite as right as "us," as if Jesus had said: "Unity is nice, but winning is nicer." Our default has been to postpone unity until everyone else catches on to the perfection we've found. But we ought to grieve any time that we divide.

We begin our annual meeting with a lavish dessert reception, where the staff and committee chairs wear name tags and mingle. Committees display pictures of their work and information on proposals they're pushing. The room is awash in PowerPoint.

When the meeting starts, we keep things moving. No one can read their reports. They get five minutes to summarize how they met their goals for the year, and their goals for next year, followed by Q&A. I'm the exception. I get a whopping ten minutes. People actually *like* our annual meeting.

We expect them to love this one. In a brave and slightly reckless move, the search committee invited Brad Davis to attend the meeting in which his nomination will be presented. He preached in the morning, was a smash hit, and will be the star of the show when the gavel calls us to order. This evening we expect a jubilant coronation.

John Barrett, our church's chairman and I had brainstormed the week before, trying to anticipate what issues could come up. Brad Davis and I talked this through yesterday; he knows there's an elephant in the room. After some reservations about this being Brad's intro to Old First, I came to see how just by being there, he could pour oil on troubled waters. We need to make a good impression on him; he's made a stellar impression on us.

We knew the budget would be scrutinized. Someone may find fault with *Line Twenty-Seven-B, Cost of Newsletter Postage*. There could be a motion to increase missions support—or decrease it, depending on who gets to the microphone first. Someone will challenge the report of the Capital Improvement Committee, which says in effect, yes a gymnasium would be nice, but fix the roof instead, then re-surface the parking lot.

What John and I didn't anticipate was the Curillo/Wood ambush.

I have not forgotten the rift between Mike and me. It's serious, and perhaps something will be said. I'm ready to publicly apologize. Not only is that politically wise—I owe him that. But for reasons I can't explain, except perhaps pigheadedness or pride, I decide to not bring it up in my report. That will prove unfortunate.

During the reports, everyone behaves nicely; we even laugh a lot. Hopeful things are said about our almost-associate pastor. Brad smiles—a bit guarded, but smiles nonetheless. No one mentions the Garraty-Curillo War. Maybe, I'm thinking, the storm will blow over.

No such luck. The first half of the meeting is simply the eye of the hurricane.

The budget is presented, seconded, and a few mundane questions are asked. We expect the usual budget hawks to wax eloquent about fiscal caution. Instead, Andrea Wood stands—and when she does, a number of people start shuffling papers, as if expecting something. Andrea is not smiling.

"As all of you know, First Community Church has a special place in my heart. I have given a significant portion of my life to this, the finest church in River Glen. And I have given generously to its financial support.

"Which compels me to address my fellow church members tonight. During this meeting, we have heard many upbeat, optimistic reports about how things are going. While I would like to be as positive as others, I can't be, and I do not think any of us should be fooled. We are headed for a fiscal crisis, one that could undermine our church. And it must be addressed."

John was getting nervous. "Where is this going, Andrea?"

"I have the floor, Mr. Chairman! For the past several years, our minister has outlined specific goals for our church's growth in the coming year. And every year, we vote to increase his salary with hardly a second thought. However, in only one year, his first, were his stated goals achieved. This is irresponsible. Therefore, I move the following resolution:

"That the Senior Minister's compensation increase, as proposed, be deferred until such time as the church's financial performance is shown to have increased by the amount envisioned in his report, and that said increase be limited to the percentage of the financial increase realized."

It helps to know something about Andrea. She's the great-granddaughter of one of the church's founders. Losing her seat on the council to a younger and newer member mightily irked her, and perhaps this is just her effort to reassert her place as a force to be reckoned with. I quickly learn that there's much more. Lo and behold, three members rise from their seats as if on cue, and begin passing around copies of said proposal, already printed with attached documentation, quoting me in words lifted from my very own reports during each year of my ministry. There's mischief afoot.

But it is hard to argue with the data, especially when I penned some of it myself. Every year, I'd set specific goals. And each year, we made progress—

often barely—but we consistently came up short. And while my pay will never make the Fortune 500, each year I get a tolerable cost-of-living-plus increase.

John is flustered, and not a little worried. He has that deer-in-the-head-lights look, wondering what to do. *Someone wants to humiliate you, Pastor. I hope they find a way to do so nicely.*

Mr. Curillo, no doubt in a sincere desire to keep business moving smoothly, stood. "Mr. Chairman."

"Yes?"

"Mr. Chairman, in order to conduct a proper discussion of this important matter, I will second the proposal."

Now it's on the floor. So are most of the jaws in the stunned assembly.

The temptation is to deflect this. Maybe it can be tabled or referred to a committee. No, that's a bad idea. That leaves it out there blowing in the breeze. On one hand, I'm confident this proposal won't pass. On the other hand, I suspect that its framers—and there are more cooks in this kitchen than just Andrea—fully realize that, and aren't worried if it meets resistance. They're planting seeds of doubt, which will be cultivated in the months ahead. This is just a shot across the bow.

If I'm smart, I'll roll the dice and push for a vote. Hopefully, it will be defeated, and I can commence damage control. If they're smart they'll table or refer it, thus hanging it like Damocles' sword over my head. It gives them a forum for pouring more gasoline on the fire. As it turns out, they're very, very smart.

Had they gone directly for the jugular and proposed that I'm an idiot who should be thrown into outer darkness, a well-defined review process in the bylaws takes over. And neither I nor they would be in control. But by planting seeds they can paralyze the church, guaranteeing a stagnant and contentious year. They know it, and they know I know it. *OK, preacher: survival is now your number one project, and we'll give you no rest. How much can you take?*

Andrea asks for the floor to explain her motion. John consents. She's brief but well prepared. Her main point: you may like the minister. But can you trust his judgment?

I'm expecting Curillo to jump to a microphone and continue the attack, yet he remains stone-faced and silent. Fred Marshall, chair of the endowment committee, takes the floor. This looks planned; he reads from notes. After expressing his "concerns" he asks the treasurer to answer a few carefully worded questions. The treasurer steps to the microphone. I'm feeling OK about this; he's always been supportive. Uh-oh. He has notes too.

Some of the folk here not only don't like what they're hearing, they're perceptive enough to see that this is a planned attack. Some are visibly shaken. They cannot believe that this could happen in the family of faith. They glance my way, and some look toward Trish and Melissa, sensing that this may be devastating to them as much as (or more than) to me.

While this unfolds, one person—to me she becomes a saint—quietly slips into an empty chair behind Trish and puts one hand on my wife's shoulder. Trish stiffens, turns, and receives a loving, knowing smile. I hardly know this person, but I love the ministry of presence she provides to a woman I desperately want to not be in this room right now.

Another saintly soul makes her way to a microphone. Her face is flushed, and her hands tremble a bit, but when she calls for John's attention there is no mistaking her resolve. She's meek in the biblical sense: strength under control. John wisely senses that she will not be ignored, and replies: "Yes, Monica?"

A forty-something single mom, high school counselor, and gifted leader, Monica speaks sparingly. But when she does, people take note. She doesn't shout, but her steady, calm spirit and a minimum of words are all the more forceful for their brevity, bringing every ear into her service.

"I do not know nor wish to know what is behind this proposal. I know that I am not pleased to see such a disturbing resolution introduced here, when such concerns should be brought to the Pastor-Parish Relations Committee. Only *there* do such discussions belong. I urge us to defeat this resolution."

Timid applause drifts through the congregation. Mr. Curillo rushes to a microphone. "I move, Mr. Moderator, that this be tabled until our church's leadership prayerfully and thoughtfully reviews this."

It is seconded immediately. I sense that Monica's words threatened Andrea's—and Mike's—strategy to keep it alive and simmering. I fear the effect of postponing whatever Andrea and company have in mind for an end game. A voice from the back—I don't turn around to see who—calls for the question, and John couldn't be happier. "All in favor . . ."

It's not unanimous; I'd guess about an 80–20 split. But tabling passes, and everyone knows that while we may have salvaged a bit of decorum tonight, we will face this monster again. The matter is decided. But it is not put to rest.

Finally, "New Business." Rarely is it much, except for an occasional motion to thank the staff and volunteers for another year of faithful service. This year, no one gets thanked. What should have been the highlight of the evening—the motion to affirm Mr. Brad Davis as our new associate pastor—is presented, seconded, and after waiting for discussion that doesn't happen in a deathly silent room, John calls for the vote. Brad is now Associate Pastor Brad Davis, by a vote of 235–6. Perfunctory applause, then a sigh of relief.

A motion to adjourn is made, seconded, and passed. The meeting is adjourned, and once again, the vote is not unanimous. A sizable minority ask John to re-open the meeting. But as soon as they make their plea, we hear words we'll hear again when this drama's second act unfolds: "Point of order!" It's Andrea this time. "According to Robert's Rules of Order, adjournment cannot be reconsidered. The meeting's over." She's right. Round One is over, and she won.

For centuries, we've perfected rules to keep us from battling each other with weapons or words. Parliamentary procedure, motions, amendments, votes—Roberts Rules. The goal: win-win. Leave your weapons at the door, follow the rules, and business moves sensibly along.

Except when it doesn't. All this time and energy, devoted to the inner workings of an organization commissioned by its Founder to be more concerned for what happens *outside* its walls. I wonder what Sophie would think. I wonder if God weeps.

CHAPTER TEN
HOME

We leave quickly. Abruptly, in fact, after I pull Brad aside and try to reassure him. He's positive but without enthusiasm. He's been extended a call, but he could still decline. We agree to talk in the morning. He must wonder what he's gotten himself into.

There are those who assume that clergy, being other than merely human, sail serenely across whatever choppy waters a congregation stirs up. But pastors are profoundly human, and the best among them are sensitive creatures, often deeply so, and tonight's public flogging could shred the strongest among us.

Our departure is an act of mercy. The sooner we are gone, the sooner they won't have to say "have a nice evening" to us. Perhaps then they can share their opinions without whispering.

Perhaps the mercy is for me. I'm angry, embarrassed, and I'm in no mood for small talk. I'm in the mood to scream obscenities.

Trish and Melissa just watched their husband and father stripped of dignity in front of people they know, and I wonder if I can ever expose them to this again. I wonder if anyone in that room appreciates that. Or if anyone there gives a damn.

As we leave, we pass knots of young people—for many, their very first church business meeting. They came to celebrate the affirmation of Brad's ministry among them. They lobbied vigorously for him, and tonight should have rewarded their persistence. But while they won the vote, a well-earned celebration was gutted of its joy.

My mind shifts into damage control overdrive: Are there phone calls to make? (Yes—well probably.) To whom should they be made? (I don't know yet.) Should I make them tonight? (Absolutely not—it wouldn't take much to push me into saying something honest, and because of that, profoundly regrettable.)

Damage control begins with Trish and our daughter. I want them to revive my confidence, to cheer me on, to say that I can do what it takes to navigate this tsunami. I try to envision a way that this could be less destructive for them. I hope they slept through this nightmare. I hope that soon I will awaken from it.

I've always had a solution. I knew my options—and always had them. I always could pull rank and stifle any rebellion. But tonight I don't know what, or how, I contain this one.

My passengers are silent. Good. I need to think of something—

"Hey—I could use some dessert. Ice cream at our fav—"

"Take us home, Dad." Melissa's tone of voice discourages debate.

"Noel?" Long before I am ready, Trish breaks the silence. I should have guessed she'd not leave me in my thoughts. She looks my way. "Noel, didn't you see this coming?"

I sensed this could happen ever since The Great Lottery Train Wreck, but I've kept my thoughts largely to myself. Protecting Trish, I reasoned. But she knew.

"This," Trish states, "is fallout from your comment to Mike Curillo."

Melissa interjects—"What about Mike Curillo?"

"Have you heard anything about this from your friends, Melissa?" Maybe she can add something to my mental damage control file.

"What I've heard, Dad, is that you insulted him, and that it was a really dumb thing to say, and beyond that I'm not hearing much at all from my friends lately. They've been strange, like they're afraid to talk to me. I'm humiliated. And after tonight, I don't want to be here anymore."

Melissa looks out the window at the receding image of the church that just betrayed her trust. Out of the corner of my eye I see Trish staring directly at me, fully expecting an explanation that makes sense of this night.

Silence. Then Trish speaks with an edge in her voice I rarely have heard before, perhaps never.

"I don't know what they taught you in seminary about conflict, but *this?* This was an attempted assassination. You cannot *not* respond."

"I know." The experts tell us to remain calm, to be an objective, non-anxious presence in a crisis. It's a wonderful theory, but for the first time in a long time, not only am I angry, I'm scared.

"Noel, let's get home. Then we will talk." That was not a suggestion.

"OK."

Trish turns to our daughter. "Melissa? What do you think?"

"You don't want to know what I think." She crosses her arms and slouches down in her seat, staring at the darkened floor behind her mother.

I'm the last one in the house as the garage door rattles down. I want to delay this conversation because I'm in no condition to be in charge of it. But I won't run and hide tonight. Captains go down with their ship.

Melissa speaks first. "I'm going to my room. Good night."

Trish objects. "I think you need to be part of this." Melissa ignores her and heads up the stairs. Trish turns toward me. "I'll be down in a minute. Wait for me in the family room."

Have I fallen that far? Don't I get to decide where I'll lick my wounds? Yes I have, and no I don't.

Trish had a marginally churched upbringing and was skeptical of my emerging call away from a maker of money and toward a keeper of souls. She rightfully saw it as a step backward lifestyle-wise (and for a time, it threatened to be a deal breaker). She's supportive of my work, but guarded about it. She unapologetically identifies herself as a follower of my Boss, but she, not organized Christianity's confusing stew of creeds and traditions, has the final say on *how* she follows Him. While the church has long held a grip on my heart, it carries in her mind a mixed history of faithful witness, hypocrisy, and often-outrageous corruption. Her heart has not been won, and tonight's fiasco will not help.

After a major event, Trish and I will debrief. Her analytical skills are crucial to me, and she is my fiercest defender. Rather than settling into the living room with wine, crackers, and cheese to lubricate the conversation, this feels more like an interrogation. No, that's not true. I'm interrogating myself, second-guessing my judgment, finding my way through a strange and frightening land.

I sit on the sofa. I turn on all the lights—this is no time for mood lighting. Ten very long minutes pass, and Trish comes down the stairs alone. Instead of coming directly to the family room, I hear her footsteps on the kitchen floor. The refrigerator opens, then closes. I can't hear what she's taking out, though I wouldn't mind that glass of wine. It would help me relax a bit, and maybe help put some distance between me and my emotions.

She walks in with two glasses of water. I want to ask how Melissa's doing, but something tells me that she, not I, will make the first move, and it won't be long in coming. As she sits across from me on the love seat, she's already speaking.

44

"Noel, please do not minimize what happened and how difficult this is for us too."

"Is Melissa going to be all right?"

"In time. But her life is much more complicated now. Her circle of friends is largely drawn from the families in that room tonight, and no one her age should have to worry about how to sort this out."

"Would it help if I talked to her?"

"Maybe. But before that, I need to know the condition of *your* head and heart." She stands, comes over toward me, and sits on the arm of the sofa, almost—but not quite—close enough for me to reach her.

"Noel, I love you. Unconditionally. I believe in you. I trust you. You know that, but tonight, I want you to hear it again so there's no doubt in your mind that I stand by you, and that will never change.

"I also want . . ." Her eyes well up. She struggles, and I'm not sure if she can continue.

"Tonight, I sat there surrounded by people I've always trusted to be faithful and kind, but suddenly not knowing if I could look at them, not sure if they were friend or foe. I was helpless to help you. I could see Melissa put her head down, her shoulders tremble, and I couldn't reach her. And then I try to put it in some kind of perspective. It's a misunderstanding. A difference of opinion. A manageable problem."

She pauses. And when she speaks, her anger grows, and grows. "But what happened in that room was hideous. Hellish. Poison. Shameful."

I choose my words carefully. I can trust this audience with the truth.

"Yes. 'Shameful' pretty much describes it. There's a part of me that wants to lash out, but that's not productive, and I don't know how much clout I have right now. This may take some time. In the meantime, I want to make sure you and Melissa are OK."

Which is true. What's also true is that I don't know what "OK" means right now.

"You did see this coming, didn't you?

"Not this. But I've been uneasy about things for a while."

"Such as . . ."

"Such as Mike Curillo's behavior—or lack of it, when I knew he had to be seething."

"And you preferred to minimize it, even when I told you I sensed something strange."

She's right. And smart enough to know what was happening in plain sight.

"This is not just about you. Don't become a combatant in a personal fight. The perception tonight that you are the problem needs to be re-framed as a threat to the whole of the church. That will be tough. But that's the leadership they need."

"I thought I was protecting you from worry."

"You've always seen me as your equal, a partner, since we began our life together. You told me that I was 'competent,' and I am. I can handle worry, Noel."

And with that, this woman whose love for me glows white hot with anger at what has just soiled the soul of her beloved, stands and walks out of the room, her eyes showing grief, fury, and determination all at once. And I am left alone with my thoughts.

CHAPTER ELEVEN
NIGHTMARES

Trish and I head upstairs to get ready for bed without a word. There's no shame in silence. She's in bed within half an hour, and I use that time to sort through my mental snapshots of the meeting. I assume I flossed, brushed, and somehow got into these pajamas, but that happened without any engagement from my mind. Now I've been here an hour, lying next to my wife who may or may not be sleeping, in a darkened room in which I cannot rest.

Every institution—even one that promises hope, comfort, and grace—can turn on the ones that serve it. My colleagues talk about it, sometimes even joke about "business as usual." Sometimes they weep, souls who have poured their lives into the very place that becomes their undoing.

I get up and head for my study but wind up in the wingback near a fireplace as cold and dark as my heart. My mind searches for an explanation.

We are to blame for some of our troubles. We are not all gifted preachers, administrators, counselors, in a world of low tolerance for the merely adequate. We make mistakes. We may even act out. Just the same, some of us receive from the community of hope and grace . . . neither. When disagreements bring movement to a halt or someone is offended—those who serve are delicious scapegoats. Add to the mix people denied power in other settings, and you have an all-too-common phenomenon in an institution with few effective restraints. The Church can be its own worst enemy.

I can't sit still. I head for the kitchen where I'm rewarded by a cup of cold coffee from yesterday morning's carafe. I warm it and head back to my wingback sanctuary, my mind still in hyperdrive.

The Church was founded by those who followed an amazing Man who envisioned a community that did not take its cues from the surrounding culture, where ambition and success measured a person. He sought a beautiful contradiction: a living laboratory, a diverse, improbable motley crew, bound with love so deep that people would lay down their comfort, possessions, and lives for each other, expecting nothing in return, confident that it led to a better world.

And, they believed, it was—is—nothing less than the Way of the God who found it perfectly suitable to lay aside all we would imagine a god should be, enter the human plight at its bleakest, take on the status of a servant, allow us to deem this servant-God disposable . . . And then, this fledgling community declared, this One rose again, promising to return—not to destroy but to embrace us and share the abundance of a healed cosmos with us, freely, extravagantly, unconditionally.

I take what's left of the coffee back to the kitchen, thinking that I may need some more. I may not sleep at all tonight.

That's what they struggled to bequeath to us, hoping that where they failed, we would not; that what they had not yet learned would be revealed to us. They attempted something so outrageous that it would take all of history to achieve, and even then only with God's help.

And yet, taking our cues from our grim culture of winners and also-rans, we seem too insecure to risk grace, too impatient to wait for God's time, or too cynical to take seriously the very Way we profess. We push and claw. We. "They" did not turn on me; we turned on each other.

Our "Christ" is a more reasonable one. We tame the beast in Him. The Lion of Judah becomes the lapdog of the comfortable. Always compliant, He never soils the furniture we've so carefully arranged in our house of cards. Respectability religion—suits and ties, spiritual zombies.

I toss the coffee into the sink and slam the mug down, nearly ripping the handle off in the process. I don't need caffeine to stay awake tonight. Adrenalin will do just fine.

And when necessary, we gather the machinery of the Church that bears the name of Christ and use it to hammer each other into submission.

CHAPTER TWELVE
QUESTIONS, QUESTIONS

It's mid-morning, and Brad Davis, now my colleague, meets me at one of the more secluded eateries downtown. He's not on the clock yet, still has coursework to complete and will head back tonight to the Big Apple. After last evening's meeting many would advise Brad to decline an offer that lands him in a minefield. So I'm nervous.

But (assuming he still wants the minefield) after we finish our conversation, he'll meet with the chairs of the search and finance committees to finalize his contract. Then he'll spend some time apartment hunting before heading for O'Hare.

I'm relieved when he speaks first. He's processing the previous night's debacle with an open mind. He doesn't waste time. "Am I in any way a complication for you in how you respond to this?"

Not a question I was expecting, but a perceptive one. "I honestly don't think so. This was already brewing, although I didn't anticipate last night's outcome."

He's quiet for a minute. There's a lot to process. "We get a fair amount of conflict-resolution training in seminary, which is good as far as it goes. But I have the added benefit of watching my dad navigate a highly competitive, risky environment. It's no secret that he faced some headwinds as a Black man—comes with the territory."

He's quiet again, looking past me, thinking. Then he looks directly at me. "I assume that in any organization as large as First Community Church there will be politics. And, please don't take this in the wrong way, but churches are not always shining examples of grace. I want you to be brutally honest with me, now, and when I begin working here. I want you to update me as things progress between now and when I start."

"You can count on it. You will have to navigate some awkward conversations. People may try to triangulate you. But I hope—and believe—you can handle it. We need you, Brad, and I think that the folk you'll be working with, regardless of what they think of the senior pastor, want you to succeed."

I like how he stated that: '*When* I begin working here'—not '*if*.' Brad's not done probing his new employer. He's also probing me.

"OK Pastor. Who's the largest demographic in the church?"

"Women, by about ten percentage points."

"You probably know where I'm going with this, but who's more likely to be involved in leadership?"

"You realize if my wife heard us talking like this, she'd ream us out."

"Which is why you're the only person I'd dare talk to like this. So who's more likely to be involved?"

"Women again. I assume, Brad, that you're not objecting to women being involved."

"I'm sure you know better. But as a rule, men in the church have some catching up to do. Many of us bought into the idea that if we're busy enough, have enough stuff, and are sufficiently entertained, we'll never have to look our soul in the face. We sometimes think that we can live without core relationships and accountability."

Brad pauses. "The point being, Pastor, that with your background, you've got the credibility to draw people like Mike Curillo back into healthy relationships—with themselves, with God, with you too. You talk their language, and you're exceptionally well equipped to reach competitive types. I think that you of all people could realistically win even Mr. Curillo's heart."

I'm surprised. That borders on presumptuous for a still-in-school rookie to challenge his future boss, but I'm impressed. So I challenge him.

"OK—I'm wondering what you were seeing last night. Was something missing?"

Again, he thinks, reinforcing a perception I'm forming of a guy who thinks before he talks, but once he speaks, doesn't pull punches. "I won't oversimplify what clearly had more layers than I'm aware of. But Pastor, here's what came to mind: I wonder if people last night forgot how tightly they are tied to each other. It's the 'body' metaphor, where each of us plays a part in each other's lives, whether we share their goals or not. Our bodies need all the organs, all the systems . . . church is no exception. There are no 'others' here. Whether it's Mike or you or anyone else—we're one living thing. I think that was missing last night."

CHAPTER THIRTEEN
ASHES

I'm half-reading a magazine, half watching the evening news, when the phone rings. Caller ID says it's my favorite caller. In these last days of February, I know the answer before I ask.

"Hi, Dad. Is the lake still frozen?"

I get his familiar chuckle. "Just barely, but yes. And I suppose down there in the Deep South you're having picnics and lying in the sun."

"Not exactly. But too bad you people on the tundra still have to wear thermal underwear."

When Dad retired, he made our summer cottage his permanent home for all but about three months of the winter. Long before development pushed real estate prices skyward, Mom and Dad purchased a couple of wooded acres on Madeline Island in Lake Superior and built the family's summer retreat. Only since my father retired to this peaceful island could someone inhabit our cottage in winter. He insulated the walls, added a bedroom and heat—a Franklin stove. It's furnished in cabin chic—well-worn mismatched furniture that's variably aged, some from my grandparents, some from Ikea. But that's the charm of it. I've gone there every year of my life, and we annually spend a week (and usually more) sharing what is now our family's holy ground. And when I see the "715" area code, I know it's my father.

Since it's Ash Wednesday, I confirm that he'll be with us for Easter. He'll spend the weekend here, our guest at Sunday dinner, and if I can persuade him to come out of retirement for about an hour, I'll give him a role in Old First's Easter celebration. A father-son team. Wish I could hire him permanently.

As usual, he digs into my psyche, checking to see if his son is still sane. "So how's the preaching business?"

"Wish I got to spend more time on that, actually. I'm still amazed at how much time I spend on politics and paper-pushing."

"I hear you. It's changed over the years," he says. "You're more like my doctor: spends too much time on paperwork and practicing 'defensive medicine' so he doesn't get sued."

"The way things are here, I don't know if I'll be the one getting sued, or the one who sues. You would have loved our annual meeting."

"This ought to be interesting."

"Remember that Curillo guy? He's on my case big time, and we've had some confrontations lately. He may win these battles."

"Are you personalizing this?"

"Maybe. I think he has, too. My review last December was pretty brutal, but the annual meeting was an all-out attack."

"What did he do?"

"This will take some explaining. Actually, there were several folk who went after me, including Curillo. Out of nowhere, they challenged my leadership and proposed that my salary be tied to performance goals."

"You think this was orchestrated?"

"Oh, it was orchestrated. Not only was the resolution all written out, but others who stood to support it had their speeches ready to go. Some serious planning went into this."

"Do they want you out?"

"No one said that, but I think that's their end game. I won't caricature all of them that way, but for Mike Curillo, it's gotten personal—he's on the attack, clearly has allies, and he's relentless. Maybe because I used to be in his business. Finance guys can be competitive, and I figure he enjoys having some clout over me in the church as one way of winning that competition." I don't tell Dad about my impulsive response to Mike's millions.

"Maybe. But Noel, one of the things I'd think you do best is to compete when you're challenged." (Where have I heard that before?)

"I try, Dad. But there are other issues occupying my mind."

"What do you mean?"

"River Glen is hardly the inner city, but I keep encountering its problems. Mostly it's people in some form of distress who drift through, and several this winter landed on my doorstep."

"How does your church respond?"

"Old First doesn't. I mean, we don't have a coherent response plan. None of the churches have on-site resources specifically for people in trouble, except maybe for fire victims, that kind of thing."

"Do you feel a need to lead your church into some kind of response? Or what is it exactly that has you thinking about it?"

"It haunts me, Dad. I know that reaching people on the margins is part of our calling. But most of the people here are here because they like this middle-class, all-white town, or left the city to escape the problems we find creeping closer to River Glen. I think I'd meet major resistance if I started pressing the issue. Honestly, *I'm* not thrilled with the idea."

"Son, if I could do my life over, there are a few things I'd do differently, and one of them is right here."

In my memory of conversations with Dad, this is new territory—I've never heard him regret anything in what, at least in my mind, was a stellar career. "Tell me more."

"When you were a kid, how often did you hear me preach about justice?"

"When I was a kid, I didn't actually hear many of your sermons if I could help it."

Dad laughs. "You were daydreaming about Kara Smith, huh?"

"Smythe, Dad. *Smythe.* She was much more interesting to me than your preaching was. No offense, of course."

"None taken. But you not only missed out on some *great* preaching, you failed as I recall to even get a date with her."

"Actually, I did get one. Worst date of my life. She made me feel like the geek I was. But I heard more of your sermons than you know, Dad. You not only preached well, you lived what you preached. You have no idea how important that was to me. But to answer your question, I can't remember anything specific about poverty, or race, or hunger, that sort of thing."

"Sorry to say, there wasn't much about 'that sort of thing.' I was a product of my age and upbringing. My preaching focused largely on our individual spiritual journey. Or evangelism. Or the church's need for support. I didn't ignore human need—but I nearly did. Compassion and justice for those on the margins was on the margins of my ministry."

"Dad, I've never thought anything other than that you preached the Gospel faithfully."

"Thank you. But faithfully doesn't mean completely. I left out the people who weren't in my flock because they were too poor, too rough around the edges, too . . . not white. I urged people to give to those in need. But I never led them *to* those in need. Ours was a hands-off kind of love. Which is hardly love at all.

"I dunno, Dad. There's a word for preachers who preach a social gospel at Old First."

"What's that?"

"Unemployed."

Silence. Then—"Could you, as a minister or simply as a Christian, tell a hungry person face-to-face that their plight is not your problem—and then walk away?"

"That's what I've been saying—maybe not in word, but certainly in deed, and the more I think about it, the more I'm embarrassed. I've had encounters with transients showing up at church looking for help. They're an increasing problem in River Glen."

Dad's response is short, but abrupt. "They are not a 'problem!'" He pauses. "Noel, this haunts me. If we learn anything from Jesus' conflicts with the powerful people of His time, it's how frighteningly possible it is to be sincerely, confidently, and completely wrong about what matters. But I won't start preaching to my son. You'll probably read Isaiah 58 tonight—read it a couple times first, and I won't need to preach."

I know what it says. But I'll read it again, because Daddy said so—and I remember its tone: *Shout out, do not hold back! Lift up your voice like a trumpet!*

I actually enjoy the Ash Wednesday service, including its somber tone. It's likely nobody's favorite day. Hallmark doesn't sell "Happy Ash Wednesday" cards. Attendance is the lowest of any service on the calendar, which I understand in a feel-good culture that sees Ash Wednesday's call to repentance almost as a betrayal of the right to blissful ignorance.

But this is the one time of the year when I can look each person in my flock in the eye—each one who attends, at least—and speak their name. I don't like the traditional words, but I remind them gently that "You are dust, and to dust you shall return." Distressing but true, a loving corrective to a death-denying culture.

And the best part? As I say that, I'm marking them with the sign of the cross on their forehead or the back of their hand, a physical as well as spiritual contact with each person who on the other 364 days in the year, I see mostly at a distance. Something in that moment almost makes the board and committee meetings, reports, and yes, conflict, worthwhile. It's a moment of grace, tenderness, and vulnerability.

But before that, I lead the gathered—about fifty souls tonight, a fairly typical turnout—in the service. I'm reading the scriptures, which, as my dad reminded me, include Isaiah's familiar words: "Announce to my people their rebellion, to the house of Jacob their sins . . ." The sometimes-grim task of a prophet, I think, as I continue.

". . . Is not this the fast that I choose: to loose the bonds of injustice, to undo the thongs of the yoke, to let the oppressed go free . . ."

So far, so good. These are big-picture subjects; the kind one writes their congressperson about.

". . . to share your bread with the hungry, and bring the homeless poor into your house"—And I am frozen in place.

For a long moment, I don't even breathe. I should be reading, "When you see the naked, to cover them, and not to hide yourself from your own kin." But I can't speak the words. I sense everyone in the room is wondering what has happened to their pastor, while I think of nameless souls at the church's door. I am seeing again 'the homeless poor' as if for the first time.

The words finally spill out, ". . . then your light shall rise in the darkness . . . you shall be like a watered garden, like a spring of water . . . you shall be called a repairer of the breach, a restorer of streets to live in . . . for the mouth of the Lord has spoken."

I continue the service to conclusion, but Isaiah isn't finished with me. All the way home, I'm debating an ancient prophet who won't give up. "Bring the homeless poor into your house . . ." I don't think I could do that. But I suppose Isaiah isn't impressed with a handout, then sending them on their way. "Shout aloud, do not hold back! Announce to the people . . ." No wonder the life expectancy of a prophet was below average.

CHAPTER FOURTEEN
UNSCHEDULED GUESTS

April brings us closer to Easter and its looming deadlines, and while the office is running smoothly, there's tension in the air. The annual meeting still echoes in everyone's ears. Plus, it's Thursday again, and what we don't need are any interruptions. Which is apparently what just walked through the front door. Again I hear those magic words: "Pastor—we have an unscheduled guest."

My job as a minister is to care, but my role as an administrator is to navigate these unscheduled, time-consuming distractions as efficiently as possible. I'm not indifferent to suffering, nor inclined to turn someone away without some sense of direction. What's more, it's cold and snowing on this early spring Thursday. It's harder to send someone away when winter refuses to admit that it's over. How can we turn this poor soul out into a blizzard?

Exactly as I expected, a disheveled stranger stands by the literature table pretending to read a paperback Bible. I introduce myself and ask what I can do for them, knowing exactly what's coming. Or so I think.

Like other transients who walk through the door, he'll at least try to be polite and respectful, introducing himself—no, as "he" turns around, he's a she. Probably about thirty-five, but from the look on her face they've been very hard years. It's easier to tell a male panhandler, kindly, of course, to take a hike. But it's harder to turn a woman away, and they often have harder hard-luck stories. Often those stories involve children. That's my mental calculation. I was never more right. And more wrong.

"Pastor, I need a place to live, and I need food for my daughter. And I've run out of ideas."

"Have you tried the Salvation Army?"

"Yes. They're full."

"I'd suggest trying the River Glen Community Center. They have a shelter too, and—"

"Pastor, please. I've tried the community center, the Salvation Army, County Social Services, and you're the fifth minister in the fifth church I've talked to this morning. All of them said the same thing, and I'm tired of getting the brush off. I need help. I'm not used to begging, but I'm desperate enough to try."

"What's your name?"

"Lisa. My daughter is Cherry."

"Got a last name?"

"What I've got is a cold and hungry daughter. Listen, six years ago I was a bank teller and a wife and a mother, living in our own house, making enough to live on. I got called up, my husband ran off with an old girlfriend he couldn't forget, and when she got busted for dealing drugs, he did too. Lost his job, went to jail. When I got back, I divorced him, found a boyfriend. Life started feeling normal again, until he was deported to El Salvador—I didn't know he had no papers. Lost the house. We lived in a shelter, shelter closed. Drove here, car broke down. I'm out of options, and you're asking what my last name is. Tell me why I should give it to you."

I don't have a good comeback for that. But I can't send her away with the boilerplate wish-you-well. She doesn't sound like she'd leave.

My deadline is racing toward me, now forty-seven minutes away. Mary is looking through the glass door, waiting to see Ms. X turn around and leave meekly. *Go in peace, dear sister. Please.* That's not happening, and the woman who is now answering the phone is still staring at me. She's getting worried—*is another deadline in jeopardy?*

"Come into my office."

I sit down behind my desk. My unscheduled guest sits across from me, eyes focused on mine, as if to say, *Mister, you better have answers. I have no time for BS.* "Look, Lisa, I'm blown away by your story. A husband, home, job, gone?"

"I never, ever, thought I'd be in this mess. It always happens to other people, you know?"

"I'm so sorry, Lisa." We are silent. Neither one of us has much to say.

"I'll be honest with you. You need cash? We've got zip here. Here's what we have. We keep a few grocery vouchers for special needs. I've got a voucher for a gas station too, but sounds like your car needs more than that. I'm not sure what I can do about finding a place for you to stay."

"Please."

I look down at my desk. I sense she's still focused on me.

"My last name's Grant."

I look up and smile at Lisa Grant.

"Lisa—I need a minute. Would you wait out in the lobby while I make a couple calls?" She looks at me suspiciously, guessing wrong about my intentions. "OK, I guess." She gets up and walks out. I follow her to the door, close it, go back to my desk.

Alright, I can get her food. I know a couple mechanics for her car. But I have no idea where she'll stay. This is not my problem, right? I run a church, not a social service agency. I'm accountable to the congregation which pays me to care for this place and its programs, not every Tom, Dick, Harry, and Lisa who walks in asking for a handout, right? I've got hymns to pick, for goodness' sake.

Except for my Boss, who probably meant it when He talked about going a second mile and whatever I do for the least of His siblings I do for Him and . . .

Well, I've got one of His sisters in my lobby who won't take no for an answer, an impatient sister in the outer office who won't be amused by another blown deadline—why not involve the other significant woman in my world? I pick up the phone, call Trish, and give her a Cliff's Notes version of my dilemma. She listens quietly, and when I'm done, silence. I don't like silence. I ask, "Do you have any idea where they could land?"

"Yes. Right here." I'm stunned.

"Trish, we don't know them. How do you know we can trust them in our home?"

"Noel, up to now, it's people like us who haven't been trustworthy. Bring them home."

She hangs up. At zero hour minus thirty-six minutes, I call Lisa back into my office.

"Lisa, you and Cherry are, if you accept, our guests tonight. We have a guest room, and we'll provide dinner and breakfast. Then we'll see. I'll look into your car situation, and we'll try to figure out something on housing."

She is genuinely speechless. Then her face changes. She hardens. "No. I'm not comfortable with that."

"Lisa, it's really all I can suggest." Then I go on the offensive, sort of. "What other ideas do you have?"

She looks down.

She looks up. But this time, her eyes are reddening. "Thank you."

CHAPTER FIFTEEN
GOOD NEWS . . . BAD NEWS

I quickly finish the bulletin and send it to Mary. I knock off work early after arranging with my mechanic to tow the Grant-mobile to his shop. I cancel my end-of-the-day haircut and take Lisa and Cherry Grant to our home on Cherry Lane. Turning the corner, I make a joke about our street being named after the younger Ms. Grant. Her response tells me that she's not into gratuitous humor. Introductions are awkward, in part because Trish has barely finished revising the menu for tonight's dinner, and in part because Lisa is embarrassed, while Cherry seems to have taken a vow of silence.

Melissa's a good sport. Less than a year older than Cherry and as gregarious as any now-seventeen-year-old around, she has a well-honed strategy for reluctant guests: they don't get to decide whether they'll join in the fun. Melissa takes Cherry's arm, and instead of asking, simply declares for the both of them that they'll be up in her room getting acquainted.

That leaves Lisa, Trish, and me. We stand in the kitchen like pillars of salt for about thirty seconds, trying to think of something nice to say when we know nothing good in Lisa's life to talk about, and Lisa knows nothing at all about us. I invite Lisa into the family room, which opens into the kitchen. That way, this person who still makes me uncomfortable is surrounded by Garratys, and I'm ashamed for even thinking that we need to.

There's laughter coming from Melissa's room. Not a lot, but some, and it's not all Melissa. In approximately three minutes she's accomplished what I failed to do in half an hour. How does she do it?

Trish invites Lisa to help with the meal. While the spaghetti noodles boil and an Italian salad is tossed, I get a chance to call the garage for a verdict. Bad news. For starters, seems there's no resuscitating the radiator. Wonderful. "OK,

Will, go ahead and fix it. I'll take care of it. Anything else?" Lord, I hope not.

"Well, Pastor, I'm really not sure I can salvage the front brakes."

"I'd appreciate it if you'd try, Will. This isn't someone with a lot to invest in an old car like that." I'm not sure I'm thinking about Lisa as much as myself, since I can already guess who's paying this bill.

Dinner is a simple spaghetti with meatballs and salad feast by Chef Trish. It's surprisingly pleasant. At first, Lisa and Cherry are nervous, perhaps feeling watched by unfamiliar people in an unfamiliar setting, but it doesn't take long for them to relax—the crystal and fine china are balanced by the simple, calm grace of the Garraty women who never fail to set our guests at ease. Melissa has broken through the Cherry barrier, and I catch our young guest smiling from time to time. Seems the girls have some interests in common. I do note, however, that she's almost as reserved with her mother as she is with us.

With the main course winding down, Trish looks to Lisa's daughter. "So Cherry—I hope Melissa hasn't bored you to death with her musical taste."

Melissa chimes in. "Cherry and I like a lot of the same music."

This gets Lisa's attention. She seems surprised, and eager to see some life in her daughter, I suspect. "Do you, Cherry?"

"Yeah."

Lisa presses her daughter for more. "Like who?"

"Oh—lots of stuff." In other words: I don't want to talk about it in front of people I don't really know, OK?

Trish rescues Cherry with a question for her mother. "Is it OK to ask what your experience with churches has been?"

Lisa looks down, and I suspect she's wondering what a minister's wife might consider an acceptable answer. "Well . . ."

"Lisa," Trish offers, "I suspect that you've asked churches for help and haven't found all of them helpful."

Lisa's relieved; she can be honest. "No. I guess they get asked a lot, right? But I thought they'd be at least respectful."

Sitting across the table from Lisa, Trish responds. "I don't know if that breaks my heart or makes me angry. We owe you at least respect. And a lot more. Someone in your situation should be treated like a guest."

I'm not sure if she's talking to Lisa or to her less than hospitable husband.

Lisa opens her life briefly to us. "I was raised to go to church, but when I started hanging with a rougher crowd, my church friends lectured me, then shunned me. Told me to my face that I was going to hell."

"They weren't speaking for the God I believe in, Lisa."

This frees Lisa to open her lived experience to us. "They taught me to be afraid of God. I'm not sure I want to believe in anything the churches I've known taught me."

Suddenly she's embarrassed; she'd been a little too honest, she thinks, telling a minister's wife that she doesn't have much use for her husband's employer. "I'm sorry, I didn't mean—"

Trish is having none of it. "Don't be sorry. We're the ones who owe you an apology."

Thanks, Trish, for reminding me.

First thing Friday morning, I've prepared my famous French toast for our guests, complete with sausage, juice, assorted fruits in pretty little slices, and coffee. I'd love to make them all a bag lunch, but Sunday is approaching, and I need to have something intelligent to say when it arrives. But first things first: get Lisa's car fixed, so they can get on their way. While Melissa and Cherry are eating, I step into my study and call my friend Will. I trust him; he's a church member and a decent guy, so I'm confident he'll keep the repairs under control. Will disappoints me.

"Sorry, Pastor. That car shouldn't be on the road. The brakes are flat out dangerous. No way she can even drive it without new rotors. Tires are barely passable, and I won't let it out of my shop in that condition. What do you want to do?"

"Sounds like Lisa gets new rotors. Do they come in a choice of colors?"

Will laughs. "Find out what her favorite color is, and I'll paint them."

Melissa calls for help from the kitchen. "Dad! We need you! Cherry, are you all right? Dad!" I sign off with Will and head her way. Rounding the corner, I smell what's happened before I see it. Sure enough, Cherry's stomach has rejected my French toast. Instinctively, I ask a question with an already obvious answer. "Are you all right, Cherry?" She's clearly not. She's embarrassed, and she looks awful.

"I'm sorry." She heads to the bathroom, almost knocking Trish over on her way. I'm annoyed, Melissa is worried, and Trish grabs the cleaning gear and gets to work.

When Lisa enters the kitchen, I let Trish handle it. "Has she been sick?"

Lisa looks defeated. "She did that a couple days ago too. I don't know what's wrong. She doesn't have a fever or anything. I feel terrible, Mrs. Garraty. Really."

"Don't worry, Lisa. I'll get this cleaned up. You just take care of your daughter."

Did I tell you my wife is a class act?

I drop Melissa at school and head to the office, leaving the Grant's at home with Trish. Will calls and asks me to run by the garage. I tell the office staff I'll be back in fifteen minutes, assuming I'm about to write a check and collect Lisa's car.

I greet Will, and he's not smiling.

"Do you want the good news first?"

"I don't want anything else."

"Well, Pastor, the radiator's fixed. Got a used radiator, so that's not going to hurt too badly. However . . ."

"Will, when I'm talking to a mechanic or a doctor, I never, ever, want to hear the word 'however.'"

"Why don't you just come with me." I follow Will into the garage where Lisa's car is still on the hoist. Will does not point me toward the brakes. "Look under here, Pastor." I look at the hole where the bottom of the muffler is supposed to be. I shake my head in disgust. "OK, Will—go ahead and fix it. This just has to get done." I'm eager to send the Grant's on their way and I'll pay almost anything to get this resolved.

"It gets worse." Will directs my attention to the various struts, shafts, and fittings that connect the front wheels to the car. He grabs one front wheel. When he works it back and forth it moves far too freely, and there are some very ugly noises coming from places that aren't supposed to make noise. "Pastor, you know what's happening, don't you?" I sigh.

"CV joints?" Will nods. "At least." He knows that I know that this car won't see a public road without some assurance that the front end will remain intact.

I can't believe it. I'm no mechanical genius, but I know that before this car leaves River Glen, about six or seven hundred dollars, or more, will leave my checkbook. It's a little more than I can handle gracefully. "Just fix the damn car."

"Pastor?"

"Just fix the *darn* car. Sorry."

"Pastor, this 'darn' car is a dying car, and shouldn't even *be* fixed. It needs to be scrapped. The engine is suspect, the transmission is worse. Nobody's paid attention to this car's to-do list for years. It's worth nothing more than junk value, and you're looking at putting nearly a thousand dollars into it? If I did everything it obviously needs, it still could give up the ghost before it leaves town. Don't make me waste your money."

I know he's right. I suspected as much but hoped for a miracle. No miracles today. No answers for our houseguests either.

CHAPTER SIXTEEN
A THORN IN THE SIDE

I need answers. Lisa, Cherry, and I are in my car. A sympathetic mechanic (with more bedside manner than some doctors) has persuaded us that his patient may be terminal. We're driving away from the last social service agency in the county, all of whom regret having nothing to offer. It's been a morning-long litany of: all our facilities are full, our resources are tapped out, we require the person to be a county resident, or some other reasons why a homeless mother and daughter don't qualify for help. I can't imagine what someone without a home must face on a cold, miserable day like this.

I've called my colleagues in River Glen's other houses of worship, all of whom have pledged to support one another in our hour of need. Mine's today, but none of my colleagues can honor that pledge. They have prior commitments. My Protestant colleagues all feel my pain, as does the local rabbi. The Catholic priest is away at a clergy retreat; the leader in our local Sikh temple is attending his own. The imam is in Minneapolis with a family emergency. I find variations on the we-aren't-available-today theme everywhere, as if there's a conspiracy afoot. Is their calling today to serve God by stranding me with an unsolvable problem? That's neither fair nor true—just the ravings of a momentarily mad man.

My last call is to my best pastor friend, the Episcopal rector across the square. As he's fond of saying, Episcopalians have cornered the market on wisdom, but today, he's wisely having lunch with his Bishop in Chicago.

Say . . . Chicago . . . Why didn't I think of that before?

Driving with my cell phone in hand and steering with my knee, I scroll through the directory. Maybe I still have that number . . . Bingo. I tap it, relieve my knee of driving chores, and someone answers. After nearly a minute and a half on hold, my callee comes on the line. "Hello, this is Sherman Jackson."

"Hey, Sherm, Noel Garraty. Remember me?"

"Noel Garraty. So whose side are you a thorn in these days?"

"You do remember! That warms my heart."

"And your memory is giving me indigestion. Say—as thrilling as it is to chat with the most clueless seminary intern we ever had, I doubt this is a social call. Either you're going to make a big donation to the shelter, in which case I'll listen, or you need a favor—though I can't imagine what it would be—in which case I'll say goodbye and God bless you and go back to actually doing something useful."

"Ah, Sherman, the years have mellowed you like the finest vinegar."

"What do you need, Mr. Garraty?"

"It's *Reverend* Garraty now."

"Heaven forbid."

"Too late. Got the shingle on my office wall. Here's the deal. I have a mother and daughter named Lisa and Cherry Grant in my car. They're homeless, broke, and need some help, and I've tapped out my resources up here."

"You know we're a men's shelter."

"Sherm, what am I supposed to do? They're decent folk, and I need someone I believe in to make an exception or give me an alternative. I'll be there in forty-five minutes, OK?" I hang up before he can respond. This ought to be interesting.

At first, I'm proud of going the "extra mile." In fact, I'm going an extra fifty, with that much more for the return trip. The little ego demon in my heart tries to convince me that it's pretty Christian of me to do all this for two lost souls. But as we drive toward the shelter through some of the meaner streets on Chicago's near south side, I realize I'm really taking the Grant family right back to what they'd left the day before. Had their car not broken down they may have found their way to a livable life. But now I'm bringing them back to where they'd landed when the bottom fell out of their lives. If they spend too much time here, it could begin to feel like this is the best they can do. A few minutes ago, I felt good about myself. Now I just feel guilty.

We park just past the shelter and walk in. It's lunchtime. The place is full, noisy, and smells of coffee and food. Sherman is sitting at a table with four or five men that I assume by their looks are homeless. He sees me but doesn't jump up to embrace me like a long-lost friend. I introduce Lisa and Cherry.

"Ladies, feel free to get in line for some food. Noel, you sit here."

As soon as they're out of earshot, the fangs come out. "What on earth were you thinking, Garraty? We don't take women, I don't do favors, and as you can see, I have all I can handle here. I don't need you suburban rich guys thinking I can mop up whatever you spill."

"Look, Sherm, I understand. But I had to find something. And while we never got along very well—"

"'Got along?' Were we even on speaking terms when your internship ended here?"

"No. We weren't. I think we were both glad when it ended. But look—my church in River Glen sees folk like Lisa and Cherry more often now. We clergy talk about it when we get together, and we know we need to figure something out. But so far, we just don't have the right resources up there. We haven't caught up to the city."

"Nice church?"

"Yeah actually. Growing a little, lots of families, decent facilities."

"People like yourself?"

"Mostly. I think I connect pretty well with them. A fair number do the kind of thing I used to do before seminary."

"Rich?"

I've been ambushed by Sherman Jackson. I know right where he's leading me, and I can't do a thing about it. "I'd say we're upper middle class."

"My, Garraty. Sounds like you got just what you wanted. Seems like you have tons of resources, not like us poor inner-city folk who are never more than a week or two from closing our doors. Say, maybe you could find me a job on your staff, so I could get a regular paycheck just like you."

"Sherm, please. I need—Lisa and Cherry need—a safe place to stay. They're good people. We had them at stay at our place last night, but it—I need at least a referral if you can't house them. Yeah, maybe we're a rich church. But we don't have any place for people like Lisa and Cherry up there."

"Then, *Reverend* Garraty, if you 'don't have a place for people like' those inconvenient poor folk, why don't you and your snobby little church build one? Sounds like you think they're encroaching on your safe, gated, fancy neighborhoods. They're not 'encroaching' on anyone. They're running for their lives. They're refugees, not invaders."

I don't appreciate being lectured in front of other people, even if they are homeless. Foolishly, I tell my former mentor something to that effect, and it's like pouring gasoline on a fire.

"Listen, Garraty. You came here six years ago because you had to. Urban Ministry was a required course, and they had to drag you here kicking and screaming 'cause you kept telling them you felt called to minister in—how did you put it?—'a setting more consistent with my life history.' Yeah. An upper-middle-class, suburban, lily-white history, right? Thought you'd never need to learn what the street is like, right? So in comes the most arrogant, pompous, judgmental intern we ever had to put up with. Your 'ministry' among us nearly emptied the place. I had, and still have, serious doubts about your suitability for *any* kind of ministry."

My ears are burning; my face is turning red. As Jackson's voice gets louder the rest of the room gets quieter, and suddenly I'm the white guy in a sea of mostly brown and black getting reamed out by the director. This is not my day.

Jackson lowers his voice and turns to Lisa, who just sat down with her lunch tray. She pretends to not have overheard my flogging. "Lisa, see that office over there? When you're done eating, you and Cherry go in there, ask Monica to call Gracie. She'll know what to do. You'll be OK. And while you're doing that, I'm going to continue to set my young suburban friend straight on a few things. All right?"

Lisa and Cherry aren't done eating, but after what they'd just witnessed, they can't wait to find out who Gracie is.

Actually, Sherman doesn't set his young suburban friend straight. He just eats, and lets me chew on what he's already said. I look around while inwardly licking the wounds on my ego. After a minute or so, Sherman speaks in a suddenly calm voice.

"So let me tell you a story—true story—about what sometimes happens in downtown Chicago. There was this blind guy, a street person, always looking for a handout. Everyone knew him. They stepped over him every day on their way from the office to this great little deli across the street. He was filthy, he stunk, and he was pushy. People hated him. Probably still do. Ever seen the type?"

"Yeah. Every time I'm here in the city."

"What do you do?"

"Walk on by, no eye contact."

"Why?"

"You're thinking I should help him, and I really want to. I *hate* walking by. But isn't that enabling him? Besides, if I try to help all of them, I'd be broke before I got to that deli."

Silence.

"You really think I should help someone like that?"

"Just wanted some clarification."

"About what?" (Do I sound defensive yet?)

"About your *modus operandi* when someone out there asks for some help."

"Well, that's my *modus operandi*. I keep moving. I want them to get help—it's just that practically speaking, money might do more harm than good. Besides, you said he was pushy—to me that's a deal-breaker. So what happened to this blind guy?"

"Some dude—pretty ordinary looking, middle class, I'd guess, modest resources at best, shows up with his buds on their way maybe to lunch. He's known as a bit of a soft touch, so our blind guy hollers for help. The crowd on the street tells him to shut up, and instead, he ratchets up the volume. We now have a very public scene. He's yelling for help, people are yelling for him to shut the blank up, and this guy is put on the spot."

"Yeah. That's how I feel when I'm accosted by these people. On the spot, needing to make an immediate decision that, a: I'd rather not make, and b: I prefer to make after checking this guy out. I hate those moments."

"So what do you think the nice guy does?"

"OK, I would guess you're gonna tell me that he smiles, takes out a dollar—maybe a five—and gives it to the blind guy. I might too, frankly. And if you must know, I'd feel crappy for doing that, and just as crappy when I don't. It's a no-win. Which does Nice Guy do?"

"Neither. He asks someone—in fact, someone who's been trying to shut our panhandler up—to go get him and bring him to Mr. Nice Guy. And when they're standing face to face, he says, 'What do you want from me?' Sound familiar yet, Preacher Man?"

I should have known.

"Could be one of a half dozen stories of Jesus coming to the rescue."

"Actually, it is—if you'll pardon some storytelling license. But unpack the story with me. Jesus comes through Jericho—lots of history, important town, and Jesus is just passin' through. But He stops for a blind beggar along a country road. A beggar who yells and screams and demands. You find that disturbing? It's always satisfying to help the less fortunate—as long as they follow the rules, fill out the paperwork, and let *us* decide when, where, how. We want to manage our charity, keep it within our schedule, not in the middle of a workday, or our day off, or during a church service, *and* within our discretionary income.

"'Many scolded him,' the scripture says. That's our instinct too. We find beggars offensive. We are offended by audacity. *Demanding* that we respond? That's not the social contract! They aren't supposed to define how we respond! The person in need should be quiet and polite so that we feel in control, as if we initiated this generous deed. Maybe if we're honest, they frighten us. They are the 'other' we don't understand.

"So what does our blind beggar do? He cried out even louder! Because the poor, my suburban friend, have nothing to lose by being brash, and nothing to gain by being polite.

"Here's the thing: I think that somehow this beggar knows enough about Jesus to know he can push the envelope. Never forget this: the people in this room—they often have a better, more practical theology than *you* do. Their faith isn't learned in Sunday School as much as in trouble. Many of these people—most of them, I think—believe in a God who acts on their behalf. Their God performs miracles. While you are preaching sophisticated theological babble, they are in constant crisis mode, so God shows up for them a lot. And, frankly, since you work for a God who shows up, they may assume the right to expect the same from *you*.

"Get this straight: It is not 'reasonable' to expect meek, polite requests from people who are repeatedly denied what they need, who are told to wait, and wait, and wait. Rebuke or lecture the poor on how they did it wrong? *That* is unreasonable, condescending, and just one more form of oppression."

"Never thought of it that way."

Sherman's on a roll. He keeps dismantling my *modus operandi*. "It made more sense, Garraty, for the beggar to ask for less. Isn't asking for his eyesight a bit too bold? Don't we get to decide how much money—how much justice—to dole out, as if it were a commodity we get to spend as we wish? This guy dared to ask for *everything*. And Jesus honors that, publicly in fact, in front of his critics. Kinda like preparing a table before him in the presence of his enemies, dontcha think?"

"I guess I need to re-think my reactions. What should I do?"

"I don't know. Really. I don't. I don't know what *I'll* do the next time. But I can't wait to hear what you do."

I drive Lisa and Cherry to a women's shelter about ten blocks away and intend to drop them off but think better of it. We park the car, and I walk with them toward the shelter. Lisa, who's been down this road before, says nervously, "Reverend Garraty, they won't let you in." She's probably right. But I'm not going to surrender just yet.

"I want to make sure they're ready for you."

And sure enough, we ring the bell, and someone who's watching us on a monitor inside says, "Ladies, I'll let you in but not until the gentleman leaves."

That's embarrassing, but I understand. I say goodbye, Lisa says goodbye, Cherry's very interested in examining the concrete. I walk away and hear the electric door jamb clicking shut behind them.

CHAPTER SEVENTEEN
THE INEVITABLE

Have mercy on us, O Lord, have mercy on us,
for we have endured much contempt.
We have endured much ridicule from the proud,
much contempt from the arrogant.

—from Psalm 123 (NIV)

Poor Brad. All he did was to tell the truth.

Church should be an ideal place for hard conversations marked by trust, respect, an open mind and heart, speaking the truth in love. But someone somewhere declared that we don't talk about politics, sex, money, or especially race, in church. Christians, it is alleged, must avoid discomfort at all costs.

OK, maybe we'll talk about race. But only briefly, because we are not racist. And we assume that Brad got that memo.

A youth meeting was ground zero. Brad has been with us only for a few weeks. He's still technically in school, but most of his academic work is virtual while he eases into Old First. Of course he and I had discussed how his Blackness played into his ministry here (Brad was, now that I think about it, less confident than I about a "honeymoon" of sorts).

While his call to Old First was overshadowed by questions about mine, Brad still came—a testimony to his courage. Stress and conflict do not frighten him. It's all in a day's work for someone raised in Chicago's urban core. Then a tragedy in the Windy City makes the news. In an all-too-familiar scenario, Gary Brown, an unarmed Black man, is shot by police, and protesters take to the streets as we watch. There's property damage, though by whom remains a mystery. A few protesters are roughed up, a few officers injured, arrests made, and the city's response: more police—all on the night before the youth gather.

Melissa joins us in watching the news, complete with first-hand witnesses, official statements, drone and helicopter footage. She seems detached from the story, focused on her phone, typing furiously. I quietly nod toward our daughter: "Melissa's doing homework on her phone?"

Trish has noticed too. "The way she's typing . . . this isn't a term paper." I watch; she types in bursts, sometimes for a few seconds, sometimes a minute or so, then a long pause, another burst, another pause . . . I get it. This is a very serious chat.

Melissa looks up long enough to say, "Later." She walks toward the stairs and her room, typing all the while. I shrug and tell Trish that Brad and I will talk about this tomorrow, and we return to watching an unfolding tragedy fifty miles away.

Half an hour later, we hear our daughter coming down the stairs, asking if we can talk. "What does Brad do with this, Dad? No—wait—I've been talking to some of the church kids about our meeting tomorrow. I think we're going to ask Brad to help us sort this out. Is that OK? We're going to do it. I just want to know what you think."

I'm calculating how this affects the thin political ice I'm standing on. Trish takes a higher road. "I don't see how you can *not* raise the issue. I do think he needs a heads-up though."

"Yeah—I texted him already."

I affirm that. "Your mom's right. You'll get to hear someone who lives with this all the time. But if you think you can tell me, what kind of buzz you're hearing?"

"Wow. It's all over the place. Some kids think the cops are trigger-happy. Others say the guy probably did something suspicious. A few, I think, were parroting their parents. I think tomorrow will be pretty tense, Dad."

Trish asks, "What do *you* think?"

Melissa shakes her head. "This breaks my heart. These people have families, and it must tear them up. This has to stop." She looks at her phone; we hear it buzz too. "Gotta go." And up the stairs she goes.

"Noel, are you going to that meeting?"

"I think so. Should I?"

"Many of the parents will want to know how Brad handles this—and you, for that matter. I think some people will be nervous and expect you to keep things, and I hate to say it—keep *Brad*—under control."

"White fragility?"

"This," she says, "is a petri dish for white fragility. And for some backlash if Brad does what I think he should do. Frankly, I think he should be honest about what it's like being Black in the city, even if it ruffles feathers. In any case, Noel, I think that this may be unstoppable."

I think she's right. "I'll offer to attend, but I have a hunch he'll feel it's an opportunity he can't pass up and frankly, he might be freer without me. This might define his time here."

Brad isn't as gregarious as usual in the morning. He's quiet, focused on getting from the front door into his office. He closes the door, but fifteen minutes later, he's at my door. "I know it's early—I'd really like to talk."

"Come in." He sits down.

"We are so sorry about last night, Brad."

"Yeah. Look. Melissa's talked to me, said she's talked to you, and along with some other kids she's pushing for last night's shooting to be our subject tonight. By the way, we know the Brown family."

"Oh, Brad . . . any word on his condition?"

"They say he'll live, but nothing's for sure." He leans forward. "About tonight. I frankly wouldn't choose to put this out there. Not this soon, before I've built some 'cred' with the congregation.

"Besides—can I be honest? I'm *tired*. Not physically—just tired of being the token Black who speaks for us all, kind of an ideal Black who eases everyone's anxiety. I'm tired of getting all this tone-deaf advice about if we'd stop burning things, or stopped marching altogether, or how we *had* a civil rights movement, and everything's OK now. Oh—and please turn down that music and pull up your pants.

"I'm sorry, Pastor. I promise I'll try to not vent like this tonight. But for me, this isn't philosophical. Another brother shot by cops we don't trust. And all we hear from the city is more cops, law and order, if only he had complied with the officer . . ." Brad throws up his hands. "Part of me wonders: What do we do tonight that doesn't blow up? But I also don't think I'll have much choice."

I sigh. "The kids have pretty much set this in motion, haven't they?"

"You wouldn't believe the text traffic. Not just Melissa, but a ton of kids, and they're arguing already."

I'm quiet for a bit. Brad wants to say something; I put up my hand to buy a few more seconds.

"You could cancel tonight's meeting so we could make sure we know what we're doing. Or I'd come to the meeting, in which case, the questions would likely be safer but not as honest. Or, you lead the conversation, just you and the kids, with no filters on what's said. But—that could be a no-win for you?"

Brad shakes his head. "Maybe. There will be arguments, and they could be lots of heat, little light. But that's not inevitable. Pastor, if we don't deal with it while it's on everyone's mind, it will be harder to address it the next time. And there *will* be a next time. I want to take the risk."

It's a gamble, but if he's willing to take it . . . "This is your call, Brad. For what it's worth, if you think you can handle a roomful of amped-up kids, I will trust you and back you completely. I think it's your moment."

"Thank you."

"I'm not Mordecai and you're not Esther, but the question still fits: 'Who knows but you have come to this place for such a time as this?'"

I don't go to the meeting. Brad and Melissa will be my ears, and I trust them. I know some of his mind here. Now, I'm seeing what I hoped to see: his heart.

CHAPTER EIGHTEEN
THIS IS MY WITNESS NOW

I t's after ten o'clock when Melissa unpacks a loud, long, and intense evening. Thirty-five youth and young adults pummeled Brad with the pent-up emotion of growing humans trying to make sense of it all. Brad, she said, was remarkably calm through most of the evening.

When I asked about the part of the evening not covered by "most," she was cautious. "Brad got pretty intense when people started preaching at him about what Black people should do. Some of them said they were, their word, 'tired' of feeling responsible for racism when it wasn't their fault. I won't say he snapped. But seriously, he got loud—not too loud—but he wouldn't let anyone interrupt. He talked like for ten minutes, and when he was done, the room got real quiet. Some kids got kinda teary."

"Do you think Brad went too far?" I don't think Brad would have—but perception is reality, and I want Melissa's sense of where "too far" begins for her peers.

"Personally, I think we had it coming. And we learned a lot. This is to me the best part . . . I think almost all of us realized we need this guy right now. Dad, I don't know what will happen to Brad if the grownups learn what he said. But you have to not let us lose him."

The next morning, I find an inbox twice as full as usual. Going through the emails, my screen is having a hissy fit. "reverse racism," "Brad-is-a-nice-guy-but," "my daughter/son/boyfriend felt attacked for something they didn't do," and on and on. But this is mixed with "this was fantastic!" "thank you for finding Brad!" and "the whole church needs to learn this." There are twenty-six phone messages. The most ominous: two that promised to bring this to the personnel committee. And we all know who chairs that group.

Brad arrives asking to talk, and once again, I welcome him in. "So—I got a quick report from Melissa. Tell me about the evening. Especially what you said, if you can."

"The conversation was everything you can imagine, and I won't try to detail it. I'll say this—of thirty-five people there, close to thirty said something, with three or four kids trying to dominate the conversation, mostly supportive of the police. But not all. By the way, Melissa's great. I mean it. She was vocal when it came to contradicting defenses of whiteness and white conduct toward minorities. She's done her homework. I can tell you what I said almost word for word. I've gone through this so many times over the years:

"'What would you do if you lived in a heavily-policed neighborhood where you have stop-and-frisk, harsh sentencing, and the risk of death for any perceived provocation (or none at all), where schools are falling apart, or no living-wage jobs nearby or public transportation to jobs farther out; where you're constantly viewed with suspicion, treated like a problem . . . how would that work for you?

"'What if you were told that the problems into which you were born (as were your parents before you and theirs before them) were _your_ fault and _your_ responsibility? What if your white neighbors gladly tell you what you're doing wrong, that you deserve poverty because you're lazy? Oh, and another thing white folk expect: never upset us. Be polite, and don't object to what we do—or don't do. Not that it will help you, it just makes it easy for us to ignore you, because we will, unless you upset us.'"

"Wow. I don't know what to say." I really don't.

"I wasn't intending to attack the kids with that, and I'm not attacking you, Pastor. But that's my lived reality."

Brad stops talking. After a moment, I respond. "You know that I've been wrestling with homelessness lately, right? Seems like we're now facing _two_ issues."

"If I may, Pastor Noel . . . no. We do not have two issues: racism plus homelessness. They are linked at their core. Start with this: half of the homeless are Black. _Half._ Far more than their share of the population. The same is true for incarcerated people. Add poverty. No health care. No mental health care. Joblessness. Homelessness. They are not separate "issues," because they all intersect." Brad leans across the space between us. "And the center of gravity to all of these things is how race bleeds into how we think and how we engineer public policy to favor one group over another."

We both catch our breath. Then quietly, he speaks before heading to his office. "One more thing. Basically, the kids were supportive. Some more than others, but you should know that First Community Church has some activists in the making. I don't know how wise it is for the pastor's kid to lead the charge, but your daughter's definitely the go-to in the group."

I think I'm proud of Melissa for that. I also think she will complicate my life.

It was a quieter-than-usual Friday dinner. It's my evening to cook, but tonight, with minds a thousand miles removed, we eat out. Beyond ordering our food, we've said virtually nothing. Plates have been cleared, and I would welcome some words. So would Melissa. She looks at me, and with a Mona Lisa smile, raises her hand. I nod.

"Something I think both of you should know . . ." She's searching for words, in unfamiliar territory. "We study things—'race relations' or 'civil rights,' but it's been cold, just facts and figures. That's not enough for me anymore. Seeing how it hurt Brad, it's personal now. I can't just let it go, and neither can a lot of my friends. We want to *do* something. Not sure what, but we're talking."

Trish asks what I also wonder. "What could you do? Personally, I mean." It would not be like Melissa to shrug something off.

"I might try to organize a march."

This is new. Then again, this is Melissa. I probe this notion of hers. "What, where, when, who?"

"Maybe outside school? On the square by the church? This is still a work in progress, Dad, Mom—hard to say who'll actually step up."

She stops, thinking. We give her time. "I think this is more spiritual than political for me. I ask myself how my faith plays into this . . . and how speaking out, marching, whatever I do in response to what happened—what happens all the time—this is how I love God and my neighbor." She pauses. Then, "This is my witness now."

We clergy offspring had a reputation for pushing against the pressure to be inoffensive. Marching in the streets, especially in this town, pushes that envelope. And yet, she's right to say that words are not enough.

While Trish drives us home, I think that we could be watching a birth, with our daughter as the midwife. Once inside the house, Trish speaks: "Just so you know, Melissa, we're behind you a hundred percent. I'm happy to help if you ask for it."

"I think this needs to be our thing, Mom."

Melissa is hearing a call as valid as my own. What's emerging isn't framed by people experienced enough to find the flaws in every new idea, and then do nothing. These are fresh, why-not-thinkers grounded in Gospel and deter- mination, assaulting a mountain and believing in their bones that it will begin to move. It happened half a century ago. Maybe it can happen again—in any case, I am proud of my daughter, and won't stand in her way.

I just don't want to be surprised. I hate it when something happens and I'm the last one to know.

CHAPTER NINETEEN
CRYING FOR CARL

I don't know why I'm going back to Sherman Jackson. I either find perverse pleasure in his contempt, or I need him to penetrate my well-insulated world. Also, I'm worried about the Grants. My efforts to find them in Chicago, northern Indiana, Milwaukee, Madison, and Rockford have failed. Maybe Sherman has some ideas. I spend part of my day off sampling the delicacies in Mr. Jackson's dining hall, as I ask Sherm about Lisa and Cherry.

"I'm sure you've been searching every shelter, hospital bed, jail cell, and underpass in Illinois, huh?"

"I take it you don't know."

"Good guess. Noel—may I call you by your first name? If someone wants to disappear, it's easy. Even if they don't want to disappear, they often do. The reality is that you may never see them again."

I change the subject. "So why are there so few permanent places for people on the street?"

"For starters, lots of these folk don't like the idea of permanence. Cramps their style."

"Yeah, but for the Grants, wouldn't something permanent be welcome?"

"Probably. And they're not unusual. Most people aren't homeless for long. Maybe a month, maybe more, but they're not permanently on the street as much as home-insecure. Some alternate between the street and someone's couch. But many of the people I work with would run in terror from anything with 'permanent' in the title."

"So give me a snapshot of the typical person you see, if there is a typical person."

"There isn't a 'typical' person in the unhoused world, Garraty. They aren't a category. These are complicated, multi-layered humans."

"OK. Sorry. Any common threads?"

Sherman shrugs. "They feel shut out by your world. Script it any way you want, but include poor, discouraged, and alienated, and you describe everyone I know. Some are victims of bad choices, but mainly, we have a housing crisis. If you're poor, you may wait a year, maybe two, maybe more for affordable housing. And that's after you've filled out more forms and encountered more bureaucracies than you can count.

"One in four renters spends half their income on rent. A million are evicted annually—not counting those evicted during the pandemic. Home ownership among young adults? The lowest in decades. We're *four million* homes short of the demand, and what exists is priced way beyond their resources. Four million workers commute three hours from the best housing they can afford. Some people with graduate degrees and good jobs sleep on a friend's couch or in their cars. That's why one in fourteen Americans has been homeless at some point."

"How many homeless are there? The—" Sherman interrupts. "Please try to *not* call them 'homeless!' They are human beings, just unable to secure an address. And I think especially you would admit that they are God's children."

"I know they are. I'd just like to know how many . . . *persons* have no roof over their head. The numbers I've seen are all over the place."

"No one really knows, Garraty, See, many of them avoid having anyone know much about them. You want numbers? Five million, maybe six, in the U.S. But that's not what you need to know. You *need* to know that twenty percent are families, and you know some folk like that, don't you? The Grants aren't just numbers in a category to you, are they?

"And eighty percent of those families—*families*, Garraty—are headed by a single woman, a Lisa Grant. Even I can't imagine what that's like. Kids trying to survive with guns, gangs, prostitutes, hostile cops, rats, using abandoned buildings for toilets, and a lot of them have an addict for a parent. How would you like to be a six-year-old in *that* world?" He throws his butter knife down on his plate in disgust.

"And guess how many people here are combat vets."

I don't know, but Sherman doesn't wait for me to admit it. Sherm's on a roll.

"Forty percent are veterans. Viet Nam. Desert Storm. Kosovo, Baghdad, Afghanistan—you name it. We teach them as little boys to respect life. When they grow up, we teach them how to be the world's most efficient killers, and they come back with blood on their souls and nightmares of the people they blew away. And if they can't handle the nightmares, the VA does what it can, I guess, with the pennies we give this chronically underfunded agency. They have good people there. VA doctors don't work there to get rich; they mostly care. They get it. But they can only do so much, so when we tell a veteran 'Thank you for your service' it rings hollow."

I toss out what I hear from a lot of people in my world. "Shouldn't the unhoused community, or the poor, be held accountable for self-destructive behavior?"

We eat in silence for a minute. Then Sherman speaks, but without the usual bluster. He's quoting Scripture. "And the Word became flesh, and dwelt among us."

"I've preached on that a few times." I have my own spin on "the Word in flesh," but I want to hear how Sherman unpacks it.

"I suggest that you, who claims to follow Jesus, re-frame the problem the way He did."

Sherman's voice loses its reflective tone, and he looks at me with fire. "When any so-called Jesus-follower sees what is crushing people, the proper response is to *follow* Jesus where Jesus always goes. Don't pontificate on how 'they' should get their crap together. You come here, dwell among us, get shot at like we do, be mugged, raped, ridiculed like we do, *die* like we do, and take your chances like the rest of us. Or nothing will change. *Nothing* will change."

He stops, sighs, and cuts a piece of ham, stabs it with his fork, and slides it into his mouth. I let it sink in for a minute. Then I offer what I've been thinking.

"I remember what you said about my church creating a place for people who need housing. I've read about tiny houses, furnished and available to homeless people. Could we build a kind of separate community—lots of security, educational facilities, childcare—"

"Garraty, I'll give you points for thinking. Here are some of the problems, and they're huge, maybe insurmountable. One: many of these people don't leave their problems at the door. They're mentally ill, mentally limited, or emotionally so unstable they can't be trusted to be on their own. Two: almost everyone here has some form of addiction. Many would bring that mess inside the gates."

I'm embarrassed that my notion is demolished in thirty seconds. "Guess it wasn't a very good idea, huh?"

"It's not bad, Garraty. Let it simmer. Keep thinking out of the box. Sooner or later, someone comes along with something that helps.

"But let me tell you what you could really do. You have influence. And the people you influence have influence. Make the white Christian community a player for the good of others. Stop using your clout to protect your privilege."

Sherm sits back and sighs, looking tired. "I just don't know, man. I dunno." He leans forward, looks me straight in the eye.

"One more thing—this is important. As bleak as their lives look, these people, despite living on the street, are *living* on the street, thriving in ways you and I can hardly imagine. Not just that—more of them than you realize are people of great faith. You think *you* love Jesus? He's their best friend. To them, He is marginalized and thrown away just like they are. Some of them, Garraty, really hear God talk to them. Doubt all you want, but I wouldn't argue the point if I were you. Their church may be a refrigerator box in an alley, but they pray, they believe, they speak of finding a half-empty box of corn flakes as a miracle, and dammit, out there, corn flakes *are* a miracle."

He looks around the room at his constantly changing flock of weary (but in this place, much honored) sheep. And for that moment there is a softness in his eyes, an unmistakable, gentle, love.

"The God who hears your soothing prayers on Sunday hears their cries for help, their rants against the system, the police, the whole world sometimes, and God listens, meets them where they are, embraces every rough edge, and delights in every one of them, Garraty, *delights* in giving them corn flakes, and calls us to give them far more than that.

"So whatever you come up with, Reverend, come here ready to partner with them, listen, learn, and walk with them—or stay home."

I've been taken to the woodshed again, but I actually feel better. Not much, but some.

I look around the room, and there's this lone individual, the only occupant of a table, facing the wall and hunched over his meal. Sherm looks over to where I'm looking. "Carl. Won't give his last name."

The name rings a bell, but I don't know why. Not yet, anyway.

"What's his problem?"

"He hasn't got a permanent address."

"I know—but what's his story?"

"That's a better question. Better, frankly, than asking what's wrong with someone, like a lot of you suburban types do."

I don't protest the jab. Jackson is like God in one respect: he's never lost an argument.

"Looks like he's got a drug problem."

"He does."

"Tried treatment?"

"Several times. Doing some 12-Step stuff now."

"Good."

"It won't work."

"Why?"

"Drugs aren't his only problem."

"What else?"

"He's Black."

"I can see that. So are most of the people in here."

"What you can't see—though everyone else in this room can spot it a mile away—is that he's got AIDS."

"Wow. That's tougher."

"And he's gay. Which is why many in this community won't touch him. A gay Black man with AIDS is about as welcome in my shelter as he would be in your pretty little white church. Drugs, poor, homeless, Black, dying of AIDS—none of the statistics give him a chance."

"Can I talk to him?"

"Be my guest."

"Sounds like you don't care about him."

His annoyance turns to anger. "Garraty—I *love* him. But in this business, empathy can eat you alive."

I'm not sure I agree with Sherman, nor am I sure what motivates me to talk with Carl. Maybe I'm trying to raise my stock in Jackson's eyes. Maybe I'm trying to prove something to myself. Maybe I actually care about this guy. Motives are funny things.

When Sherman says, "Carl's not crazy," I believe him. I walk across the room and sit down across from Carl. "Hi. Sherm told me your name's Carl. Mine's Noel, and—"

He looks up, glares at me, and resumes eating. Now I know why he's not interested in talking to me. He tried that once, not long ago, and I blew him off. I make a feeble attempt at feigning innocence.

"You come here often, Carl?"

He continues eating.

"Look, I don't want to bother you. I'd just like to get acquainted."

"Why?" A minor triumph: he talked.

"I used to come here a lot when I was going to school. Tried to help Sherm and the people here. I care, I guess."

"Great. What made you suddenly care?" Carl seems more interested in some horrid-looking macaroni and cheese than in this successful, arrogant, very white guy who suddenly is ready to treat him like a real person.

"So where do you go after you've eaten?"

"None of your business. I'd just as soon be left alone, OK?"

I surrender and retreat to Jackson's office just long enough to say goodbye. I'm thankful that he didn't ask me how my conversation with Carl went. He probably knows anyway, but hopefully won't discover that Carl and I have a history.

No one knows why Carl rejected the treatments that could extend his life. Carl himself may not know. He lives on the margins, not as much by choice as by the collective verdict of a world that disqualifies people like him from the pursuit of happiness. Perhaps Carl simply surrendered to that collective verdict as his destiny. Only God knows, really, and I suspect that God weeps.

At least Sherman's not laughing at me. If I had to guess, I'd guess he too is crying for Carl.

CHAPTER TWENTY
HAND IN THE COOKIE JAR

Brad catches me in the parking lot on our way into church. "Something I need to tell you, and it needs to be now."

"In my office?" Brad nods. We head for my office; I close the door.

"I'm listening." I'm also worrying. There are so many moving pieces to my life and work right now, and they all need to work together if I'm going to salvage this uncertain year for First Community Church, and for me. I don't need any surprises, especially from Brad.

"Pastor, I love working here. I love working with you. I love these kids. It should come as no surprise, though, that I'm getting some pushback over my race."

River Glen has hit some hard spots over me, but it's heartbreaking to see how Brad's color—and his willingness to address it—has been costly for both of us. The pushback reveals some intrinsic cracks in the congregation. But also, potential growing edges as well. A delicate topic, but I need to hear him out. "Tell me more."

"There are two things. One is implicit bias. We can work on that. Well, the church needs to work on that. But there's another piece. I'm finding that my heart is sometimes—many times—somewhere else. I'm drawn . . ."

He stops. He's struggling for the right words. Which is why I'm worrying.

"It's frankly a surprise that this, right here, is so right for me. It uses my gifts. It's a breath of fresh air to be in a smaller community, so close to open country. Still, I think that being here is clarifying that even though I've found joy in River Glen, at heart, I love Chicago. It's my hometown.

"Partly, I think, to be among people who look like me. There's a special kind of ministry that can happen there. It's rougher, more life-and-death, when people worry if their kids will come home tonight. Where young men like me are as likely to wind up in prison as they are to find a job. I hope to give First Community Church everything I've got. Still, at the same time, that other world energizes me too."

The look on Brad's face changes to that of a kid caught with his hand in the cookie jar. I'm sensing he revealed more than he wanted to. He's direct, so I follow suit. "So you're thinking that you won't be here very long?"

He pauses. "I have thought that, to be honest." He takes a deep breath. "My work here may be difficult, but it's also just beginning, and I want to follow through. Hopefully I can find a way to also minister to the city that I love—and draw our church, or at least its younger cohort, into working with me there. But it all depends on whether this church will still want me in six months, a year maybe. Right now, that's not clear."

I want to contest that, but Brad shifts gears. "OK. I maybe shouldn't have raised that now."

"Don't ever think you can't tell me where your heart is, Brad."

"Thanks. All right. Here's how I see . . . I'm still not used to saying 'Old First,' but anyway, what I see is that we are 'First Community Churches.' I see two or three, maybe more, sub-congregations with lives of their own. One of them, certainly, is made up of younger members, with their own values and networks. Another is, for lack of a better term, the white-collar cohort, defined by social status. There might be more, the older generation maybe. But this church holds all of them in a fairly happy tension, at least most of the time. Our job then in a conflicted time is to keep them from spinning away from each other. You and I are, right now, the pivot point for all this." He's right, I tell him. He's put into words what I've seen but not named.

"I hope we succeed, Brad. I hope we can sustain the 'happy tension' you talked about."

Brad pauses, like he's forming a response—the kind that takes this conversation in a new direction. "Funny thing, hope. Isn't it amazing how we use one word in two vastly different ways?"

"I assume you'll enlighten me . . ."

"There's hope as in 'I hope it doesn't rain on our picnic, but I'm not sure.' But there's hope in our faith that's more like *confidence*—that in whatever God is up to, God won't fail."

"OK, Brad. I like that. So which 'hope' applies to Old First's 'happy tension?'"

"Pastor, there are risks ahead. There are no guarantees that either your path or mine or the church's are what we envision. We need careful, reality-based planning with little room for error. But we may try so hard to be 'realistic' that we tame our capacity to imagine truly great outcomes. Even in the church. We have a long history of surrendering to what seems to be 'inevitable.'"

"So if I apply your logic to right here, right now: our plans to keep our jobs may or may not be realized, but Old First may become a thriving multi-cultural church?"

"Pastor, even *that* is too small a vision. Listen, Doctor King, Sojourner Truth, Harriet Tubman, all of them—the apostles for that matter— they all worked toward specific goals, knowing that visible outcomes are subject to uncertainty. But behind it all, they knew on some level that the ultimate prize was more than they had capacity to imagine—and yet for them, absolutely certain. They bet their lives on it.

"So should we, Pastor. Every time we have the audacity to pray 'your will be done on earth as it is in heaven,' we're claiming something both impossible and true anyway.

"And that should drive us to be rather stubborn." Brad pauses, looks away, smiles, then looks back at me, smiling. "Ever get a pebble in you sock?"

"Oh, yeah." I don't know where he's going with this, but what Brad describes is painfully real. "It's annoying, but you keep walking, and every step reminds you that it's still there, and I've paid the price for not taking off my shoe, taking off my sock, and saving myself from a blister."

"Exactly. Pastor, when people seem eager to settle for lesser outcomes, our job is to remind ourselves and the church of what we're called to do. And why. We do not let setback or even failure derail our hope—that God gets what God ultimately wants. We're stubborn, maybe even irritating—"

"Like that pebble."

"'Pebble?' Brother, we're a rock in their sock."

Once again, Brad amazes me. His faith is forged in a furnace that refines and clarifies more starkly than the privileged world which shaped me, and I learn from him what no seminary textbook offers.

This kind of hope is revolutionary—an insurrection that refuses to end in a tie, much less lose. And I hope I will not run from it.

CHAPTER TWENTY-ONE
THE INSURRECTION

I pull into an empty parking lot. Early Sunday morning, and my heart is singing. It may have something to do with how I spent the day before. Nothing in a minister's life has more moving parts than a wedding, and by the time the loving couple is saying "I do," we've navigated pre-marriage counseling, wedding planning, communicating with musicians, wedding coordinator, custodian . . . it takes a lot of people to marry someone.

And yesterday, we accomplished just that. I did my part reasonably well. But it wouldn't have happened without a few surprises—a delayed flight into O'Hare carrying the Maid of Honor, a predicted shower that turned into a fifteen-minute monsoon as guests arrived, and an unraveling seam on a wedding dress. My team, which at the last minute included Trish, the Calmer of Rattled Nerves, performed magnificently.

In the end, a nearly flawless wedding was followed by a reception that gave Noel and Trish an opportunity to prove that we can still dance. It didn't erase the horror of this week's shooting or the gathering of our younger members. But it was a gift of grace for me, balancing reality with the greater reality of hope.

I'm there early on Sundays, rehearsing my sermon in an empty sanctuary before the building comes to life. I hear people showing up—musicians, Church School teachers and the techie who prepares to stream the service. But there are more cars than usual. I look out the window: a couple dozen young adults and youth are huddled in the parking lot. Nothing on the calendar—did Brad forget to mention something? Melissa's there too, and she seems to be leading whatever is going on. My rehearsal may not happen just yet. I head to the door.

Melissa confronts me before I'm off the sidewalk. "Dad—this is our idea. I didn't tell you or Brad because we don't want either of you to be blamed for this. I know it's going to be controversial, but this is our statement, and we want to make it in our own way. Just head back inside. Please."

"What statement are you making?" I'm pretty sure I already know.

"We're responding to the shooting, and we want our church to know that." As she speaks, trunks and back seats are emptied of protest signs. Some support Brad. But not a few also say, "Justice for Gary Brown," "Jesus was a person of color too," even "Black Lives Matter." Which they are soon chanting, along with "This is what democracy looks like!" in front of our prestigious, traditional, respectable church, louder than the bell that rings at noon. Black lives may not matter to many in this mostly white town, but to a determined group of young adults, they had better matter to Old First.

My first instinct is: *Please, no.* This may not end well. It ratchets up the tension and could cement people's positions for and against, and in some cases against each other. It makes Brad's position more difficult, more fragile—mine too. And my daughter is one of the ringleaders of this . . . insurrection.

But this is already a critical moment. These kids are using the blunt instrument of public protest (though some may say they're using a sledgehammer to crush a mosquito) to confront deeply rooted bias. Whether it's Brad's future or mine, this is a moment of conscience for this faith community. What they are doing in our parking lot, a public witness in our overwhelmingly white community, may be a turning point. We may actually *need* this.

They picked the perfect Sunday. Next week, Palm Sunday, Brad is preaching. Protest then and it would have seemed choreographed. Picking this week set the stage beautifully.

I'm not going to stop this. On the contrary, while I have "deniability" by not knowing beforehand, I'm all in. I head back toward the office, smiling. Bring it on, people. Still on the margins power-wise, these kids can exert soft power through direct, unapologetic persuasion.

It's a frequent pattern in history, I muse. Those on the margins often become the mainstream. The ragtag disciples of Jesus built a worldwide faith, starting with little more than shameless witness to what seemed a foolish message that re-shaped history. Bill Gates and Steve Jobs were marginal people just a handful of years ago, weird dudes tinkering in their garages. But it hasn't taken long, really— neither Steve Jobs nor Bill Gates ever ruled the world, but their inventions run it.

The kids are handing out flyers, talking with arriving parishioners. This rattles the nerves of a small cadre of board and committee members who find me watching the insurrection. Dan Costello, chair of the trustee board, speaks first.

"Pastor, should we be worried about this?"

"Are you worried, Dan?"

"Yeah, a little. Maybe the kids should have asked us for permission—they're on church property, and we're supposed to approve—"

"Dan, I know." I'm sympathetic. Yes, they should have followed the *Scheduling Events on Church Property* guidelines, which warn that "applying for approval must be made at least twenty-one days prior to the event." Plus, there's the liability issue. Always, the liability issue. What if someone falls down. Will our insurer cover it?

Dan's standing next to me, looking at the protest while the rest of Dan's fellow leaders wait for him and their pastor to make this problem go away. Apparently thirty seconds of silence is too long. "OK, Pastor, I know it's difficult for you, so I'll be the bad guy and tell the kids to wrap it up." He steps forward. I put my hand on his arm and hold him back.

"I'm asking you not to. We can talk later, but this is way too important to interrupt."

"But—"

"I mean it, Dan. Frankly, I'm proud of them. Nobody's being hurt, and this could actually be a very good thing for us."

Dan's incredulous. "This can be a good thing?"

"This is witness. This is leadership. This is—these kids of ours, who we taught to love their neighbor and to be compassionate—they're *doing* it, peacefully and effectively. After all, it's got us talking, right?"

"But what if there's press coverage? What if they inadvertently block traffic and someone gets arrested?" Dan is clearly worried—he's nearly panicking. About nothing, I'm thinking.

"Dan—they're good kids. They've organized this so it won't spin out of control, and I've got their back. Don't shut them down."

He walks back to his peers. Out of the corner of my eye, I see some heads shaking. This will cost me. But policies sometimes are like pie crust: made to be broken.

People walking by stop to look. Occasionally one asks what's going on, and a conversation ensues. There aren't many people driving by on a Sunday morning, but those who do slow down, look—occasionally, someone honks and waves, apparently liking what they see.

Public witness. For maybe the first time in our history, First Community Church is declaring a bold Gospel call to set the captives free. We're speaking out. Whether we like it or not.

CHAPTER TWENTY-TWO
BAD NEWS

I t's midday Friday. Palm Sunday's coming. Next week's Holy Week, and it will be busy. Between now and Easter Sunday, I'm responsible for six services, and anything not directly related to them is in my "Do Later" pile.

But I still wonder about Lisa and Cherry. They remain lost to us, and while I may have little chance of success, I call someone who probably doesn't want to hear from me.

"Any word down your way about the Grants, Sherm?"

"Zero, and I'm not in the mood for conversation, Garraty. I'm having a very bad day."

In a place like his I can't imagine a good one. "What happened?"

"Carl died last night." I stare at the monitor, seeing but not seeing what's there.

"Sherm, I'm sorry. Wasn't expecting that. He didn't seem that sick."

"It wasn't AIDS that killed him—well, not exactly. Carl decided not to wait for the indignity of an AIDS death, so he checked out early. Hung himself under a bridge. His next of kin wants nothing to do with him."

Suddenly, a terrible thought: *I turned him away. What if . . .* Just as quickly, I brush it aside. *Don't go down that path, Garraty—there's nothing you could have done.* But I'm processing this long enough for Sherman to wonder if I'm still alive myself.

"You still there?"

"Sorry. Something about him really got to me. Who does his funeral?"

"Nobody. He's a ward of the county."

"So what happens?"

"Pauper's burial. A Cook County special."

"Sounds dreary."

"Garraty, there are simply too many of these to handle with much grace. People who never knew him give him a respectful but perfunctory burial. Then they move on to the next one and forget about him by the end of their shift."

"I'm sorry, Sherm."

"Yeah. Catch you later."

For half an hour, I think of nothing else. Even in death, Carl still has a chokehold on my soul. *I turned him away.* I pick up a book, and put it down. *But what could I have done?* I look at my Palm Sunday service, leaving it untouched long enough to awaken the screen saver. Carl. Burial. No funeral. It's just wrong.

"The poor you always have with you," Jesus said. We tend to interpret that fatalistically: there will always be poor people, so don't worry too much about them. That's *not* what Jesus meant. In saying "The poor you always have with you," Jesus could just as easily be pronouncing the sentence for our crime of tolerating deep poverty. It means at least this: the poor—and the moral obligation they place on us—cannot be evaded. Sherman prepares a table for any deeply wounded soul in the heart of a city, in the heart of a country that often wishes the poor would just disappear, leave, die, and not bother us.

I shouldn't care so much. This fixation on a dead transient—a dead, gay, inner-city transient fifty-plus miles away. A dead, gay, Black, inner-city transient in the county morgue, killed by a modern-day holocaust, with no one to love him or claim his body or mourn his passing. *There was nothing I could offer him. We don't have resources, expertise, food or lodging for people like that.* A precious child of God with an eternal soul. The least of the least.

But what if we *had* prepared for him, or Lisa and Cherry? What if we made space for them before they showed up on our doorstep? What if unexpected intrusions became opportunities to practice the love of the radical movement that has, some say, devolved into an institutional, self-preserving machine? What if the Carls of the world were embraced as siblings, as guests? Maybe it's here—not in members or dollars—that we validate our existence.

I call Sherm again, and when the call ends I make several more, while Sherm makes a couple he agrees to make. I have started something I don't know how I'll finish. Or even how I'll pay for it.

I had six services to prepare in the next nine days. I now have seven.

CHAPTER TWENTY-THREE
A DAY THE LORD HAS MADE

We begin Holy Week with Jesus' defiant entrance into Jerusalem the Sunday before His crucifixion. The events of that week testify to a visceral tension that put everyone on edge. Palm Sunday in River Glen may feel a lot like that.

I arrive early as usual and notice that the usually deserted town square is populated by a dissonant gathering. Not a lot of people, but most of them carry guns.

In front of the church, a River Glen police cruiser and two officers. Across the square, two cars and three pickups fly American flags. Several of the occupants in camo and body armor carry semi-automatic long guns. Others carry signs: "I back the badge" and "All lives matter" are among the tame ones. Last Sunday's protest was small but noticed, and now we face those who want to set the record straight. This will be an interesting morning at Old First.

I walk to the police car. "Are we expecting trouble?" The officer in the passenger seat smiles. "We don't think so. Just want to make sure."

The faithful begin arriving. Most of them cautiously enter the parking lot. I notice one, eventually two, who drive through the lot but don't stop. They'll skip church today. Others cluster on the sidewalk, looking out toward the street. For the first time I can remember, casual laughter is missing. Nobody shakes hands; conversations are brief. They want to get inside, where conversations are barely above a whisper. I wonder what they think of last week's protesters now.

We could observe this as Passion Sunday, with its more reflective tone, anticipating the events that led to Christ's death. But it's more upbeat, my worship committee says, to celebrate the "Triumphal" Entry. Old First has a host of leave-your-hands-off-me traditions surrounding children, processionals, festive hymns, and, of course, palms, so only a minister five minutes from retirement would dare challenge the day's theme.

As people arrive, some are unnerved by what they see and suggest canceling worship. A few, including parents of young children, go home. In an impromptu meeting among leaders, Garraty, Brad, and "those activist kids" are blamed for being divisive. But others defend them: "The division was already there," someone says, "in a society unwilling to face its history."

I won't tolerate canceling and assure folk that we have no reason to worry. "What we see," I suggest, "proves that we need to do what we're doing."

Most of the time, a parade commemorates a holiday. On Palm Sunday, the holiday commemorates a parade. Jesus, the gospels report, entered the city at its busiest time of year to the cheers of hopeful pilgrims and in full view of His critics, daring them to take Him on. That set in motion the events that would push them past the breaking point. He would pay for His audacity with His life.

Some who welcomed Him may have joined the mob on Thursday night and Friday morning. In that sense, "*Triumphal* Entry" seems dubious, but in the lexicon of Christian tradition, Triumphal it is, and we celebrate accordingly. Children lead the choir into the sanctuary, climaxing a parade that starts in the parking lot (rather than the town square, which is today a less-than-inviting space). There are more pickups now, slowly circling the square. Some have Confederate flags, one has a bumper sticker across the back of his F-150: "I believe in God, Guns, and Guts."

As the children march, they sing, accompanied by guitars and cymbals: "*This is the day, this is the day, that the Lord has made . . .*" When they enter the church, we join their singing with "*We will rejoice, we will rejoice, and be glad in it . . .*" The children circle the sanctuary, most waving palm branches while some distribute palms to the gathered faithful. The energy builds; the tension that began the morning eases, as for a joyful minute, it *is* a day God has made, and we *will* rejoice. The parade encircles the room.

The music stops, and I stand and read again the words we'd just been singing from Psalm 118, words that always lift my spirits: "This is the day the Lord has made; let us rejoice, and be glad in it!" Then I lead in a responsive Invitation to Worship, where I begin the alternating lines between pastor and congregation:

"What's the commotion? Why all the shouting?"
Who's this intruder, disturbing our peace?

"Why has He come here? We were contented."
But others, imprisoned, are seeking release.
"Bound by despair, alone and forgotten"
Years without number wasting away;
"Longing for someone with love and compassion"
Who would walk with them and show them the way.
"Today He arrives, and stands here among us."
Today, we rejoice; our Savior is here!
"But will we receive Him? Will He find welcome?"
We open our hearts to God-coming-near!

The organ hits full volume, and we sing "All Glory, Laud, and Honor."
There's a welcome, and a few notes about the week ahead. Then music
from the children's choir. A college-aged liturgist reads a longer rendering from
the Psalm that opened the service. I read Matthew's telling of the entry of Jesus
into the last and most turbulent week of His ministry. People have high hopes
for this Teacher, this Rabbi, whose reputation precedes Him. The choir sings
its anthem, up-tempo, celebratory. Then Brad preaches.

He wonders aloud why the reactions of people to Jesus' entry fade so
quickly as the week wears on. Never forget, he says, that less than a week later,
Jesus is executed in a heinous act of premeditated murder by the most respected
religious leaders in the land. There was cheering again, only this time, for the
death of the One some had welcomed just days before. Brad says this well. One
can feel the tension of ancient Jerusalem during that week.

"Did all those who called for His crucifixion," Brad asks rhetorically, "really
want him dead?" Probably not, he suggests. "But how many of us would have
the courage to stand up to the mob?"

With that, he makes a perfectly appropriate this-world comparison,
reminding the congregation of our nation's grim history with lynching—
thousands of African Americans tortured, shot, hung, burned, often by good
church-going Christians, many of whom were afraid to call out the hate and
venom on display—every bit as horrendous as on that fateful day in Jerusalem.
As he continues, he slides from eloquence to passion in the authentic tradition of
Black preaching, as if every word is fueled by knowing: *This happened to my people.*

I can feel some folk getting restless. I can already hear them saying, "How
dare he get political in church? Yeah, we know Palm Sunday led to Good Friday,
but we're used to the idea of Jesus being crucified. Wasn't that a good thing?

After all, it benefitted us! Why dredge up something as disturbing as lynching? It's in the past. Let sleeping dogs lie."

History matters—because history isn't over. This morning's counter-demonstration proves that the stubborn ethos of the Confederacy survives even in places that once shed blood to defeat it. Places like River Glen, Illinois.

"Would we stand firm today?" he asks. "Or are our convictions all too often like sandcastles, eroded by the slightest wind or wave?"

Brad ends by asking us, "What would we do if Jesus entered River Glen today? Would we welcome Him? Would we even recognize Him?"

Toward the end of the service, I share our prayer concerns, concluding with one of my own.

"A couple months ago, I asked you to pray for a man named Carl. Thank you for praying. I wish I could report that because of our prayers, Carl was healed. Carl died this week in Chicago of complications related to AIDS. He has no family.

"I know that Carl never worshiped with us, but I have asked to officiate his burial. We're told that if we reach out to the least of Christ's brothers or sisters, we're doing it to Him. I am inviting you to attend if you can the funeral of a man you never knew, because he deserves at least to be mourned as a child of God."

Even if some of them come, I don't know why I'm asking them to do this. Carl won't know, so who benefits? I will. And Old First may benefit as well. This may thaw a frozen heart or two.

Then I lead in the Pastoral Prayer. But for some reason, I pay less attention to the congregation who hears this prayer and more to the God who already knows what overflows from my heart in recent weeks.

I end with, "As those who preach One who emptied Himself until only His love was left, may we not leave this earth with love left over, unused. May we practice for the day when your realm comes, by living in ways that at least dimly reflect it. In the name of Jesus, who taught us to pray, 'Our Father, who art in heaven . . .'"

No one thanks me at the door today. They affirm Brad—at least, most of them. The best I get are polite formalities. I suspect Brad's sermon may have been inadequately comforting. And I may have been just a bit too forceful in raising up Carl's death. *Thanks, Pastor, for raining on our nice Palm Sunday parade.*

CHAPTER TWENTY-FOUR
HOLY WEEK

On Tuesday morning I head to Sunrise Coffee for a twenty-four-ounce black coffee and a bagel. At the last minute I decide it's to go—much to the surprise of the barista who knows me as a talkative eat-in customer. I head to the office imagining a myriad of possible outcomes Brad-wise, not all of them good for my church, for Brad, or for me. The bagel's long gone, the remaining coffee cold, while I look blankly at the email on my screen—the one that greeted me when I checked my phone before getting out of bed.

I'm the only one here. At seven-thirty, no one's likely to disturb me, and I would love another hour to sort this out. There have been alarms in the background noise of the office, a sense of foreboding that I couldn't shake. *Something isn't right. Something just isn't right.* I've learned that those feelings can be what I label (often in retrospect, and not in jest) "nudges of the Spirit." In my theology and experience, God didn't finish speaking 2,000 years ago. There is still a Voice, and I'm wise not to ignore it until I'm sure it's just me, and not something—Someone—more.

This morning, I know why.

> Dear Rev. Garraty,
> This is a difficult note to write, and I regret the need to burden you with this during Holy Week. I have taken time to reflect on my experience at Old First. Some of this won't be news to you, but you may not be aware of much of what I need to outline here.
> Being a person of color in a nearly all-white congregation presents inherent challenges. I understood that when I pondered a call to First Community Church. In retrospect, I wonder if the people

understood it, or assumed that merely calling a Black man to serve here proved the absence of racial bias. It grieves me to say this, but I think this includes you.

You have been genuine in your desire to bridge the divide that has separated Black and white people. So have many in the congregation, especially among its youth. But the fact remains: I have been subjected to implicit (and at times explicit) bias during my short tenure.

In conversations with adult youth sponsors, there has been pushback against proposals to discuss racism with the youth. In our music ministry, I've offered the rich heritage of African-American spirituals, and encouraged the incorporation of contemporary Black music—rap, hip-hop, and more—in both worship and youth ministries. It has been almost always resisted, usually flatly rejected as not fitting "our tastes here."

In social settings, I've often been asked for my perspective on race in America, or in River Glen. While I've occasionally interjected my understanding on matters of race, I've been reticent to offer unsolicited views. When I did, I've been the recipient of contradictory opinions, often being interrupted, even lectured on what I should think.

Several River Glen church members have called, emailed, or confronted me, urging me to back off what I believe are my core convictions about race, racial justice, and the Gospel's response to racism in all its forms.

I have tried, Pastor. But though I truly want to continue serving people I have come to love, I question whether I should continue to serve here. I believe I am facing a hostile working environment, due in large part to the fact that I am a proud African-American man, a proud African-American Christian, and that is threatening to many, perhaps the majority, in the church family.

I look forward to an open, respectful, and honest conversation about these matters.

Thank you.

I draw several conclusions. One: Brad isn't making this up. Two: Brad's heart is breaking. Three: This isn't just Brad talking. I have no doubt he wrote this and meant every word, but it doesn't fit his usual writing style. He's organized and concise, but there's a formality that tells me that someone was looking over his shoulder as he wrote. Then I remember that his sister Molly is an attorney. The phrase "hostile working environment" bears the mark of legal jargon. Four: If this is how Brad Davis is being treated, I'd have a hard time defending the church should he take legal action. I'd want justice to prevail, and when an individual is being unfairly treated by an institution, I lean toward the individual. Five: I am part of the problem. Six: I pray it can be resolved outside a courtroom.

I schedule a meeting with a handful of church leaders and a few others for what I hope can be a grace-driven, healing response.

Hollywood couldn't have scripted a more perfect pauper's burial. Two local news outlets show up. A cold spring rain adds to the mood. I had hoped for a crowd, maybe a hundred people honoring the memory of a man born for a better fate than this one. Even fifty would have made a statement. But here we stand: eight parishioners, one minister, one director of a homeless shelter, a county burial detail busy elsewhere and behind schedule, and two disinterested journalists who hope this dreary assignment proves worth their time. Maybe I'll be on the nightly news. My fifteen seconds of fame.

I need to write a thank-you to the eight members who showed up. Whether for me or for Carl, it was a labor of love, and I love them for it. But still . . . eight people. Yet they came, on a dreary day in the middle of the week, for someone they did not know. I ask myself if I would have driven into the city for an anonymous unhoused man, rather than staying warm and dry at home. Or would I have excused my indifference? He made poor choices. He ran from his problems. He was gay. He had AIDS. He was a junkie, mentally ill, a loser, a lost cause.

Yet the faithful from Old First, the funeral director, Sherman, and I, stand under the shelter by Carl's soon-to-be-filled grave. Through no fault of their own, the crew tasked with bringing Carl's casket to the open grave isn't here. A prior service for a Viet Nam veteran can't commence until the honor guard arrives. Without the crew to carry Carl to his resting place, I wonder how long it will be before we can start. Sherman decides that we'll start now.

"Garraty—let's do this." He looks toward the hearse twenty-five yards away and in the rain. He turns back toward us and says with Sherman Jackson authority: "People, we need some help carrying the casket."

I begin to say "Gentlemen"—but I realize that my eight parishioners are five women and three men, all older than I am. This is not promising, but I hope that they are a deep enough talent pool despite their age. So I amend my almost-uttered request: "Friends, could any of you help us as pallbearers?"

Several of the women whisper; two of them start walking into the rain. One of the others points to her husband, who joins her. That makes six: three women, three men, including Sherm and me. Make that seven. Harry, eighty-something and more fragile than he'll admit, walks my way. Unsure that he could carry the weight on the rain-soaked earth, I suggest Harry take the lead at the front; Sherman and I will make sure that our end of the casket isn't dependent on Harry's questionable strength. We approach the remains of Carl, child of God. These members of Old First, at ages where they shouldn't be lifting things, carry Carl across soft, wet ground. Harry sees a small lake between us and the grave; he guides us wisely in a clockwise detour around the left of the water. Our shoes and the cuffs of our slacks will require attending to when we get home. But Carl is gently lifted above the earth, before being lowered into it, and I am honored to be among the saints who came and carried. Nine people, only two of whom knew him, took the time to honor him. How is that not love?

I begin: "We gather to honor God by honoring this man who was God's precious, much-beloved child. He was someone's son, brother, friend, a man for whom Christ died, embraced in God's unbreakable grace and love."

I've officiated at funerals for people I knew as friends, for members of my own family, and never been overcome by emotion. But I am grieving a man I barely knew. Could it be because I love him? Love: sometimes foreign to my professional life. But here, today, I never knew him, and I'm feeling the loss of a man I could have known.

The God I worship pitches heaven's tent in places I never wanted to go. If I entertain going to places I've always avoided among people I've not wanted to know, Someone else is the Force driving this reluctant lover of the unloved. No one except for Sherman wanted to "shepherd" Carl. I guess shepherds like me prefer our sheep spotless—or pretending to be. Carl had one advantage: he had no pretense left. *Let the children come to me*, Jesus said. Was not Carl a bruised, broken child?

Sherm concludes the service with an impromptu prayer and benediction better than any I could have spoken. We walk away saying nothing until we're in the car and out of the rain. My parishioners drive away, and the journalists leave without speaking to me, and for that I'm grateful. I'm especially grateful for those eight saints from River Glen. We witness the casket slowly settle into the ground, awaiting the backhoe that will push the dirt into place.

"So, Garraty, what you gonna say on Good Friday?"

Good question. Jackson sees the breaking of something hard and brittle in me. So Sherman acts like Sherman, which is like a shark to blood. He's driving home a point. *How could anything done inside your warm and dry church match this?*

Yeah, Sherman Jackson, I see. Everyone thinks it's Wednesday, but I know better.

"As far as I'm concerned, *this* is my Good Friday."

On the evening of Wednesday in Holy Week, while the choir rehearses in the background, we convene a hastily arranged meeting. Most of our personnel committee meetings are benign. With our staff, these meetings are usually a love fest. This time, we have guests from our denomination's clergy oversight team and our church's legal counsel. They, along with Pete Harris, the pastor-parish relations committee chair, are the only ones who know, but that will soon change. There is water at the table, and copies of the email I received from Brad Davis. Pete introduces the church's attorney and turns the meeting over to me. I get to the point. "Monday, I received a note from Brad Davis." I ask them to read it, and let it sink in for a moment. No one speaks.

"I've consulted with our guests, and we all agree that this is serious and potentially litigious."

Mike Curillo leans forward. He's livid. "This could ruin First Church."

The attorney responds: "Mike, it could have long-term implications, but we don't know that yet, and we can't afford to react."

Curillo isn't satisfied. "Just the allegations could tear First Church apart. Do you realize what you've unleashed, Pastor?"

"Believe me, Mike, I take no pleasure in this."

Mike presses—it seems that I'm more in his sights than Brad is. "You're head of staff. How could you not see this coming? How could it have deteriorated to this point without your intervention long before putting us all at risk of being sued?

"Precisely because I share your concern, Mike. I had my ear to the ground, or at least genuinely thought so. This did not emerge until just the last few days."

"Sounds like mismanagement to me, people."

Our attorney addresses Mike. "Mr. Curillo, the issue before us is our response to Brad's email. Note that this was more of a warning rather than a formal accusation. Later, we can talk about what was done before, but we have options short of litigation. Right now, we need a united, strong response." Thank you, legal counsel. But I suspect this will come back to haunt us.

The meeting ends with an agreement to invite Brad to a follow-up meeting on Friday. Of all days, Good Friday. With input from our attorney, I will draft a response to present to Brad. In this already intense week, I will need something like a miracle.

CHAPTER TWENTY-FIVE
THE TOWEL AND BASIN

O n a Thursday 2,000 years ago, love was defined. And it is unbearably hard. The "maundy" in Maundy Thursday comes from an archaic Latin word for something like "mandate." It recalls that while Jesus uttered very few explicit mandates (people already carried a crushing load of them), He did utter this one: *Love one another as I have loved you.* John's Gospel tells us that on the night before His crucifixion, Jesus modeled the love in question by washing the disciples' dirty and conflicted feet. I will reprise that model tonight.

I start with something Jesus was passionate about:

"In Jesus' final prayer, He asked that we would be 'one.' Jesus knew that we would argue, and we would divide. And we have. And we will. But our first calling and greatest obligation is to love, and to see Christ in each other. No matter our point of view—we are still one body, one community, one family."

That week began with defiance—Jesus, disloyal to Imperial Rome, publicly mocked power itself. When Herod would ride pompously into Jerusalem on a white horse, Jesus rode into the Holy City on an ass. Exposing the hypocrisy of the religious elite, He trashed the Temple's marketplace, up-ending tables, spilling cash and goods across the stone-paved floor. Day after day of drama Hollywood could never match, led to Jesus' trial, beating, and torturous death.

We wish we knew more. We'd love one complete, satisfying narrative. What we have are four distinct re-tellings. Yet they all converge on Thursday. It seems quieter, the eye of the hurricane. But at that first Last Supper, Jesus openly identified what was mere hours away: Judas would betray, Peter would deny, and that whole motley crew would cut and run (except for some women who dared to witness the crucifixion—perhaps the only real heroes on that horrid day).

In the midst of that unpromising mess, He told us precisely what love is.

"A new commandment: Love one another as I have loved you." His followers understood that as 'a new *commandment,*' love stands on equal ground with even the Ten Commandments, not merely an additional eleventh mandate, but a gathering of *all* the ancient laws into one new, overarching Law of Love. That is the template for the love Jesus expects from *us.*

The "new" part? . . . *as I have loved you.* No exclusions, no conditions. Love without sentimentality, without the false love that's blind to shortcomings. Jesus sees them in all their shameful, cowardly, and vulgar inadequacy and washes their filthy feet hours before He is executed—and submits to it explicitly *for* them, and for us. Love? All in, no exceptions, impossible to break, pouring all He had including life itself into these hopeless, clueless, religious failures.

"Love your neighbor as yourself" seems easy; some people are lovable. Some are so much like us that when we love them, it's like loving ourselves. But we also know another parallel but more disturbing command: "Love your enemy." In fact, Jesus doubles down on enemy-love: Pray for them; do good to them, He mandates. Turn the other cheek; go the second mile. When they curse you—*bless* them.

That distresses us. So we become religious lawyers, looking for loopholes. War must be an exception; how can we love someone we're shooting at? Didn't St. Augustine give us a template for killing each other appropriately? Nor, we protest, do we have to love someone who breaks into our home, terrorizes and robs us. No love for criminals, and thank God we can execute the worst ones. And if they belong to *that* political party? Take them down. Paint them as monsters. Jesus must have never thought of "those people." If we look long enough into scripture, we can find verses here and there to support—we insist—our exceptions, diluting His hopelessly idealistic, can't-be-serious suggestion. Or if necessary, gutting it altogether.

Yet this love above all, not some lesser timid imitation, must define them and us. Because even those hopeless failures—and in time, ourselves—are beloved children of un-boundaried grace, filled with our Master's own Spirit, who will turn history around.

At least in the first four decades-plus of my life, that love has not described me very much. Even now, I can't imagine loving anyone outside my family that way. Do we, in our relative wealth and comfort, find that we simply have too much to lose to love like that? Including love for the Mike Curillo's of the world? Do we ask: What will I get in return? Will this love make me happy? And can I stop loving if it doesn't?

Maybe that "love" isn't enough anymore.

After Communion, I wash the feet of the willing. Folk who wish to partici-
pate will remove shoes and socks and sit in front of half a dozen pre-positioned
bowls and towels, where I will kneel before them and simply wet their feet and
gently dry them. It's intimate, even cringe-worthy for some of us to have our
feet seen, and especially touched. It's also what Jesus literally told us to do, as a
reminder of our true stance before others, friend and family alike.

Among the two dozen or so who come, there are a few leaders: John, the
council president, Brad Davis, and at the last second, Mike Curillo. There
are two people between Mike and me when he takes his place. It is difficult to
concentrate on these two precious souls before I move to the feet belonging
to Mike. I'm hopeful. I try to not look him in the eye. I'm aware of the irony,
kneeling before this person with whom I have clashed. Still, I wash and dry
his feet. There's no eye contact, no smile. He stands and walks away, carrying
his shoes and socks toward the empty front pew. I try not to interpret what just
happened.

I lead worship tonight in a multi-million-dollar church with the finest
stained glass and woodwork in town, filled with music that's at the pinnacle
of art and performance—and I talk about the love of God shown in Jesus.
But it's very possible that the greatest demonstrations of this costly love may
be elsewhere: where ordinary people risk their lives to bring medicine in and
refugees out of war zones. In a hospice room where a soon-to-be-widowed
man wipes the brow of his comatose life partner. Where a single mother of a
profoundly disabled child cares for her year after year after year. Do we find
that love lived out, and not merely discussed, *here?*

Meanwhile "Jesus," St. John says, "loved them to the end."

CHAPTER TWENTY-SIX
ULTIMATUM

I simply argue that the cross should be raised again at the centre of the marketplace as well as on the steeple of the church. I am recovering the claim that Jesus was not crucified in a cathedral between two candles, but on a cross between two thieves; on the town garbage heap; at a crossroads so cosmopolitan that they had to write His title in Hebrew and in Latin and in Greek . . . at the kind of place where cynics talk smut, and thieves curse, and soldiers gamble. Because that is where He died. And that is what He died about.

—George F. McLeod, *Only One Way Left*

On the afternoon when Christians around the world recall the crucifixion, I meet with Brad Davis with our attorney and the personnel chair at my side. This gathering won't be the last; there are many moving parts on our journey to learn and un-learn, to discover how we relinquish our claim to an innocent whiteness.

I have drafted what our counsel considers an acceptable start along the way: a mutual understanding between Brad Davis and his employer that his call to Old First will be honored, his position among us secure, and that we will not impose on him conditions or expectations beyond those in his signed call covenant. This is on us, not Brad.

After a prayer I take a deep breath, and I begin.

"Brad, I have no reason to doubt that what you described is your authentic experience among us. It breaks my heart to think that we could inflict harm on someone we love, but I know that it can happen. I'm guilty of inflicting pain; I have done so with more than one person in this room. It grieves me.

"I am committed to listening, learning, and seeking clarity. I still believe in your ministry here. I think we all do. You've read our response to your note; I would like to first hear from you."

I expect some pushback from the lawyer, perhaps, or from Mike. I'm surprised; neither seems eager to speak. After a few seconds, Brad takes the floor.

"Thank you, Pastor. This is a good start. But this road is longer than you may know. Old First needs to understand that half a millennium of history built the gulf between us, no matter how well-meaning we may be. It would be easy to say, 'Brad, tell us what we need to know.' But it does not work that way. To be blunt: you need to do your own homework. I can't be your teacher. You need to tap the best resources you can find in order to understand how firmly whiteness is rooted in our country at every level, including the church. Our faith does not grant us immunity. We speak of influencing the world around us, but the world influences us too. It's like having an accent: we carry the stamp of our history, consciously or not.

"This will be costly. Including, perhaps, costing Old First some members. But you cannot compromise the truth to please everyone."

Now, Mike speaks. "I'd like to know, Pastor Garraty, if all this is true, why didn't we know this before now? Did you or did you not do your due diligence in preparing us for bringing a person of color into an admittedly white church? Shouldn't you have known, Sir?"

The attorney's not happy with this, and tries to rein things in. "Let's stay focused on our response to Mr. Davis' letter, Mr. Currillo." Good advice, but I can't let Mike's question linger unaddressed.

"It's OK. Mike, you're right. I should have known more than I did. I assumed that sincerity and good will would be a sufficient guide. And we were wrong. But I think we're ready to learn. In fact, I'm sure of it. I know I am."

"I don't share your confidence." Mike says. But then his tone shifts in a way I've not seen in him before. "I hope you're right. I'd like to see this work."

"This *is* asking a lot," I acknowledge. "But we've met challenges before."

The attorney again: "Mr. Davis: Are you hearing anything that eases your concerns?"

Brad is silent for a few seconds. Then, "Somewhat, yes. Please know that my letter was not a threat. I needed to be heard. But I also need to see concrete steps. That won't be easy. But it's not negotiable, gentlemen. And I don't think it's too much to ask."

The attorney looks my way. "Pastor—I'm sensing the start of a path forward. How do you see this playing out in the near term?"

I've thought about this and offer what I hope can walk us back from the edge. "A couple of things. One: I will speak to matters of justice in my own voice—sermons included. Also, I'll build a working group to guide a whole-church look at race. Brad's right, there will be opposition. Mostly, I think, discomfort, fear perhaps. I know because I've personally been resistant to looking at my own bias, but there's no longer the option of ignoring this. My goal: buy-in from the First Community family across the board."

The attorney addresses Brad. "If this happens, would you be satisfied?"

Brad knows that his answer could pivot the future one way or the other. "I will be as supportive as I can be," Brad says. "But know this: If this church wants to be part of the answer to a racially divided world, it will take more than just effort. It will have to be Spirit-driven and Spirit sustained—sustained, because it may never reach a tidy end point. It will take a miracle. But miracles happen."

When we gather on Good Friday or any other day, we ought to be as open as we can be. Maybe this service really should be in the town square, stopping traffic, disrupting business as usual, *life* as usual. The Gospel is not captive to a church. It is for offices and street corners, wedding chapels and junkyards, studios and machine shops, mansions and refugee camps with mud for streets. The message especially of this day is for all who will hear. We do not hasten to Easter. This day must exhaust its message first.

Tonight I will lift up a part of the message we often overlook. For 2,000 years, Christians have traced their spiritual heritage through Mary, this Palestinian peasant who is the mother of our Savior. Parents long to be with their children in pain. Astonishingly, Mary is present at the crucifixion, a dangerous place for the mother of a convicted and soon-to-be-executed criminal. Mary is kindred to mothers whose children are in the ICU, or fathers with no food for their starving families, or parents in refugee camps or on our streets who have dreams for their children, but who must watch their children suffer tonight. I count Lisa Grant, wherever she is, among them.

Mary knows that pain. I cannot imagine watching your child die, yet she stood watch that horrid afternoon, while her Son bore our griefs and carried our sorrows.

CHAPTER TWENTY-SEVEN
SEEKING SABBATH

Those who say, "I love God," and hate their
brothers or sisters, are liars; for those who do not love a
brother or sister whom they have seen, cannot love God
whom they have not seen.

—1 John 4:20 (NRSV)

Holy Saturday began on a promising note. Dad is here. He will have a part in tomorrow's service. More than that, I may need his strong shoulders. I came home last night to a refuge. Trish met me at the door, said nothing, took my hand and walked me into the family room. There were few lights, no music, just the two of us. This woman who knows me intimately gently stroked my shoulder, waiting for me to speak but letting me remain in my thoughts.

On her own initiative, Melissa had a friend take her to a movie. Dad was busy at the basement workbench doing something that didn't really need to be done; I suspect his instincts told him not to force a conversation. Each in their own way surrounded their son, father, and husband with quiet and gentle grace.

Saturday breakfast is almost funeral-like. You've walked with me through these last days, and you know the state of my soul. Thankfully, no one asks questions. They know that I'm not ready for tomorrow. I play the confidence card as well as I can, but I excuse myself as soon as the dishes are cleared from the table and head to the office to work on Sunday's message. Or try to.

Easter is not easy for preachers in the best of times. Our greatest story tests our faith's credibility. It defies what we think we know about life—that those we have lost are not coming back. To preach the rising of the Christ to a well-educated crowd is a tall order, and in my current state may be out of reach.

While reading the resurrection story on Monday, the word "garden" caught my attention. Jesus was buried in a garden tomb. On Thursday night, Jesus took His disciples to a quiet place to pray, also, a garden. Mary Magdalene is the first person to talk to the risen Jesus. Where? Well, she mistakes Him for a gardener. Then there's the Garden of Eden and a host of garden-like references peppering the biblical narratives—is something afoot here? I wondered: *Where are we planted?* But in the end, nothing came. And that's where on this Sabbath day I find myself.

Defeated, I'm home for lunch, in no mood for chatter. I sense Trish looking toward my father, who nods once. Seems they've been talking, conspiring, really. Dad breaks the silence. "Son—can we talk?"

I surrender. "Maybe some fresh air?" Dad agrees; we head outside.

"Dad, I'm sorry, but I'm not ready for tomorrow. Having trouble concentrating."

"Not ready to preach, or does it go deeper than writer's block?"

"Deeper, but I'm not sure why. Fatigue maybe. A hard week—I'm sure you know some of that from Trish."

"She filled me in. I don't envy you right now. A crisis surrounding your associate, your ongoing debates with some lay leaders . . . I don't need to know the details. I'm sure confidentiality limits what you can say. She told me you had an unusual funeral."

"I don't know which of those was the more difficult, but the funeral hit me, and hard."

Dad's quiet for a long minute. "You're grieving. You remind me of what I was like when your mother died."

He's right. I am grieving Carl. He was my brother—I lost a *brother* under that overpass. I don't think tomorrow can resolve itself until I pay attention to that loss. I don't say that to Dad. I'm not ready to unpack it with him until I sort it out for myself. "I need to get back to the office, Dad."

"After a week like this, I wonder if you'll find anything there."

"I'm not going to ask you to fill in, if you were thinking that."

"I was not, and I would have said no if you'd asked. Noel, I know you, and I trust your gifts. If you have to stand up there tomorrow morning and wing it—I really think you'd be OK. You'll get energy from the gathered faithful that you're not feeling now. Plus, I'm old school—I really think the Holy Spirit shows up when we need help.

"Here's what I will say: Prepared or not, don't go back to church today. It's a Sabbath. Honor this day as such. You're clearly in no place to be creative—so don't try. Rest. Enjoy your family. I doubt that the disciples were very productive on that first Saturday after their world imploded. Why should you be any better?"

After a low-key afternoon filled with a jigsaw puzzle and an innocuous documentary about wildlife someplace far, far away, I sneak away to my study, carved out of a dormer in what once was our attic. There's a guest suite behind me: bedroom, bath, stairway, and open area (a play space for the grandchildren we hope for). Then there's my office. If you walk in, you'll see my back; I prefer my view to be through the west-facing window. The ceiling's peak is lower here, dropping off quickly on either side. When walking around my desk to my reading chair and lamp, I have to lean a bit to avoid the drywall. Desk, chair, lamp, reading chair, wireless speakers, and a low row of books—welcome to my sanctuary, where I find myself holding a one-way conversation with my late brother.

Carl . . . I am grieving your death. The funerals I usually conduct—like Edward Kaskey's—are comfort-giving celebrations of lives well lived. But no one is saying that about you, my brother. Your death wasn't one of those "good" deaths, nor do we think that you did your best. No—we have our judgments, our opinions, our disapproval of the choices you made. I'm sorry, but you were unworthy. Yours was not a good death.

But how do we know that you didn't do the best you could? Did we forget the headwinds you faced, the limited welcome we offered you as a Black, gay, addicted, and sick man? We disrespected you; we dismissed everything about you. Even your body failed you as we stood by and watched.

Yes, you found—or were found by—Sherman Jackson and perhaps others who did all they could to undo our indifference. But *we* should have been there—*I* could have been there—and I chose deliberately not to.

I am grieving your death and what I know of your life. I am grieving what the world that has been so good to me did to you. We despised you and let you disintegrate right before our eyes. I despised you in my presence when you asked for my help—and I counted you unworthy. I closed my heart to you.

Your death is not the only cause of my grief. I grieve what I have become, dear brother. I talk routinely about love and hope and Jesus, but I'm also capable of closing my heart to a precious and beloved child of the same Creator who gave us both breath and life, and kinship. And I did that based on a few seconds—seconds!—of first impression, when what little I saw in you reinforced my already-present biases.

I helped to kill you, my brother, and I am sorry.

CHAPTER TWENTY-EIGHT
EASTER

As Easter dawns, the sun is nowhere to be found. I haven't slept. The recycle bin near my desk gives witness to my failure to find my voice. This void is virgin territory. I thought I had an Easter sermon. But that was Monday. I need some spark, something to offer a congregation needing hope as much as I do. The time when I need it is barely four hours away.

Old First mercifully does not hold an Easter sunrise service. But I re-read the local weekly for churches holding one. Episcopal—check. Lutheran—check. Methodist—nope. Presbyterian—yes. Several good choices. Unfortunately, led by pastors I know, and today I seek anonymity. I know, it sounds crazy.

Community of Hope, about whom I know almost nothing, holds a sunrise service in Forest Park's amphitheater. New church start, about three months old. Independent, on the contemporary side I'm told. But we don't know each other, so Community of Hope it is. I shower, dress, whisper to Trish that I'm attending a sunrise service and try to leave the room before she wakes up enough to ask what on earth I'm thinking. Instead, I hear her say something I didn't expect: "I hope it feeds your soul, Noel. Love you."

The praise band starts some pre-service music; it's contemporary all right. Good drummer, using bongos and a box drum—maybe a full set awaits the later service in their rented worship space. Three acoustic guitars, decent but not really familiar with each other, so it's rough. Two on vocals, male and female, one is clearly the band leader or the pastor—won't know until they identify themselves. Not great singers, but it's ten minutes to six in the morning, so I applaud their efforts.

I stand atop of the grassy semi-circle around the band shell on a chilly rise overlooking our small lake. The sky to the east is overcast with lingering mists from an overnight shower. I see about fifty worshippers, mostly young but some heads are grey; definitely come-as-you-are. I'm the only one with a tie, and I wonder why I bothered. Several invite me in closer. I smile and shake my head. Everyone's disappointed by not seeing a sunrise, but the clouds match my mood on this resurrection morning. The tomb isn't empty yet. The stone remains in place, and I'm begging God to roll it away, or I may end this day feeling barely more triumphant.

There's no liturgy, just a welcome before we sing a song I don't know. Not specifically Easter-like, but upbeat and catchy despite lacking the refinement I'm used to. Their voices occasionally hit a note that I'm not sure exists.

But why am I being a critic? They owe me nothing. I'm the one crashing this party. It's six in the morning, these people clearly love Jesus and each other, and they're enjoying their first-ever sunrise service. I may not be in a clapping mood, but while my hands are firmly thrust into pockets, I pick up the tune, albeit without enthusiasm.

The band leader isn't the pastor, who steps out of the crowd at the foot of the stage. He takes a hand-held mic and after some light-hearted comments about the service later this morning, reads the resurrection story out of John and begins preaching.

I suppose you *think* you know how this turns out: at the last minute, the sun miraculously bursts through the clouds and this exhausted, crumbling minister is transformed with the Good News that Christ is risen, and filled with the joy of Easter, he can't wait to tell his congregation that all will be well. Hallelujah.

That only happens in novels, people. Bad ones at that.

The reality is that at 6:33 a.m., the precise astronomical sunrise comes and goes with the sun nowhere to be seen. And by 6:45 a.m., I leave pretty much as I came, still desperate for some thread of hope, some sliver of inspiration—even some caffeine.

In fairness, there's a glow in the sky. Not enough to say, "There it is—the sun!" Just a hint of orange . . .

I drive away replaying something this rookie preacher said. He noted that yes, the resurrection of Jesus Christ is the core of Christian belief and is affirmed in all four Gospels, repeatedly highlighted in Acts, the letters of Paul, the Apocalypse of St. John, and more. And yet, the rookie said, there is nowhere in the Bible an actual description of it. I could argue that Matthew comes close, at least closer than Mark, Luke, and John. But he's right—no explicit narrative of Jesus getting up, shedding the grave clothes and walking out of the tomb.

Not one. Jesus appears after rising, but apart from the Roman guards who may or may not have seen The Event, no one we know of witnessed it.

There is, he said, nothing on YouTube that shows Jesus actually walking away from the grave. Everyone thought that was hilarious. But I can't get past his next statement.

"The sun is hidden, but it always wins the battle to be seen. Jesus had already won the battles over fear, rejection, hatred, disappointment, betrayal, and Jesus wins the battle over darkness and death, every time."

The sun *is* there, whether I see it or not, lurking behind a veil of mist. And as I get to my car, I hear myself saying, *And the sun will win the battle to be seen.* To be honest, I don't even know what he went on to say. I just keep playing that over and over. I drive home wrestling with this intriguing statement, wondering if it means anything to me.

My first words of the morning liturgy, printed in the bulletin, are "Christ is risen!"

The congregation lifts its collective voice and reads the next line: "Christ is risen indeed!"

Mercifully, most of what I need to say this Easter Sunday is scripted—thank heavens for printed bulletins—and I can recite even words I do not feel. I hope the people attribute my lack of enthusiasm to the weather. I understand what the disciples must have felt. I too have witnessed death this week. They encountered an empty grave and had no idea what that meant. In time, the story became clear, and I stand as beneficiary of that amazing day, but today, I am still grieving a days-old death.

I do not have the luxury of time. I have this present moment in which to bring long-awaited Good News to life: Christ is risen, and as Christ was raised, we too shall rise. Hallelujah.

Brad Davis has been betrayed. I have unleashed a firestorm. Hallelujah, Christ is risen.

The liturgy, hymns, and choir proclaim the Easter message, and provide me with perhaps twenty minutes to find my way. I will be ever grateful that this day's reader knows when I need some cover, offering to handle the pastoral prayer this morning. He should know. He raised me. As a pastor himself, my father can sense when a relief pitcher is needed.

But I still need to preach. I have no manuscript—just that page of Monday's first ideas with a few meager cross-outs and a few hand-written phrases that should have been developed by now. Carl's death and Brad's outrage sidelined any focus on this moment. There is some good stuff there, but un-researched, un-developed, unworthy of the biggest Sunday of the year. Yet it's all I have as I step into the pulpit.

After reading the text, I set the Bible aside and look down, I assume, to my notes. I see wood, not paper. In the rush of the morning, Monday's scribbled notes did not make the trip from my desk into the sanctuary and onto the pulpit. As gracefully as I can (can you see my hands shaking?) I begin:

"Many of you are gardeners. There are flowers in this space today and almost every Sunday that you lovingly provide. Whether flowers—or berries or tomatoes—you who love getting your hands in the soil are rightfully proud of what you can do there. You love what you bring forth in your gardens, don't you?

"A few of you are farmers, and you love the land too. You *must* love it, to take the risk of planting and nurturing crops that must sustain your farm and your family, year after year. When this fall's harvest comes I pray that you gather an abundant crop that rewards your love for the land.

"Whether farmers or gardeners, do you realize how honorable and beautiful your labors are? It's true that a farmer can nurture a field large enough to feed a community. It's also true that a gardener can nurture each plant as if it were their child. Either way, you are linked to the first labors of humankind, tending the earth in the Garden of Eden. Not only that—your labors are reflected in almost every story in the Bible—including the story we celebrate today."

It's at this point that my memory of Monday's scribbling is exhausted, and I'm on my own. Except that a message actually unfolds, a thought at a time, and I'm hearing it just as my congregation does: for the first time. I remind us all:

"Creation was nursed in a garden called Eden. All through the written Word, gardens and fields are woven into our salvation story. Jesus' last hour of freedom was spent praying in a garden. His followers, facing the sundown deadline for burial, hastily placed Him in a garden tomb, from which on Easter He emerged more alive than ever before. And the first sighting of the risen Messiah? When Mary, standing near the garden tomb, thinks He's a gardener."

Which, I say, suggests that in that first Easter hour, Jesus may in fact have been genuinely tending Creation—as if beginning the renewal of all things. "Gardens," I tell them, "are more than a backdrop. They challenge us to see ourselves in a garden where *we* are tended, where our lives can be re-birthed as seeds bring forth new life. And if we are willing, to lay down our lives as seeds of new life for others."

And then: "Most of you were still asleep when the sun came up. Which is fine, because it was a cloudy, gloomy start to Easter. But let me tell you about the sunrise you didn't see. 'While it was still dark,' our text says, there took place a resurrection that as far as we know, none of Jesus' followers witnessed. They were too late. While they were sleeping—though I suspect they did not sleep well that morning—God was already at work turning history upside down.

"The universal symbol of the Christian faith is a cross—the weapon of state-sanctioned torture, humiliation, and gruesome death. And a grave. In a garden, yes; robbed of its dead, yes. But still—a grave. Strange symbols for a religion that speaks of love and joy and peace. We would have picked flowers, or an eagle, or a star, or—a rising sun banishing the darkness against a bright blue sky.

"But we don't get a vote. Our faith is defined by cross and empty tomb not as bleak symbols of gloom, but defiant symbols of a supremely confident God.

"In the cross God holds a mirror before us, reflecting back to us the evil of which we are capable. Then and only then, God bursts through our grief and shame with the promise of forgiveness and new life out of dry bones and broken lives, from which God creates incredible beauty. Without our effort or even knowledge, God turned us and the world toward confidence, courage, tenacity, and hope. Christ is risen. We too shall rise."

I pause. Something I haven't articulated before—maybe not even to myself, comes from somewhere within me:

"Today we focus on the resurrection story, as we should. But we may be overlooking something. Easter is also a *love* story. There are many debates about the resurrection: how did it happen, did it really happen, what does it mean? Those are important questions. But for this moment, let's let the theologians debate them. Instead, let's remember that at the root of all that happened on that morning was witness not just to God's power, but to God's unbreakable love. A love that went to cross and tomb. A love that did not abandon Jesus even in death. A love that will never abandon us.

"Out of whatever loss, or the death of whatever dreams we cherish, as surely as the sun has risen, Christ has risen, and we are bathed in grace and love before we even know we need it.

"Jesus once asked a grieving woman—and us—'Do you believe this?' We face the same question today: Do you and I claim that promise?"

And with that, this message that has carried me—that still seems too short, that in my mind needs to go on—simply stops. My instinct tells me that I'm not finished, but I have nothing more to say. I pause, hoping for a tidy phrase, a sentence, to bring it all home, but nothing comes. Lacking a memorable, well-honed conclusion, I surrender. I simply shout, "Christ is risen!"

There's an awkward pause. Tradition tells us that a unison response is required, but it's not in the bulletin. A handful of people accustomed to tradition dare a somewhat muffled, tentative, not-quite-in-unison "Christ is risen indeed," followed by equally awkward, nervous laughter at the surprise. I smile. "You weren't expecting that, were you?" This brings more laughter, a welcome release.

It's OK. I'm OK now. The Word in unscripted words has been proclaimed. Not what I would have written, barely a third of what I'd have considered sufficient. But it's done, and I am free.

I pause. Then, "This time, join me in recalling the good news of Easter—Christ is risen!"

"Christ is risen indeed!"

"Amen."

The congregation stands to sing "*The day of resurrection—earth, tell it out abroad . . .*" The offering is taken; my father provides a pastoral prayer. I cry through it while the choir leads and the congregation joins in a rousing final hymn. I prepare to give a memorized benediction, but as I stand before my congregation—among them really, near the front but about two rows into the center aisle, arms outstretched in blessing—I speak from my heart.

"Today we celebrate again not our strength or brilliance or wealth or power, but our weakness made perfect and holy, because our confident God delights to reclaim the world in ways we can hardly imagine. Dear ones: You are God's beloved. Go in peace and joy."

Somehow I survive the handshakes and Happy Easters at the door, and it dawns on me: not only was I carried through this morning in strength not my own—what matters is not simply that I was able to stand and deliver—but that God graced us flawed but faithful followers of Christ in myriad guises with hope while it is still dark. A gift offered, to be received.

CHAPTER TWENTY-NINE
PAID IN FULL

I should be driving away from River Glen this morning. Holy Week and Easter in a normal year are exhausting. This year, on Easter Monday morning, I am numb. But I promised Dad, Trish, and Melissa, who are packed for the vacation that should have already started, that I *will* be done, and we *will* be on the road after I resolve one nagging matter. But it might be a time-consuming task, beginning with an awkward phone call to my friend the funeral director. I don't really want to know, but I need to find out what the costs for Carl's funeral will be; then I need to arrange to cover them. The costs aren't huge—it was a taxpayer-paid pauper's burial, after all. But Carl has a casket worthy of a brother, and will have his own grave marker, for which we are (or I am) responsible. Plus: *flowers*. He clearly loved beauty and color, and it was fitting that he be laid to rest under a generous spray of the best the florist could create. There are memorial funds, emergency funds, none of them likely to fund something like this without asking for favors I have little right to seek. But I promised to make sure the bills get paid, and now I have to untangle that mess.

He tells me it's been paid in full.

By whom, I ask. He's not sure he can tell me, but I suspect he thinks I need to know, so he tells me without telling me: "An elderly woman," he says, "stopped by on Good Friday. Said she had come into a little extra money after her husband died and just knew that paying for Carl's funeral is what her late husband would have wanted."

After I hang up, I smile and offer a truly heartfelt prayer of thanks. Then on a hunch, or perhaps a divine nudge, I pick up the phone again. It's been a while since I've talked to Margaret Kaskey. I should check in on her.

She answers the phone; I ask her how she's doing. Fine, she says, and you?

I say that it's been an unusually hard week. I could tell, she says. You looked so weary yesterday morning. Yes, I reply, I was very tired. But I add that this morning I am profoundly grateful for how God has refreshed my spirit. And, I say, "I just want to tell you that I am grateful to you, Margaret."

She tells me that she can't imagine why, but I'm welcome. And then she says she's so glad I called, and she's happy that I sound so much better, but she needs to fix breakfast, and she hopes I have a wonderful day.

Before I hang up, I simply say, "Thank you, Margaret. You don't know how grateful I am."

"I love you, Pastor Noel. You're a good, good man. God bless you. Bye."

I think she meant it. And I'm certain that we both shared a knowing smile when we hung up.

CHAPTER THIRTY
OUTRAGEOUS

> So what I have tried to develop first of all, in myself, is the
> mentality of the subversive. The subversive is someone who takes
> on the coloration of the culture, as far as everyone can see. . . . He
> has committed himself to Christ's victory over culture. . . .
> He is always carrying secret messages, planting suspicion that
> there is something beyond what the culture says is final.

> —Eugene Peterson, *The Contemplative Pastor*

We came north in a two-car caravan. Dad set the pace, and I was amazed that a man past seventy is still comfortable matching his speed to his age (while generously interpreting the speed limit). This trip brought us from River Glen to his home on a legendary island in a Great Lake, and we're finally here. There is no more beautiful place than two acres of marsh and forest on Madeline Island, the Garraty's personal Jerusalem. The cottage my father built was once a simple two-room affair. He added electricity during my childhood (I miss the candles and kerosene lamps), and eventually, indoor plumbing (I miss *nothing* about the mosquito-rich path to the outhouse).

Easter is behind us, and we're enjoying early hints of spring with Dad, who has joined me on the screen porch tonight. A soft rain clears the air following a thunderstorm that can still be heard in the distance. I'm still consumed by storms brewing back home, and in my mind. Despite the confidence that carried me through Easter, I'm once again unsettled about how—and if—we serve those who count themselves among the unhoused.

A reckoning is coming. The postponed vote is scheduled for mid-May before everyone scatters for the summer. Time is my adversary, giving Andrea and company room to reinforce their opposition. But time is my adversary in another way. I've got an emerging vision, but there's little time to put the pieces in place before a congregational vote seals my fate, and with it, my dream.

"Sometimes, Dad, I am ready to pour all my energies into this project, and I'm energized by what could be. Other times like now, the road ahead seems exhausting. Serving people so far from our world is risky, Dad. Maybe too risky. In the meantime, I still have a congregation to care for."

Dad says nothing. Just keeps watching the rain. He's thinking, and I hate it when he just thinks. It forces me to keep talking, which provides the elder Garraty with information that can also be ammunition.

"I dunno, Dad. I thought these encounters with people on the street were headed somewhere. Pastors should push the envelope, and I thought maybe I was called to push that one."

My father doesn't move, but he does speak, softly. "'Push the envelope.' For you, or your church?"

"Both, I guess. I like challenges; my church needs one to stretch itself. But if experience is any indication, it's an outrageous idea." I turn to look at him; he reciprocates. "Dad, I've been a suburb-dweller my whole life. White collar, comfortable, secure, pretty safe. Same for Old First. As conventional as it gets. To minister to the poor, hands-on, large-scale? Great idea. But maybe for us, outrageous."

Dad abruptly stands up, and the old rocker creaks in relief. He walks to the railing and looks through an oft-patched, fifty-year-old, rusty wire screen. I'm about to remind him for the hundredth time that it should be replaced when he interrupts the silence. "OK, Noel. What is feeding your soul right now? Unpack it for me."

Dad's not smiling. He's on the clock now, a minister-father mentoring his son. This has often been uncomfortable, but I like comparing notes with Dad. I also know that he has an agenda.

"Dad . . ."

"Noel, you may be an adult, but I bet I could still get you over my knee. So humor me. What's at the center of Noel Garraty's spirit?"

I sigh and lean back against the cushion on the wicker wingback. "Initiating a healing space for unhoused people. I think I'm saying that out loud for the first time. I don't have a plan, a place, anything specific beyond that. I'm almost afraid to define it; politically it makes no sense to push. A lousy cost/benefit ratio. I could wind up with a credibility deficit even deeper than the one I have now—and that assumes I keep my job."

"So, I guess you just pack your things and move on. Is that anywhere in your thinking?"

That has crossed my mind. But . . .

"No, Dad. What I'm saying is that to make this work it will have to be a full court press, a no turning back thing, and no surprise roadblocks. This is huge under ideal circumstances, and borderline crazy right now. I believe in it, and I'm not sure I can say no. Just not too keen on saying yes."

Dad waits, takes a deep breath. It's as if he's not sure he should influence my thinking, while at the same time he's convinced that I need his counsel. On that he's right, and he'd disappoint me if he kept it to himself. He doesn't disappoint.

"Here's my view—admittedly from the safe distance of retirement. Reverend Noel Garraty expresses his faith by risk-taking, not risk avoiding, knowing that God's commitment to him is unchallenged no matter what. You say this is an 'outrageous' endeavor. Noel, your core message *is* outrageous. All of it. The Gospel is counter-intuitive, absurd, illogical, even to us who believe it. There's that 'wildness' to our faith, its un-tamed power. We may try to rein in, to manage it, but when we tame it, we lose it. You *know* that. I've heard you preach that, and when you do, I see how it animates you. 'Let the Gospel loose and watch it change us,' you've said.

"But you've also preached that our tendency is to run from our message because we're afraid of an open-ended, risky vision. It may cost everything for the vision holder. But faithfulness involves believing outrageous things and praying outrageous prayers and living outrageous, out of the box, push-the-envelope lives.

"And therefore, declaring an outrageous dream and pursuing it. Even when there's pushback, or when it changes with new information, or when it inevitably gets more complicated than the vision you had at first, because it *will* be messy.

"Look—you're a rational man. We raised you to use your mind, to make evidence-based decisions. You made a good living by being rational and objective. But even in finance, you took risks. Reasoned, but risks nonetheless. And this sense of calling that troubles you? Same thing, really. You have evidence to back up the need. You can craft a rationally sound plan, and you know how to sell a good idea.

"Failure is always possible. So what? Noel, caution and reason matter, but they can't take you across the finish line. So they hand the baton to faith, which runs the next lap. That's how we love, son. We dare to risk in love.

"Remember what I used to say: 'Ask, and you shall receive—whether you want it or not.'"

The day before driving home, I get a call from the office. Mary is upset enough to call me on vacation but won't talk specifics over the phone. I won't force the issue with her. So I call Brad.

"Hi, Pastor. You home now?"

"No—not leaving until tomorrow. Brad, a question. Mary called and asked me for a face-to-face as soon as I get home. She won't tell me until then, but if you know what it might be about . . ."

"I can understand her reluctance. There was a board meeting last night; I was there. They voted—not unanimously—to postpone the special meeting. It's now set for September or October—that wasn't decided for sure."

"'Postpone?' Why?"

"It was presented as necessary because things are so busy here, too many people will start vacations by the middle of next month, we need more time to discern—"

"That's nonsense."

"I agree, Pastor. I thought it was a thin veneer to cover some political mischief. Mary's really upset about it. So are one or two council members.

"Pastor Noel—maybe I flinched here when I should have challenged it. I didn't. All I had was this surprise motion, and my gut telling me it was dirty. Am I wrong here?"

"You're not wrong. But thanks for telling me. Brad, the sky isn't falling. Don't worry; I'll respond when I get back."

My mind is working overtime wondering how I'll clean up this mess. I also think this may be a gift in disguise. Yes, there are people who will leverage this time to make my life interesting. But it also gives me time to flesh out my vision. I have some ideas. They're, well, outrageous. But they address an evident need—and maybe even capture enough hearts to turn the tide.

Like they say: sometimes, the best defense is a good offense.

CHAPTER THIRTY-ONE
HOME, AND HOMELESS

After any absence, home feels good. I'm thankful when someone opens their home to me. Yet our *own* home—with its familiarity, safety, and refuge, is a place to simply *be* without pretense. At home, we can unburden. We can snack or feast as we wish. We can sleep whenever we want; we can rearrange the furniture, leave the dishes in the sink, complain about the décor, leave books or shoes or unfinished projects wherever they land. We can change the channel or turn off the TV or crank up the stereo with Brahms or Beyonce whenever the whim strikes (with of course the consent of our spouse).

I wonder what it's like for the unhoused. I raise the question with Brad. I get more than just an answer.

"They lack more than a warm and dry space, Pastor. They treasure privacy as much as—perhaps more than—we do, yet their life is frighteningly public. We have some control over our private lives. But when you are not only seen, but constantly and cruelly judged, what's *that* like? You seek to be left alone but know that you must be on your best behavior despite being reduced to a label. You absorb hostile messages directed at you until you become your own most ruthless, merciless judge. You just know that on some level, you have failed yourself, God, and humankind, to be living such a dismal life.

"For some on the streets, though, being homeless is itself a kind of home. In time, it's your normal. You learn the rules and how even your vulnerability can be useful in getting what you need. Plus, there is a seductive simplicity: all you need worry about is surviving the coming night."

Sometimes, an off-hand comment changes one's life. I say, "I wonder if *I* could survive out there," expecting no response. Brad starts to say something and then stops, thinks for a moment, then speaks.

"This matters to you, doesn't it?"

"I guess it does. Can't get it out of my mind for some reason." I suspect the "reason" may have something to do with the Spirit's nudging, but I keep that suspicion to myself. Maybe Brad guesses it anyway.

"Pastor, if you want to find out, I have a suggestion. What if you and I—I know this sounds crazy, but what if we did some first-hand research?"

"Okay . . ." I sense he's not thinking Google or the library. Nor am I thinking what he's about to suggest.

"Why don't we—you and I—spend a night or two living on the street?"

My initial reaction is . . . curiosity. Once, I would have dismissed the notion without a second thought. Talk about high-risk. I'm fully aware that Trish—and any sane person—would question such a venture.

And yet, I'd be with someone familiar with it—more than me, at least. "Let me think about it, Brad. 'Crazy,' maybe. But . . ."

A piece of my heart is in the outdoors; a bigger piece of my *life* is in the commotion, contention, confusion, of modern America. There are rarely visited, remote places where one can be enveloped in solitude and silence. They offer relief from our contentious world—if you can get there. And I have the luxury of doing just that. I'm the embodiment of privilege: white, American, financially secure. I can travel as I wish.

Meanwhile, many of my neighbors are held back by family, work, disability, poverty, and no way out—even if just out of town. My pondering highlights the divisions in American life. I'm in a system where privileges flow down to me but not much further. *Is that OK?*

I sit with this for a while. I close the laptop. *What if,* I ponder, *I really do make a pilgrimage into the heart of the city? Am I prepared to battle its demons on their own turf?* Brad has opened an enticing, terrifying door. Maybe it's the Spirit leading me to do something absurdly holy. In any case, the question is shifting in my mind, from "Does this make sense?" to "What should I wear?"

CHAPTER THIRTY-TWO
RESEARCH

One great reason why the rich in general have so little sympathy
for the poor is because they so seldom visit them. Hence it is
that one part of the world does not know what the other suffers.
Many of them do not know, because they do not care to know:
they keep out of the way of knowing it—and then plead their
voluntary ignorance as an excuse for their hardness of heart.

—John Wesley, 18th century

"This wouldn't be the first time I've lost sleep over you." I'm trying to persuade Trish that this will simply be research, in the same Chicago neighborhood that Sherman Jackson stalks during his working hours. "I need to experience life on the street, up close and personal. To see how people survive out there."

"I'll be honest," Trish confesses, "this scares me, Noel. Yes, risks you've taken have often been worth it. But you've never risked your life before."

I already know that, but when she says it out loud . . . "I don't think I'm taking that great a risk. I'm not doing this all on my own. The key is having Brad with me. He knows what we'll be facing. He'll be my guide." (And, I think to myself, my bodyguard.) "And I hope to have Sherman Jackson's shelter as a fall-back."

"You *hope* to?"

"I haven't talked to him yet. He's not very fond of me."

"So you've said. What if he falls through?"

"I doubt that, frankly. He'll be OK with it. That's what he does."

"If he says 'no' and you'd wind up actually sleeping on the street, will you back out?"

"I don't think so, Trish. Some uncertainty is kind of essential to make this work."

I'm researching myself as well, to see if I have what it takes to survive in this foreign land with its unfamiliar dialect, its concrete jungles filled with dangerous beasts. I consider myself a risk-taker, but in business all I ever risked was someone else's money and my pride. In the ministry I risk rejection. But am I truly risking my life? Maybe not, I tell myself. After all, I'll have Brad. But it feels riskier than I admit.

Sometimes we must immerse ourselves in what we believe. "So," I tell Trish, "I need to make this as real as possible. I'm taking about two dollars. No car, no extras. I'll have my cell phone and Social Security card for ID." *In case my body turns up floating in the Chicago River,* I muse, but I don't tell Trish that either. "I want no crutches except someone who was born and raised there."

Something about this echoes my faith. We often take for granted that our Gospel is birthed in unprecedented risk by "taking on flesh and dwelling among us," because Love considered us worth it all.

My two-day foray into the unknown, accompanied by someone for whom it is at least partly familiar, is not much different from what believers are called to do on a daily basis: to be wholly *here* in the world, with only faith to sustain us. We will see if that's enough.

I left my watch at home. I think it's about one thirty p.m.—traffic's lightened up a bit, which tells me that lunch hour is over. It's a lunch I miss. We're homeless, you know.

Everyone is looking at a scruffy old white guy in the worst clothes in my closet, with a scruffy younger Black man in torn jeans and a sleeveless tee. Nobody approves of what they see. The non-homeless see "homeless" and write us off. The truly homeless? Well, I'm not sure. I think they have their doubts about us too. So do I.

I'm not used to feeling incompetent. I have a whole arsenal of weapons for my world: technology, titles, authority, and more. But on the street I feel inept, exposed, and, even with Brad, alone.

While I'd rather be home, I made a commitment. But another temptation is harder to resist: I could simply hide. Avoid everyone. But without entrance into the unhoused community, this is little more than a very bad camping trip. I'm here to learn through the eyes of those who have no shelter.

It dawns on me that I'm somewhat invisible. When I was "Reverend Garraty" twenty-four hours ago, I could look someone in the eye, smile, say hello—and I'd get a response: eye contact, a smile in return. I was dressed a little nicer: a suit on Sundays, of course. But even in a polo shirt and khakis, people smiled back, said hello. That isn't happening here. I miss the eye contact the most.

The change happened on the train as soon as we stepped aboard. Brad and I agreed beforehand to take our seats separately. People looked away. The seat next to me stayed empty all the way into the city. We got off the train, and people kept their distance. It was subtle, but I could feel the disdain. No one said "excuse me" if we bumped shoulders—a few almost did, until they looked at who they'd bumped.

I asked directions at the Metra station for the men's room. No one offered any. All I got was "Can't help you" as they kept walking. Nervous laughter from some high school kids. The conductor just pointed and looked away. I'm homeless, therefore invisible, or worse: dangerous.

Lesson #1: you don't exist. Or shouldn't. I'm a bum, a druggie, a drunk, a panhandler, someone who smells. So people simply pretend I'm not here, and thus make a powerful statement about my worth.

"So this is what is like," I say to Brad after half an hour walking a block ahead of my fellow clergyman-in-disguise.

"Welcome to my world, my dear white friend. This is still me sometimes, when I'm just Brad Davis in River Glen, Illinois." Were we in my office back at Old First I'd challenge that. Now, in my first hours here, I'm tasting Brad's world.

It's a bit early for drawing conclusions, but I share some mental notes with Brad. "The unhoused are about as rough-looking as I expected. Dirty, some clearly struggling with mental illness. They all look . . . old, I guess, though many of them are younger than me. The street takes its toll." Their eyes, I observe, are often blank. But sometimes they seem continually alert, almost hyper-vigilant, even frightened. They are overwhelmingly people of color, at least in my first ninety minutes of research. "It bothers me to see some in or barely past their teens. And what I'm not prepared for is how many don't *look* homeless. Many of them, with perhaps a shower and a shave, would fit into my social settings without anyone raising an eyebrow."

Brad's response haunts me. "Each one of them has a story as real as yours or mine. The difference is their story at some turn became overwhelmingly painful."

I watch their interactions with others on the street, and I see fear, impatience, short tempers, timidity, bullying, depression. The street takes its toll. You may become hardened, suspicious, anxious, discouraged. I see selfishness, but selflessness too. For most—not all, but most—even here there are touches of grace: a smile, a hug, a "thank you" for simple kindnesses. Some are rude, others humble and gracious. While some don't even know you're right there in front of them, others smile when you say "good morning." Just like in my world.

But not *from* the people in my world.

CHAPTER THIRTY-THREE
ROUGH-HEWN GRACE

Our new best friend is Freddie. If he has a last name, he's not sharing it. Freddie has not played a round of golf or owned a car in a long time. He doesn't own a home, says he don't want none, and I'm beginning to talk like him.

Just when I was wondering if I'd survive the night, Freddie reaches out. Others on the street had the decency to not kill me for my New Balance runners, which I was ready to throw out but were in better condition than some on their feet. But that is about all. Hospitality, I was beginning to think, is present but precious on the street.

Yet Freddie invites us to share his fifty square feet of floor in an abandoned machine shop, and actually talks to us. He tells us his story—very selectively, I suspect—and I notice uncomfortably that he's not inclined to bring Brad into the conversation. Brad plays along. I think he knows that he can't escape his Blackness even here, and this is primarily a graduate course in reality for the Rev. Noel Garraty. Brad Davis is my chaperone, and this only works if Brad stays off center stage.

Freddie focuses largely on his successes at obtaining whatever he needs by whatever means necessary. He likes to brag, even while having little to brag about except this: despite questionable choices, an inability to control his slavery to chemicals, a cruel and seemingly permanent rejection by his family—Freddie has survived. And for that I salute him. I am captivated by this bent-but-not-quite-broken man. He spins a wonderful yarn, he's funny (though I could never tell his jokes in church), and he has not yet lost his humanity. His love for people, especially those who are vulnerable, is inescapable. That's why Freddie befriended me.

There is one awkward moment to this friendship. I've been expecting it for the past two hours, and it is now upon me.

"Hey, No'l—you need a beer."

No, I don't. But Freddie isn't going to be persuaded if I protest—only insulted, and I might need this guy tonight. "Y'know Freddie, I don't want to take your beer. You worked hard for that bottle. It's all yours, man."

"When you get drunk last? I mean, real stinkin' wasted?"

"Can't remember." (Yes I can. The correct answer: not since college. Although I suspect Freddie wouldn't believe that, so a poor memory is the best, if not accurate, answer.)

"You don't remember?" Freddie laughs, despite the fact that nothing I've said is funny. "Prob'ly 'cause you were too drunk to remember!" Now he falls backward, laughing convulsively. The bottle slips from his hand and tips over; I quickly grab it before too much spills onto the dirt. Freddie suddenly sits up, his face the picture of seriousness.

"No'l, I worry about you. Really. I don't think you're a street guy. Maybe that Brad fellow with you. But this ain't your world, is it?"

I respect Freddie and won't lie to him. "No, not really. I just needed to see what it's like." He stares at me, starts to say something, and then just looks down at the bottle cradled between my hands. "You let go of it, and it was spilling," I explain. I offer it to him.

"Why?" Good question, and I don't know if I can answer it. "I knew this guy who lived around here. He died a few weeks ago. I wanted to know what it was like for him, I guess."

Freddie's eyes soften. "That's beautiful, No'l. Have a drink." This time when he hands me the bottle, it's not a casual gesture, and I know it. Something is passing between us of which the dirty bottle in his hand is a symbol. I have ample reason to refuse. I have no idea where that bottle's been or what's really in it, or what has migrated from Freddie's lips to the rim of the bottle. But there are times when hygiene gets in the way. This is more than a flat, warm, cheap beer. It is a sacrament. So from the hands of my brother Freddie, I receive a gift of rough-hewn grace.

Freddie, Brad, and I hear someone scream. I don't think much about it, but Freddie reacts like a dog who just heard a wolf. Suddenly he's sober.

"Someone's in trouble." I don't respond. I'll learn more by watching Freddie in what may be a common street event. "It's a woman. Let's go." By the time we're on our feet, Freddie is out the door. We jog (slowly—Freddie's a bit out of shape) about half a block and around a corner, to a group of other unhoused people gathered around the entry to a boarded-up drug store. There's what I'm guessing may be a twenty-year-old woman, clearly pregnant, clearly in labor.

The strange thing is, no one in the group seems to be taking charge. Everyone's watching, talking, smoking, offering some encouragement. But there she is, desperate and in pain. I have no idea if Freddie knows anyone here. He acts as if I'm the only other person around. "No'l, we're gonna have a baby." My hand starts to reach for my cell phone, which has disappeared. Suddenly I realize that I'm in one of the world's great cities, in a crowd of a dozen other people, and I have virtually nothing to offer this precious soul on the trash-filled concrete.

It may be spring, but I'm thinking Christmas, for this is what it looks like when there is no room at the inn. In the ancient story the cattle were lowing. Here, the only creatures are an occasional squirrel and rats. Were there rats around the manger when you were born, Jesus?

Freddie is barking orders like . . . well, like a doctor. "I need four blankets, people. And I want the guys to hold them around us so this young lady has some privacy. And I want you guys to be on the *other* side of the blankets and no looking, understand? Now you—" Freddie points at a youngish Caucasian girl who seems to be the most sober, least burned-out person there besides Brad and I—"I want you to go call 9-1-1 and get an ambulance here. We're on Fifty-fourth, south of Hancock."

"But I ain't got a phone."

"Then borrow one. Or flag down a squad car. Whatever—*get moving!*"

I decide to help Freddie assemble his medical team. "Any of the rest of you got any nurse's training?" Doctor Freddie is irked. "No'l, *you're* my nurse and no one else. You're not drunk or stoned." I should feel complimented; instead, I feel conspicuous. Again, Brad is ignored. Others there may want a piece of this chance to be a hero, and I'm the one invited to go to the head of the class.

Freddie isn't done. "No'l, I'm gonna need a few things. I need a sharp knife—any kind, razor, whatever. I need a way to clean it real good, like a cigarette lighter. I need some string." Brad finds a knife, though the owner was reluctant to part with one of his most prized possessions. I can't find any string and tell Freddie, who's busy getting the pregnant girl positioned for delivery. He looks around, and his eyes lock on a sixty-something woman sitting on the ground with two large garbage bags between her and the wall. "Hey,

Grandma—got any twist ties?" She's briefly motionless, then slowly reaches inside a filthy brown coat and pulls out a half dozen twist ties. I retrieve them and give them to Freddie. The girl's contractions begin again. I frantically obey Freddie's commands, and I'm shaking like a leaf.

It's a girl. She looks healthy, and thanks to the efforts of about half a dozen people, some under the influence of chemicals, we have saved at least one precious human life. One of Jesus' sisters just gave birth to another one, already judged as "least" in the eyes of almost everyone, but I would not have been anywhere else in the world than right here, right now, as time is invaded by eternity, and I am here to see it.

The paramedics take her and her mother away before I find out who she is. No one else in that doorway seems to care. A few comments, a few jokes, life returns to, not normal by my standards, yet a kind of normality for people who live in doorways and old machine shops. And as we walk away, I remember that my phone is missing. It was there twenty minutes ago when I wasn't in a crowd of people.

Freddie, Brad, and I are back where we started, and I share my suspicion that I'd just witnessed more than everyday street smarts at work, so I ask him how he knew what to do. "I was a medic in the Army. Kosovo, Iraq, parachuted into Bagdhad, spent some time in Kandahar."

I briefly wonder if he knew a medic named Sophie. "I wouldn't think you'd have delivered many babies there."

"True enough No'l, true enough. Didn't see many babies 'cept the ones some fool blew up. Saw lots of those." His voice turns bitter, angry. "Mostly I saw lots of blood. Lots of good people, lots of innocent people . . . lots of good men, limbs missing, insides all over the street, burnt, screaming . . ." It's as if he's remembering an all-too-familiar scene. "No wonder I got out. Too bad it was a million years too late. Too bad when I came home nothing made sense anymore." He throws his half-empty bottle; it shatters and bleeds in slow motion over the graffiti in the long-vacant shop. We sit and watch.

Suddenly his tone turns cheerful, a contrived, mocking kind of cheerful. More passive, empty, as if resigned to the inevitability of a life devoid of hope. "But I can still do it. There's nothing I've seen that I couldn't handle. I haven't forgotten a thing, right, No'l?" Freddie's not looking at me. Neither he nor I are fooled. His mournful eyes contradict his words. Freddie has surrendered to what he cannot forget and cannot conquer. I think I understand. Sherman talks about the Freddies that eat, sleep, and mourn the life they've surrendered. What service to his country did to him—what war and gore and death and a return to a homeland that felt like a foreign country did to him—helped put him here.

We sit in silence for a few minutes. I sense that maybe there's some kind of connection taking place between me and Freddie, and my Minister instincts kick in. I want to get closer to this man. There is much he could teach me, and much I long to share with him. What could I say to him? How can I—

"No'l—it's been nice knowin' ya. But you'll have to go now. I need my privacy and I need my sleep." He huddles in the corner and wraps himself in his tired sleeping bag. Within thirty seconds he's snoring. I wonder if I'll ever have a chance to talk with Freddie again. And I no longer wonder how a doctor winds up delivering babies on the sidewalk.

Dawn—I think it's dawn—emerges without much fanfare. We've walked, dozed, walked some more. A heavy overcast reflects the gathered glow of the city, a glow that can be seen most nights from River Glen.

River Glen. There's a warm bed there, and if I were in it, I'd be getting the sleep I didn't get here. I'm anxious, looking constantly around, unable to keep my eyes closed no matter how tired I am. Every sound is unfamiliar and might be announcing a threat, so we keep moving and watching. Freddie was my security blanket for a while. Brad is still here should anything happen for which I'm unprepared, which is pretty much everything. But he won't push himself into the experience unless I ask, and if I lean on Brad too often, the "research" will be tainted.

I'm lonely. There are people around, but I'm not brave enough to introduce myself. Nor do any of them seem to be interested in making a new friend. That was Freddie's gift, and I may not qualify for another. We're about a mile from where Brad and I left him, crossing under the "L" tracks into a new neighborhood, hoping it's the boundary between the alien world we're walking through and someplace less alien.

There's a free meal site not far from here that Freddie told us about. We head that way. It will at least be secure, even if only for a couple of hours until they close down. We have options there. If I want to continue my research, it can be a place to study my fellow unhoused friends. If I just can't deal with this anxiety anymore—and that's tempting—I can go home. Or I can hang there long enough to revive my flagging courage, and tough it out for another day.

That's my hope. I bargained for two days and nights, and I can't bring myself to call it quits. Much remains hidden and mysterious in this distressing yet hauntingly beautiful world. Maybe Freddie will be there, enjoying a meal.

He isn't, but my education continues over a breakfast of pancakes, scrambled eggs, juice, and coffee, served by a cadre of volunteers from what appears to be a synagogue, two white churches, an African-American congregation, and a handful of people who just love the poor.

About those who serve us—a few are nervous; must be first-timers. But they're all pleasant, welcoming a herd of about ninety men, women, and children without an address, as if we were guests at a White House banquet. An oasis in the desert, where people are refreshed by kindness.

It was strange, though, to be served as if I were—as if I *am*—homeless.

A thirty-something male in jeans and the T-shirt of a suburban congregation comes by to refill my coffee. I've been watching the way he moves around the room, especially as he interacts with other volunteers. My guess: he's a minister. He cheerfully asks me if I want a refill. I nod yes. As he pours, he says his name is Mark and asks mine. I tell him I'm Phil; Brad uses his own name. I don't know why I didn't use mine. Asks me if I've been here before. I say no. I work hard at not making eye contact. He moves along, not realizing that if he'd pressed the matter, I may have told him who I was and what I was doing, and the whole experiment might have collapsed under the weight of two preachers comparing notes before I ask him for a ride out of the city.

CHAPTER THIRTY-FOUR
SAINT PAUL

No such luck for lunch. The soup kitchen was at capacity when we got there. People who live here know to arrive early.

I know where I want to be for a free dinner (not counting the one Trish would have prepared), and head that way, only to get lost just long enough to miss out. We've not eaten, and I'm starved. Then I remember—I've got two dollars with me plus a few quarters. I'll find a convenience store, hoping for maybe an apple or a banana, forgetting that I'm in a food desert where produce is all but nonexistent. But I wait as long as I can stand it because on two bucks, I won't find enough to get me through the night if I eat now. We walk, and we walk some more.

Finally, I purchase my meal. Tonight I will live on a candy bar from a closeout bin, and a small bottled water. It will be a long night, I decide, as I carry my precious cargo through the darkening streets.

I didn't know this little park was here, roughly the size of a city block, with a basketball court, a baseball diamond, some picnic tables, some trees. Fairly Spartan, but it gets a lot of use. I'm conspicuously white but keep to the shadows when I can, watching some pre-teens playing baseball and some late teen/early twenty-somethings work through a fairly boisterous pickup game of hoops. Brad joins them, completely at ease and without the reserve I usually see. He laughs, trash-talks, even swears when the urge strikes him—this is his element. I almost ask if I can join the fun, but my skills are no match for this bunch. The park seems relatively safe, and we stay until the lights are turned off and everyone drifts home.

I notice two things. One: when the game winds down, Brad leaves with the group. That was pre-planned, sort of. When we plotted this scheme Brad suggested—and I reluctantly agreed—that if all went well the first day, I'd be on my own for the last night of our adventure. So here I am. I've done the in-class work; now it's my independent study.

Two: there are some flashes of lightning to the west, and I need a roof over my head. I walk away, but not the way I should have. Instead of a residential area, I'm in a rather tired industrial patch devoid of anything except high concrete walls marked by overhead doors, all closed. I feel vulnerable to the elements of course—and to more.

The rain starts about three blocks later. I'm walking alone and don't like feeling so exposed to both the elements and the unknowns on this barely lit, deserted street. This night turns out to be more disorienting than the last. I'd rather find some shelter and stay dry, but I keep moving, away from whatever might be behind me.

Part of my concern—my paranoia—is that I think I'm being followed by a trio of guys who paid a bit too much attention to me when I walked past. As I walk faster and then jog across the street, they match me step for step. I think it's time to run, betting my life on my guess that they're not as frequent as I am in making use of a health club.

They're not gaining on me, except for one guy who's thirty yards ahead of them and less than that from me, and I need to lose him. For the first time in my life, I'm not just nervous; I'm terrified. I have no weapon, no skills in self-defense, and it looks more and more likely that I may need them. I'm not thinking; I'm reacting, panicking. I see an opening, and before knowing where it leads, I make a sudden left into an alley. It's gated at the end. I have nowhere to run. I wonder what it is like to die violently.

I turn around. The footsteps rapidly become louder. A twenty-something in black jeans, a long-sleeved tee and a stocking cap enters the alley running at full speed and stops abruptly ten feet away, surprised to find me standing, facing him, hands empty, resigned to my fate.

We're both gasping for air after a three-block sprint, saying nothing. The other two catch up and speak first. A tall, forty-ish bearded man, rough-faced, long-haired, and of uncertain ethnicity but clearly the general in this three-man army, walks toward me. "Whatcha protectin', fool?" He pushes me—punches me—in the chest, and I stumble backwards three or four steps before regaining my balance.

"I've got nothing."

"Then why you running, huh? We're just trying to be *friendly*." He emphasizes his friendliness with another push, and this time I'm on my back. I get up slowly and silently. I have no idea what to say and certainly don't want to escalate an already fragile confrontation.

The third man in the group, Latino, I'm guessing, says in a soft voice that is more unnerving for its softness, "We're going to find out what 'nothing' looks like. Turn around." I comply, feel something hard on the back of my head, and wake up on my face, suddenly alone in an empty alley. I can barely move.

I carefully turn my head, which hurts like nothing I've ever felt before. I see and hear nothing except the distant white noise of the city. It's been raining. I'm soaked, shoeless, my shirt's been pulled up to my shoulders. I told them I had nothing, but it appears that they didn't take my word for it. I presume they made off with the change I had.

It takes me . . . twenty minutes? an hour? to put myself back together and begin thinking about what to do next. My mind, like my body, knows only slow motion. It's still dark. I'm wet, cold, and in pain, which confirms that I'm still alive.

Standing up takes a while; staying up will be a challenge, but I need to walk, to get . . . somewhere. I make my way back to the street, seeing no one. I turn to the right and retrace my steps. I'm not thinking clearly. I may find my assailants now where I found them before, but all I can think of is that park—the last place I remember as safe and familiar. I want to find that park . . . that park . . .

Everything is fuzzy, dreamlike. The only clarity is a splitting headache and a dim memory of finding myself face-down in a wet alley. Only fragments of memory recall what transpired before that. I try and fail to string together a coherent sequence of events. I sense that it's the pre-dawn hours, but the day of the week, or the month or the year or precisely which city this is, eludes me. Maybe Chicago. The rain has stopped, not a hint of breeze, and the streets are filled with a fog that matches the one in my head, making any movement disorienting. Every wall, every curb, every light, is strange, alien, disturbing. I keep walking, looking for that park.

"You look lost."

I look up into a massive smile surrounded by a full, clean-shaven, very black face. I'm on a park bench. It's not the park bench I remember, and I don't remember finding it. But it's—yeah, it's the same park. The sky is grey now. Dawn has arrived, but the sun is masked by clouds, fog, and mist. I have no idea what happened to the intervening hours or how I got here.

"I'm fine," I say, hoping that ends the conversation.

"No, you look lost. You *are* lost."

I'm uncomfortable, and say nothing.

"Son, who were you before you wound up here?"

"Why does that matter?"

"Because you're new to the streets. I can tell. You're shaking and a bit scared, and you're——" he looks me over, and chuckles "soaking wet. Son, this is a foreign land to you, isn't it? Who were you once?"

I lie, sort of. "I worked in banking."

"Bet you dressed better then." This time, I chuckle. "Yeah—a lot better."

"Kinda nice to be free of all that." He's got a point.

"Does the ex-banker have a name?" Again, I don't reply.

"They call *me* 'Saint Paul.'"

"Odd name," I say, although I'm really the odd one here. Saint Paul takes a seat much too close for comfort, sees something behind me, and bends toward the back of my neck, gingerly touching whatever is back there, and I flinch—it hurts to be touched there.

"What happened to you? You've been hit—you *were* hit, weren't you?"

"I dunno. I guess so. I don't remember much."

"Can you walk?"

"I think so."

Saint Paul gently lifts me to my feet. "C'mon, son. We can talk on the way, but I know where you need to be right now."

I let him lead but he wisely walks slowly; I'm in no shape for more. He picks up the conversation as if it hadn't been broken by the discovery of a nasty blow to the head.

"Actually, 'Saint Paul' fits. Name's Paul, and I was called" (sweeping his hand around the park) "to reach this beloved community with the Gospel."

I can tell he's just warming up. I'm about to become his next project. I try feebly to regain control of this encounter. "How did *you* wind up here?"

"What's your name, son?"

"Noel." I couldn't think up a fake name to protect my identity, and why try? He'd probably know if I lied anyway.

"Well, Noel, let me tell you how the God of heaven called me to serve among the Lord's most beautiful children!" He leans toward me, arm through the crook of mine to steady me, his face now six inches away but looking straight ahead at nothing in particular, as if gazing at a mountain on the horizon. He's relaxed. His tone is conversational, easygoing. "I'm a minister, Noel, trained and ordained. Served a nice congregation just down the road in Gary. Had it all! Home, money, success, the things of this world." He's told this story before. Its well-rehearsed cadence and volume intensify, and though I couldn't get away if I tried, I don't really want to. I'm mesmerized. If nothing else, my foggy brain tells me it's pretty good street theater.

"But God, brother Noel, *God* called me to leave it *all* behind, and like Abraham of old, I walked into this very *community*, and like *Jesus* I pitched my tent in the midst of the lost and suffering, and now, I proclaim Good News to the *poor!*" Saint Paul looks at me and expects a response. Mine's not quite what he may have wanted.

"So who pays you to do this?" He waves me off.

"You don't understand, my friend. I don't get paid—who gets paid to be homeless? It is my honor to live as you, and" (pointing around the park) "like her, and like him over there—I am proud to be a homeless man for Christ. Hallelujah!"

Whatever else Paul the Saint tells me, I don't remember. I keep fading in and out. The next thing I remember, I'm waking up indoors, this time under a dry blanket.

CHAPTER THIRTY-FIVE
HOUSE RULES

I still have a splitting headache, and the noise in this place, wherever it is, doesn't help. I keep my eyes closed and listen to voices I've never heard before.

"So who's the new guy?"

"Who cares?"

"I don't like that he's got Frankie's cot."

"Frankie's not coming back. Let it go, Junior."

"Where's Frankie?"

"Detox. Then a halfway house."

"So he's gonna go half-way again, and wind up back here, huh?"

This is followed by some very coarse laughter. I open my eyes. It's not the Emergency Room that I expected. Nothing in this place is sterile or staffed by people in white smocks. On the contrary, what's more obnoxious than the voices is the smell. I want to gag. Someone here needs a bath. No, on second thought, someone here needs to run buck naked through a truck wash.

"Hey! You on the cot! It's wake-up time!"

Maybe for them, I muse. But after what I've been through, I need more sleep. "I'll pass. Let me sleep, OK?"

"You know the house rules, pal. Everyone gets up at 6:30. No exceptions. Or the whole floor misses breakfast. Now get your sorry butt up, or we'll soak your head in the toilet."

"Yeah—*before* we flush it!"

"Let him be." I think I know this voice. It sounds a lot like Sherman. He speaks again. "You guys head down for chow. I'll get the new guy up." They leave, I roll over, feeling for the first time in two full days genuinely relaxed and at peace. It's a wonderful feeling, and it lasts about two seconds.

"Get up, Garraty."

"Excuse me?"

"It's wake-up time. Your roommates are right: no exceptions to the rule. You wanted a taste of life on the street. Well, you're on my street, you're at my mercy, and our schedule applies to stupid preachers too."

Sherman Jackson . . . I'm beginning to realize where I am.

"Hi, Sherm. Hey—I understand. But last night was pretty rough, you know? Just another half hour, OK? Then I'll get out of your hair." Next thing I know, I'm on the floor, and my tongue tastes several decades of deferred housekeeping.

"Garraty, you're in my hair, and you're staying there until I say so. What on earth were you thinking, Garraty? Got a death wish?"

He's livid, glaring at me like I just ate his pet hamster. In language both colorful and memorable he's commenting on my intellectual limitations. He's also suggesting that perhaps he will inform all of North America of his assessment.

"Now get up and get in line for chow. You're eating breakfast with everyone else, then you're doing chores like everyone else, then you and I are talking. *Then* you get out of my hair."

Sherm's being totally unreasonable, but since I'm alive, dry, and reasonably safe, I'll humor him.

On the way down I remember (or at least I think) that sometime in the very recent past, my head met a solid object. I feel gingerly back and find a rather large bandage. I begin to ask him what happened, but he sees my hand discover the bandage on my head and speaks. "You were a mess, I'm told. Saint Paul got you here. We called for an ambulance, they took you to the ER, patched you up, and you said you wanted to come here."

"I did?"

"Yep."

"I was at an ER?"

"About two hours ago. You should have stayed."

"Why didn't I?"

"You insisted you wanted to be here."

I try to remember the night before. I was running . . . three guys . . . looking for a park. Even that's sketchy, as is anything about Emergency Rooms or Saint Paul. Sherman's watching my deer-in-the-headlights moment, and his glare slowly becomes a mischievous grin. "Didn't you feel a bit of a breeze last night?"

"A breeze?"

"Yeah. Like something was missing? At least I would have wondered why my legs were so cold."

I look down. I'm wearing a pair of baggy, old, very unfamiliar pants.

"When Saint Paul found you, you were dazed, barely coherent, and wearing just your shirt and your boxers."

I'm still processing things slowly, wondering what on earth made me choose the wrath of Sherman over the safety of a hospital. Or better yet, the warmth of home.

"Does Trish know where I am?"

"As a matter of fact, she does."

"How does she know?"

"We called her. Pretty good woman, your wife. Better than you deserve. She's coming down later."

Sherm refuses to elaborate. But after breakfast, he tells me how he heard the night staff talking about the loopy guy Saint Paul dragged in. But first, he asks me what I had told her about my plans.

"I told her. I didn't want her to worry. The first night I was with my associate pastor who grew up here. It was important to me to really experience this world. Boy, did I. I remember my phone disappearing, I remember it getting dark and trying to find a place to be . . . I don't remember much more."

"What she told me is that she worried when you didn't call. By about nine last night she was seriously worried. And pissed. She called your associate—he was horrified. Felt guilty, came downtown himself looking; St. Paul found you first. Meanwhile, I'd love to watch this loving reunion."

"What made her call you?"

"Well Reverend, she'd called all the other people and places she could think of. After we talked, I told her to check the train stations between River Glen and here. She did, and about midnight she calls and says she found your car still at the Metra station. I promised her I'd look around, but it's a big town."

"But you don't work here all night."

"I did last night."

"You stayed up all night looking for me? Why?"

"I don't know. Maybe it's because I'm so fond of fools like you. Or maybe it's because there was this Guy who used to tell stories about lost sheep. Ever heard of Him?

"And I'm the lost sheep."

"And sometimes, I'm a shepherd. If someone's out there, I've pledged my life to finding them and bringing them home. Garraty, I refuse to stand by and watch even one soul disappear into the void out there. Even if it's you, son."

"Sherm, I had no idea I'd cause so much trouble."

"While you're cleaning pots and pans, I'll call Trish again. Then I'll work the living daylights out of you, and you'll attend a twelve-step group like everyone else. And when I'm through with you, I'll kick your butt back to the suburbs."

Sherman thinks for a moment. "So white boy, what did you learn?"

"Humility. It's tough out there."

"Excellent! You learned that unhoused doesn't equate with stupid; it takes skills you with your MBA know nothing about. Not a bad start."

"For the first time, I genuinely feared for my life."

"Remember that. The most dangerous thing you typically face is tennis elbow. My people know that their lives are on the line every day. They're rarely the best educated people around; a lot of them couldn't hold a job if they could find one. At least as often, they were screwed by a legal system that eats minorities for lunch and a social service system that's reluctant to actually care. Still, they have amazing survival skills."

"You know Sherm, I met a few real gems out there. Angels in disguise. I might not have survived that first night without a guy who shared his cheap beer with me."

"'I was a stranger, and you took me in,' right?"

"I thought about that."

I just handed my soul to Sherman on a platter, and I expect him to devour it. This is his chance to attack every preconception, every prejudice, every privileged white attitude. Instead, I see . . . is that just a hint of a smile from Sherman Jackson? He looks at me and says, "Good." It was a wonderful, refreshing, healing moment. After a few seconds of silence, I spoil the mood.

"I also learned how lonely this place is. Pretty God-forsaken place."

"Well son, your B just dropped to a D minus, and I'm being lenient. Two nights and you're forming judgments about an entire city?"

He stares at me. I don't move. Sherm moves his chair back an inch and leans toward me, his face a foot closer than I'd prefer. What's coming will be painful, and I decide to let it come.

"You came down here to 'experience homelessness.' Isn't that what you called it? *Isn't it?*"

"Yes," I answer. Sheepishly.

"You had your one night with a chaperone, then a second for God knows what reason, and then your plan was, 'OK—now back to the 'burbs.' That's not homelessness. That's a *campout*. These people have no home to go back to. No wife and daughter to welcome them with open arms—although tonight, that might be more than you'll get.

"It's really simple, Noel—you're a theologian. Understand the notion that God didn't just drop by for a one-night visit? God entering the world's shit, because nothing less would do? And that's what *you* would have to do, Mr. 'experience homelessness.' To experience homelessness, *you have to be homeless!*

"And never call this a God-forsaken place. Any place where people face brutality, disease, hate, and condescension from people like you, where they cry and die alone and hungry—that's where the God I worship *lives,* man. This is God's country. These are God's favorite people. And *this*, my friend, not your cushy suburb, is God's hometown."

CHAPTER THIRTY-SIX
HOMECOMING

I have no ID, no car keys, and no money. Sherm pays my Metra fare. I ride to the station where my Jeep is parked, and Trish meets me there, gives me the spare key fob, and I follow her home. I need time to sort out my story; even now it's not clear.

I am not welcomed with open arms. I was hoping for a hug, some "I'm glad you're OK," and I *really* need a shower. That would give me more time to sort out what I tell Trish. I get the hug, but it's less than enthusiastic. She says she's glad I'm home, but she's not interested in my hygiene just yet.

"You almost died."

I say nothing.

"You promised to be faithful to me, and I promised the same to you. You don't see what you did as unfaithful, do you?"

"I wasn't unfaithful."

"Yes, Noel, you were. I feel that you dishonored our relationship in this."

"I lost my phone."

"You still had options."

Before hearing my story of life on the street, Trish tells me what my antics had put her through. "I haven't slept for two days. When you lost your phone, why didn't you just flag down a police car? I was scared, Noel. Really, really, scared. I respect your passion for this. I support you when you take informed risks for something you care deeply about. But I cannot support you when you won't keep me in the loop."

That hurt. But I'm inclined to agree now.

"Noel, not knowing is worse than knowing. I am competent enough and strong enough to share whatever life throws at us. So treat me like your equal, your partner—as we always were when we started our life together. Don't shut me out, Noel."

I'm finding out how slowly time passes when I have nothing to say in return. She isn't finished, but this time, she speaks softly. "One more thing, Noel." It seems these words will be hard to say. Her voice breaks when she says, "I'm sorry too."

I am genuinely confused. She needs some time—a breath or two—before she can speak with the decisiveness I love in this woman.

"I am sorry I didn't challenge you more forcefully when you told me about this plan. I saw how committed you were to this, and I knew that telling you how I felt would be a very hard conversation. I bit my tongue and caved without telling you the truth. Even if you had gone anyway, you went without knowing my heart. In that way, I was unfaithful to you. I'm sorry."

She doesn't need protecting. I need her to walk with me on this journey, and all I did was push her away.

"So what do we do now?"

Trish simply shakes her head. "Welcome home." We embrace.

Saturday morning, still in our pajamas, coffee in hand, Trish and I are alone. Melissa's being spoiled by her maternal grandparents, so we're enjoying a glimpse of empty nesting. The nightmare of my ill-conceived adventure, now four days behind us, has at least this in its favor: we can talk, and listen, knowing how precious is this relationship we share.

I'm unpacking my conversations with Sherman while Trish listens. Sherman's the drill sergeant I need to put me in my place. Trish does that too, but she's the medic. She'll tell me the truth, but then offer me a safe place to land. They may not know it, but they're blessed co-conspirators.

Today, she does more than listen. "Noel, I like what he says about the limits of changing someone's circumstances. All I know is what I read. I get that he's got wisdom we don't, but I've studied this on my own, I have something I'd like us to consider."

"Tell me more." Full disclosure: I'm a mediocre listener. But Trish has an expansive mind and has influenced my thinking far more than I either admit or know.

"This may be more intuitive than objective. But my reading about the homeless led me to some data on homeless veterans—"

"Sherman's mentioned that there are a lot of them."

"Did he mention how many homeless vets are women?"

New news that frankly shouldn't be new to me. "No—why?"

"Lisa Grant."

I think for a minute. She's connecting some dots for me. "She never told me she was a vet."

"Me either Noel, but reading about their battles with PTSD or sexual assault while serving their country, or the difficulty of returning and starting life all over—something subtle in what she said and didn't say. I just wonder."

Then I remember. "When she and I talked that day at church—she said she was 'deployed.'" Trish smiles, and I say, "Thanks for complicating my life again."

Once in a while, like right now, I'm struck by the furious love that holds us, and I remember that my life could have been so much different. A week ago today, my life could have ended. But a very long time ago life tried its best to get in our way, before it brought us together.

"I should have been there." It's nineteen years ago, two forty in the morning, and the woman I don't know I will marry is speaking.

Trish and I started college the same year and became sort-of friends in our loose social web, though for the first three years we didn't like each other very much. She was more focused on education than I, whose social calendar often sidelined my scholarship. In any case, we were polite but distant, enjoying our mutual friends more than each other, until this early morning call interrupts my sleep and changes my life.

I'm barely awake while she's on her third cup of black coffee. She was in danger of breaking something when I found her, hands clasped around her cup in a corner booth at Denny's. Up to now, I've failed to get an explanation for why she'd dragged me out of my cheap student apartment in the middle of the night. An hour ago I began with "Are you OK?" and her response was "OK? Have any *more* stupid questions?" I've been asking questions ever since, most of them beginning with "Why?" and "What?" while her responses have largely consisted of, "You don't get it." There's been a lot of silence in between until now, when she volunteers that she should have been somewhere. It doesn't take a genius to know where, or with whom.

Near the end of our junior year, two months before our Denny's rendezvous, Trish's sister Maria ended her life. And whether or not the overdose was intentional, it almost broke the woman who now shares my bed. We who cared about Trish took her by the hand and walked her through the last weeks of class and finals. I shared two of her classes, so our friends volunteered me (the vote was 9–2, Trish and I the lone dissenters) to be her study partner, designated pest to make her eat something besides chips and chocolate, and her advocate with teachers displeased with blown deadlines.

She was a difficult charge—argumentative, defiant, and prone to tears. She had a hair-trigger anger, plenty of should-have-been-there guilt, and a broken heart. Her boyfriend had zero empathy and no patience for grief. He disappeared; I fell in love with her. I broke my romance with a brilliant and beautiful girl I'd been dating since the fall semester, whose only flaw was that she wasn't Trish.

Trish would not fall in love with me for another year, the longest of my life. Somehow I had enough sense to keep in touch without pressing my case, until finally, she calls me at one thirty in the morning and demands my presence. "Now!" she demands, "Denny's," where we meet in the middle of the night, our first "date," in a very dark place. I will remember this sleepless night as the most pivotal of my life—one that started with coffee, a donut, and tension. We finished five hours later in the same booth, with breakfast and a first hug.

Losing her sister drove Trish to shift her coursework from education to mental health. She was a good student, fierce actually, driven to save every person in the land from every form of addiction. We married at spring break in our senior year, graduated together, and as I started my job counting money, she started grad school.

Her drivenness and singular focus *almost* made me question our marriage. But good friends and a good therapist brought us back from the brink. Of the two of us, she now has the better work/life balance. And I am the luckiest charm-deficient man alive.

Apparently, our conversation about unhoused veterans is winding down, because Trish looks at me over her glasses, grins her patented "Gotcha" grin and says, "Well . . . since I've complicated your life . . . I would love to complicate it some more." I surrender, look down at my coffee, take a sip, and put the mug back on the table. Ten seconds have passed, maybe less. I'm sensing that she's still looking at me. I glance up; she is. And this time there's her other special smile, the one that invites me to enjoy pleasures that are only ours. She holds up her phone and with a flourish, puts it on silent.

I lay my now-silenced new phone next to hers on the kitchen counter, and follow her upstairs. Melissa's gone until tomorrow, and we have the house to ourselves. My coffee will be cold when I return, and that may be a while. Nothing personal caffeine, but you are far less rewarding than this.

CHAPTER THIRTY-SEVEN
FINDING THE PERFECT PLACE

"**S**o what properties can I show you, sir?"

I'm in a realtor's office, and I'm not looking for a new home. This agent specializes in rural properties. Make that farms.

I'm way ahead of the curve—and there isn't even a "curve" yet, as far as my employer is concerned. Normally, I'd first present this concept to a committee, preferably formed by people already on board with the overall goal: a retreat of sorts, a shelter, a home for the unhoused on River Glen's perimeter. Better yet (my personal dream), right along the river. But given my complicated relationship with Old First, I don't want to propose something if there's no place to make it happen. I'm saying nothing to anyone not named Trish until I've done my homework. This is me testing the water before inviting others to dive in. I need hard data: what's available, potential costs, an actual plan and rationale for *why*—this needs a much better rationale than "Noel Garraty wants it."

I'm haunted by Sherman Jackson's comment: "Why don't you and your church build one?" A city-based shelter like Sherm's is vital, but some of his folk need more than a bed for a few nights. They need a complete change, long-term, away from the pull of the city where they are vulnerable to its lures, and often unwelcome. I imagine a farm-like setting where beds are clean and soft, where sleeping on alleys and sidewalks is a distant memory, and with no intoxicants around the corner. A place where they can till the garden, fish along the river, walk among the trees, surrounded by the sounds and silence of creation. Where they can find some peace. A home for people who need months or even *years*, not mere nights, of refuge.

I tell the realtor I'm looking for a "hobby farm." I don't tell him what my "hobby" is. I have my criteria, though. Maybe forty or better yet eighty acres, on or very close to the river. Some of those acres must be wooded. A farmhouse would be nice, but we'd probably need more suitable housing for an atypical farm family. Outbuildings would be great. I want a workable farm where people can nurture their spirits by coaxing life from the soil, working in a woodshop or at a potter's wheel, in seclusion, beyond easy walking distance of a town or a highway.

This close to Chicago, he says, hardly anything like that exists. Agribusiness and exurbia have eaten up most of the real estate. But if you want to be a distance from town and farther from the Windy City, he says, there are some possibilities to the west and north. He hands me some files. I look first at the price. Suddenly, Mike Curillo's tithe looks rather inviting.

After reviewing his files, I see one that strikes my fancy. A satellite photo shows the river, some woods along its banks, a scattering of outbuildings, a big, ancient barn, and a farmhouse with a full-length front porch, at the end of a winding driveway through some trees. I hand the file back to him. "How about this one?"

He looks, and I'm expecting that he'll at least pretend it's a fine choice. Instead, he sighs, stares at the summary page and clearly hopes I'll find something else. "Yes, it seems to meet your criteria, Reverend Garraty. But up close, you may have some reservations."

"Such as?"

"Let me be candid. Yes, it's for sale. But the seller has been driving potential buyers away for the past five years."

"He doesn't want to sell?"

"Depends on the day. Or maybe the time of day. One minute he's on the phone calling us names 'cause no one's been by to see it. Next minute he's got an interested party on the property and he's doing everything he can to sabotage the deal. I'd tell him to find another realtor, but there are so few of these properties left that I keep the file active."

"So if we stop by there's no telling what he'll do?"

"Don't make too much of my reservations. He's not dangerous; at least I don't think so. He's just not put together very well. Inherited the farm from his parents who died twenty years ago. Sort of a leftover hippie. Lives off the land; has some very crude home-made solar panels, a home-made wind generator. He farms—if you can call his operation a farm—organically. At least, that's what he says."

The realtor shrugs. "If you want to see this property, let's take a look. But don't assume that this will be simple. And please, Reverend, be prepared for some buildings that are structurally OK, but, well—he's saved a lot of money on paint over the years." I surrender to his reluctance and review several more files.

When my Boss said that the first shall be last, He may have been thinking about real estate. The agent offered to show me several properties he thought I might like. He almost begged me to find some options other than the one that had first caught my eye; something makes my first choice his last, where the owner sounds like a piece of work.

We visit one that's too small. Forty acres doesn't provide enough of a buffer from the rest of the world, and it's close enough to town so that you can see what passes for River Glen's skyline: a few steeples and a water tower. His other offering is the perfect size, but all the trees have been harvested except for a few along the riverbank. The outbuildings are too far gone, and the farmhouse is a 1950s ranch. Nope. Try number three.

This one's better. A few acres of undisturbed, mature hardwoods, and it might do except for one thing. Its river access is only about fifty yards or so of riverbank—and you can't get there anyway. To reach the ol' fishin' hole you have to cross nearly a city block's worth of marsh. By the time you wet your line, the mud would have swallowed you up.

"Well," the agent says as we drive back out to the road in his Escalade, "I'll at least drive by that first property you wanted to see."

Good, I think. He's finally doing what I wanted to do three hours ago.

He was right about the paint. It would take an archeologist to find even traces of it. But I like the fact that you enter through a stand of mature oaks and maples on a winding driveway that isolates the buildings from the road. To the west is the river, just beyond the trees and brush that thrive along the bank, which is dry, rising almost eight feet above the water. A decent acreage for farming or large-scale gardening. The barn needs urgent help, but I think it's salvageable and might be worth the effort. Fix it, paint it red, and you've got a postcard. One of the last nineteenth century barns in the county, Realty Man says. The farmhouse shares the barn's vintage—and unfortunately, its condition.

Out of the corn shed comes, I guess, the owner. Hard to tell if he wants company or not. I sense he hasn't smiled since Reagan left office, and probably won't do so today.

"Good morning, Jesse." My realtor walks nervously toward the man in coveralls, boots, and—nothing else. "Jesse" doesn't say anything. He nods almost invisibly, turns his head to the left and spits. After a perfunctory handshake in which all the enthusiasm was on the realtor's side, Jesse glances my way and says, "Who's that?" My agent introduces me to Jesse Ryan, farmer, who gives me the shortest sales pitch in real estate history.

"Good dirt. All black; no rocks. Full price."

CHAPTER THIRTY-EIGHT
MAKING THE CASE

F rank Lloyd Wright . . . Santiago Calatrava . . . Paolo Soleri—masters in the art of sculpting unforgettable structures, cathedrals in a sense, awe-inspiring in size and beauty, defying the crass, utilitarian boxes that often celebrate little more than the invention of concrete.

Cathedrals are equally unforgettable. They're like the Grand Canyon, or the Redwoods: you enter a space that you cannot overpower; it overpowers *you*. They are also theological statements, shaped by a message that seeks to shape your soul. Simply by entering, you feel swallowed up, humbled in the presence of an Other who, unlike frail mortals, endures forever.

But today, cathedrals may be the emptiest spaces in the city. The institution they celebrate is being dethroned by the surrounding culture. Even First Community Church has seen its numbers and influence wane . . . and no amount of cathedral-building or technological trickery will reverse the decline of what some of us so dearly adore.

That traditional model works for us, but is propping up a Sunday-centered identity the future we should seek? Is that what "church" should be? What does the world need that we uniquely offer? I envision one answer.

First Community Church needs a different kind of cathedral—not a massive building, but a majestic *vision*. Not to impress, but to transform human lives. A project so grand that it drives us to work together, so ambitious that what we begin we can invite our children and grandchildren to continue.

Grand in scale, outside the lines, costly, risky—my vision has all the hallmarks of a Noel Garraty vanity project, the kind that drove me in my business years. But this is the last thing I would pursue if personal glory were my intent. If we can recover a sense of what is truly beautiful, we may see the image of a beauty-creating God not in brick and stone, but in the rejected and powerless. This is my vision. I will present it to my church's leadership tonight.

It's late July, and there are watches and warnings all over northern Illinois. We're having a fairly impressive thunderstorm at the moment; at least no one will be tempted to skip this special meeting to play golf. I called this a "leadership retreat" after giving John, the council chair, a snapshot of what I wanted to talk about. I also asked him not to say too much before tonight. I wanted a chance to explain it before too many council members made their minds up beforehand.

I'm on edge. My precarious standing in the congregation is the subtext to everything we talk about. They have a fifteen-page proposal in hand to back up what I'll describe, complete with statistics and charts. We're gathered around a conference table. They look worried. My guess is they think this hush-hush agenda may be about something ominous—the minister is confessing something scandalous, or worst of all that the church is broke. The chair turns the meeting over to me.

"Thanks for coming out tonight. We have had a painful journey recently. Because of that, I know that the less secrecy and intrigue, the better. Some of you are worried about my silence surrounding tonight's agenda. Let me assure you that in spite of what we're going through, especially since Easter, First Church is doing well. In fact, our summer income and attendance are running ahead of last year. The people of Old First have risen to the challenge and pulled together in many ways. I'm encouraged by some of the plans for fall and winter that a few of you have shared with me." I pause. Then—

"I have a proposal to present. It's substantial, so after I give you a general overview, I want you to take whatever time you need to digest it."

This may be a defining moment for our church. For my ministry, definitely, as it should be. Even without the conflict that makes my future here fragile at best, a pastor should think carefully before putting forward a vision for which they're willing to risk their future. But in a time when "business as usual" puts churches in grave peril, a vision beyond what seems safe may be the God-driven risk that's the safest of all.

"Not all holy places need pews. Ministry can make any place sacred, if it is furnished with tables on which we feed the hungry. Or beds, or simply a quiet place away from the distractions and temptations of the city where the addicted can begin recovery, or families without a home can find one. That can be holy ground, the 'cathedrals' of the twenty-first century, and we have the capacity to build it. We've gone through some difficult times, yes. But there is great pain all around us crying for a bold response. Even wounded, we can still be Christ's wounded healers in the world. Perhaps this can begin our own healing, by redirecting our eyes toward the future.

"I am asking our church to embrace the most ambitious mission project in our history. We've always been seen as leaders in River Glen's faith community, and with good reason. Here's a way we can continue that legacy of leadership.

"The proposal you're holding concerns a piece of local property and a vision for putting it to work. I'm asking you to withhold judgment and let me lay out my thinking. I believe we could imaginatively serve some of God's choicest children by providing a refuge for the unhoused. It could serve unhoused men. Or it could shelter abused women and children. I've learned firsthand that a lot of families without a home wind up on the street because there aren't enough shelters to accommodate them.

"There are about twelve million Americans who are or have been homeless; there could be well in excess of half a million on our streets right now. Twenty percent are homeless adults with dependent children. One third of these children have no school experience. Eighty percent of the single parents in the unhoused population are women in poverty. And those numbers are growing."

I'm not finished, but I'm challenged anyway, and was ready for it. "Yes, but are any of them connected to any of us?"

"Probably not," I tell them. "The hardest for me to accept are the tens of thousands of women who served their country, and then came back to a country that offered them, if they were lucky, just enough benefits to qualify for food assistance, but little to ease their physical or emotional wounds. They tend to congregate in cities like Chicago. And the street's a dangerous place to raise a child—"

"The homeless people I've seen in Chicago seem to be mostly drunk."

"It isn't all booze or drugs or welfare-dependency. There are the disabled who have no benefits or were wiped out financially by medical bills. There are the trades people who were downsized. There were those who sought to escape an abusive or dangerous home but had nowhere to go. Many of the children are runaways who find a substitute parent in a pimp who sucks them into a life of abuse and shame."

Finally a question about bricks and mortar: "So you want to build a shelter or something out here? Don't they need the help in Chicago, where they are?"

"Some of them need to get *out* of the city. They often need long-term housing and help, and most shelters can't keep them beyond the immediate crisis that got them into trouble. We could assemble, I believe, the resources to create a refuge for them. People, this could be the 'cup of cold water' Jesus talked about for some people who have been battered, broken, and cast aside."

"OK," our treasurer asks, "What will this cost us?"

"I would estimate about three million dollars to start, and perhaps three hundred thousand dollars a year to sustain it. But that won't be all our burden. We can find grants and other funds to support the costs we'd incur. We'd very likely find others—other churches in River Glen for instance—willing to share the burden with us. I really don't think funding is insurmountable. But I do think we should take the lead."

I'm not a gambler, but if I were and had bet a year's salary that the next question would come up, I would have won big.

"Would this involve a significant number of minorities?"

I wonder if that question would have surfaced if Brad were here. I asked him not to attend, so that question could be out in the open. "Yes. Of course it would. Almost half are African American; others are Hispanic, Native American, and other minorities as well." I could see an almost imperceptible change in his expression, and I knew—this will not get his vote. Not any time soon. Probably never.

"Pastor, are we sure we're providing enough resources for our own people? Isn't that our first priority before we go out to save the world?"

"Our first priority is to follow where we're led. I believe in this. Let's find a way to minister to some of the world's most desperate people. And let's do it hands-on. Remember Carl? I can't get him out of my mind."

One of the newer members of the council is Al. He's more evangelical in his theology than many in the room. He's prayerful, a student of the Word. He's a man of impeccable integrity and has been a loyal friend to me through our crisis, but he speaks against my proposal.

"I'm sure there are exceptions, but a lot of them are what Proverbs often calls the 'slothful,' who are poor because they aren't willing to work. Pastor, you know I believe in the scriptures. And the Bible makes it very clear: "If they do not work, then they should not eat." I don't want us to enable behavior like that."

There's a smattering of approving nods, even a soft "Amen" from someone in the room. And it is followed by a deafening silence, as happens when someone reveals aloud what many are ashamed to actually say. Hearing it out loud, it's like broken glass going down the throat.

I wait, then reply. "Al, I've always appreciated your love for the Word. It's a love I share. But that one sentence is part of a much larger conversation that's not talking about society's poor. You will not find in the teachings of Jesus or the rest of scripture a judgment on the worthiness of the poor. They are not lazy. If they are, they're dead, because you don't survive on the street unless you're an incredibly inventive, courageous person.

"People, this is not something I would have chosen. I spent the first half of the year fighting this. But I believe in this project as something we are called to do—and I hope I can lead First Church in bringing this vision to life."

The room is silent for a minute, which is usually good. What's not good is that virtually everyone's looking at the floor. Finally, a personal response, and an honest one.

"You're making me nervous, Pastor. We have no experience with homeless people. Besides sending money, what can we offer them that they can't get somewhere else?"

"Besides," another long-time member adds, "Pastor Garraty, I have a problem with them on principle. They're a safety and liability risk that I'm not sure I want to expose First Community Church to."

I let the people object to my proposal. Most apparently don't like it. Then I respond.

"Let me tell you about an experience I had a couple weeks ago." For the next ten minutes I recount my nights on the street. I leave out a few things, such as the verbal flogging I received from Sherman Jackson. I tell about helping bring a child into the world, about the living conditions, the despair and alienation. And the people. I tell about the Grants, and Freddie, who is still out there somewhere trying to find his way, and about how as a minister and as a Christian I have unfinished business with them, because God has unfinished business with them.

"Druggies and drunks? Many are. Liars and thieves? Some almost made me their victim. But there are also women with children. Disabled veterans of Viet Nam or the wars in the Persian Gulf. People who worked hard for twenty years and watched their job move to Indonesia. Women whose husbands beat and raped their own children. People our world all but ignores. People for whom Jesus died. People He called His siblings. People He explicitly made us responsible for. People that we can, in every sense of the word, *minister* to."

"Pastor, our church didn't become the success story it is by messing with a pretty sound ministry plan. Even starting small is a 'death by inches' that could eventually entangle Old First with a rather rough crowd that, frankly, I don't want my children exposed to."

They keep raising objections; I try to answer them. But it's clear that my idea is on life support. Few hearts seem moved. Instead, they opt for adding a small line item in the next budget for "homeless outreach"—mercifully we punt the meaning of that phrase to our social concerns committee. And in an attempt to let me down gently, they vote to "allow" me to bring one or "no more than two" unhoused youth to church camp with our kids. No doubt they think I'm giddy with joy over such an expansive outreach. *Aw, come on, folks. That's 'death by inches.' Why not do something so extreme you can't go back?*

CHAPTER THIRTY-NINE
LITURGICALLY CHALLENGED

Nobody loves Jesus more than James. A thirty-something single man who lives with his parents, James (and don't you dare call him "Jim" or "Jimmy") has a radiant spirit, loves Old First, and never misses a chance to serve. Frank, our custodian, considers James his right-hand man, and has declared James Flower Keeper in Chief—even had a name tag made with that title on it; James wears it with evident pride.

James is developmentally challenged. He is also our most faithful usher and greeter. And today, James is greeting a most challenging guest.

Fashion matters here. As I sit in front of my summer congregation, a fashion show parades before me as the flock enters the fold. Lots of white, plenty of pastels. Vanity should bother me, and I'm looking at a sea of it, but I'm no less fashion conscious than they are. I like the view from where I sit. It's bright; it lifts my spirits to see people celebrating the all-too-short season of warm days, long evenings, and weekends in the sun.

One worshiper didn't get the fashion memo. He's getting a lot of attention in spite of—no, because of—his failure to exhibit proper style. It's not every day that we see someone in this church wearing a baseball cap with *John Deere* embroidered on the front. We have "greeters" at every door on Sundays, volunteers who make sure everyone coming in gets a smile, a handshake, and a pleasantry or two. In the case of a first-time visitor, a special welcome packet is provided by a smiling face saying, "Can I answer any questions about First Church?"

My guess is that when James saw Jesse Ryan pull up in his mud-caked pick-up and walk toward the door, he was less enthusiastic as he welcomed ol' Jesse. He offers Mr. Ryan a bulletin—Mr. Ryan hands it back. James isn't used to that, and looks troubled. Jesse Ryan walks down the aisle; James follows, not sure what to do, because he expects to lead our guests to the pew of their choice. The first-time visitor in coveralls walks past any pews with someone—even just one worshiper—already there, until sliding into the second row, right in front of the pulpit. No one sits there if they can help it; people prefer sitting as far back as they can. Not Jesse Ryan, who sits by himself, second row, left side. James looks anxiously toward me. I smile and nod. James seems relieved and quickly returns to his spot by the entrance.

Jesse settles in, apparently wanting to soak in my every word. He'll have no trouble soaking in all he wants; the only person closer to me this morning is the organist. Sitting directly in front of me on a lightly attended Sunday, he'll have no distractions. But sitting in front of the pulpit, dressed in a relatively clean white shirt and tie (under his Osh Gosh coveralls), he'll be a serious distraction to the rest of my congregation. And to me. How does one ignore the only person within thirty feet of you when he's the first thing you see when you look up from your notes?

Mr. Ryan turns out to be liturgically challenged. Since he can't see the rest of the congregation, he's typically about five seconds slow to stand when it's time to stand and sit when it's time to sit. He's conspicuous, especially when he's the only one left standing. He makes no attempt to sing, nor does he lift the hymn book from the rack. And when the scripture is read, he sits impassively, ignoring the Bible in the pew. Not because of inattentiveness. On the contrary, he never takes his eyes off me, focusing on every word.

Worship is over, and I make my exit down the center aisle. Mr. Ryan, not knowing that the unspoken rule is to wait until the organist finishes the end-of-service chimes, simply slips out and follows me. I meet Trish at the pew where she's sitting. She glances back at my follower, grins, and we walk out with Mr. Ryan behind, a three-person parade. When we reach the door, the minister and his lovely wife greet the faithful as they leave. Naturally, the first hand we shake is Jesse's. I introduce him to Trish; he's short but polite. "Nice to meet you. Nice sermon, Reverend." He walks away.

But he does not leave. He scans a literature rack, looking up occasionally to see what we're doing. We're shaking hands, saying have a good day, while he watches.

Trish and I do more than shake hands. We occasionally put an arm around each other as we chat with our church family. At one point, Trish playfully leans over and kisses me on the cheek. We think nothing of it, but our most interesting first-time visitor witnesses this moment, and it apparently triggers a plan in his mind. We finally head toward my office; we notice that our farmer friend has disappeared.

The next day, I'm standing by the gas pump at the local convenience mart. I hear my name, turn, and find myself face to face with Jesse Ryan. "Reverend, remember what you said yesterday?"

I try to smile earnestly. "What are you thinking of, Mr. Ryan?"

"You said," he queries, "that God cares about every part of my life, right?"

"That's right. God cares deeply about our daily lives." My mind clicks into overdrive. When someone quotes my sermons back to me, I'm usually in trouble.

"So, if there's something I need, God is concerned about it too."

I want desperately to launch a full-blown explanation of the difference between needs and wants, and that God may not agree with us regarding what's in our best interest. But control of a conversation with Jesse is probably lost before it starts. "I really believe that, Jesse."

"You said that *your* goal is to care about what God cares about."

Now I'm in trouble, though I haven't the slightest idea what kind of trouble I'm in. *Note to self: I need to be more vague in my preaching.* "Jesse, what do you think I should care about?"

"Reverend, does God care about me?"

"Jesse, I—"

"God has a lot to do. It's like my farm—it's harder every year to care for my fields; I'm not a kid anymore. Does God feel tired too? I worry that God might have forgotten about ol' Jesse."

"What makes you think that God might have forgotten you?"

Jesse shrugs. "Dunno. Just that every year I work harder, make less money, get more tired. And I've always wanted a wife, you know? Someone who could work with me, keep me company, but . . ." Looking down, he shakes his head.

"I am so sorry, Jesse. But I promise you this: God never forgets us." I start to say more, but for the moment at least, Jesse seems satisfied. "I hope so. Thanks." He walks away.

Standing next to my wife later that day, I'm chopping onions for her trademark meatloaf and debriefing on my day's most interesting encounter. "Got a cousin you'd like to marry off?"

"Huh?"

"The mysterious Mr. Ryan wants a wife."

"Excuse me?"

"Seriously. He heard me speak yesterday about God's care for daily life."

"So his lack of a love life is your problem?"

"I apparently mumbled something about sharing God's concerns for the above-mentioned daily life. This is all your fault, you know."

"Once again, excuse me?"

"Your little public display of affection after church. Not that I minded. But I wonder if, when he saw you hugging and kissing me, he realized what seems to be missing in his life.

"I shouldn't kid about it, Trish. He raised a larger question about God's capacity to care. I kind of ache for him, really. Getting older, less able to manage a fairly large farm . . . I think life is closing in on him, and he's asking hard questions, like a lot of folk we know, and not just at church. Declining strength, a changing world—people wonder where the joy has gone. And they have every right to wonder if their faith matters at all."

Trish shakes her head. "So what on earth are you going to do?"

"Try to stay in touch. Just how, I haven't figured out yet."

CHAPTER FORTY
INTERLUDE

The next skirmish in the Garraty/Curillo War will be fought with silver-ware. It takes place as usual in a restaurant. I wonder if Mike ever eats at home. He said it was important, though I can't imagine after my three-million-dollar pipe dream—Mike's words—that any meeting between us would be casual. I insist on paying; for Mike, paying the bill is not hospitality but a power play, and I'm having none of it.

He encourages me to order the special. Ribs, ribs, and more ribs. I like ribs, but they're messy, and I could embarrass myself by spilling on my tie; one more point for him. I choose a sirloin. Less risk of spills, less likely to distract me when I need to stay on task. Which isn't eating—it's sparring with a cunning adversary.

After forced pleasantries, Mike gets serious. "We're concerned about how you're creating distance between yourself and the people at First Church."

"Who is 'we,' and how am I distancing myself from the church I love?"

Curillo shifts in his chair. He studies his salad fork. "We really don't want you to hurt your family, or your professional reputation, by pushing that home-less farm idea. It will kill your effectiveness as a pastor."

"Thanks for your concern, Mike. I know you mean that, and I'm concerned too. But what I'm doing is being honest about where my heart and head are moving. And I think I can take care of myself."

"But I'm sure, Pastor, that you know the church's right to terminate a pastor it thinks is no longer serving its interests."

I know some people are thinking that. But nobody's been that blunt in saying so. Mike is correct; there's a dismissal process spelled out in excruciating detail. And while Mike doesn't know my heart here, I have no interest in letting things get to that point. If I leave, it will be my call, not the church's. But I keep that unspoken.

"Mike, First Community is free to exercise that right. You're free to seek that outcome. But before you do, have you calculated the costs of my leaving under those circumstances? Will people leave when I do? How long would it take to call a qualified candidate to a wounded church?"

"I'm not afraid of whatever happens. It's kind of liberating, really. You're good at what you do because you're passionate about it. I get that. But why should I compromise the passions that get me up in the morning?"

"But does anyone at church—anyone besides you—share that passion?"

"Not many, Mike. At least, not yet." I pause. In a sense, Mike's forcing me to face the downside of my idea: there *is* serious pushback, and I might not overcome it. What then?

I decide not to debate this man who opposes not only my proposal, but my credibility as a leader. Instead, I give witness. "A couple things these street people taught me: risk is OK, because security is an illusion. The safest place to be is wherever God is, no matter how dangerous it looks. Mike—I can't do anything else without compromising my integrity."

"And I," Mike replies, "can't stand by and watch this un-doing of River Glen's finest church, all for a pipe dream. Unless you put this nonsense to bed, Reverend Garraty—I will devote the weeks between now and the special business meeting to preparing a resolution of no confidence in your leadership." Once again, he gets up and leaves, leaving me stunned at the reality of it all.

I'm entitled by contract to an annual study leave, and I usually take it in late summer, which is now. But this is no time for a leisurely trip to, say, Colorado. Maybe this fall, maybe next year—assuming I'm still employed, and that is no longer a hypothetical question. That's why I need time to pray, think, to clear my head and discern whether this place and this calling remain my path. How committed am I to this dream? Are we as a family ready for that risk?

I awaken early, four hours after hitting the pillow beside my muse, lover, and loyal critic. Good thing I can navigate a darkened bedroom. I won't disturb her with lights, and there is still no trace of dawn.

I have only the morning for this. An early start is crucial. I face a full day once I enter the church. My to-do list will keep me there until ten o'clock tonight or later. I hit the shower, dress more casually than usual for a workday, grab my day pack (minus the folders, pens, and laptop) and within fifteen minutes, I back out of the garage. I grab a cup of coffee just before the on ramp—three bucks with a tip to a near-sleeping clerk—and I'm headed west.

I stop outside of Rockford for more coffee before continuing toward a destination an online hiking blog identified as relatively remote. Relatively, because even this far from Chicago, the towns can almost see each other. On my way home, I may stop in Galena for lunch. But what matters is that for a few precious hours I'm away from calendars, clocks, and phones.

It's still fairly dark when I park my Jeep at a primitive trailhead off a gravel road two hours west of home. It's hill country out here, land that drains into the Mississippi River farther west. I suspect that before long I'll be joined by others: couples, families, lone hikers like me, some with day packs like me. I'll be just another hiker to them, but I am not hiking. I'm seeking Sabbath. Just driving here was strangely restful, as if I knew I would find "daily bread" when I arrived.

What surrounds me is beautiful, and almost too quiet. I love this open-air sanctuary. I greet the dawn under a brightening sky and hear the first of the morning's birds. I also hear trucks on some unseen highway, a plane still climbing out of O'Hare on a westward journey. But it is still a wilderness, where each tree has its place in a rhythm of life, death, and life from death, a dance begun at creation. In places like this, ancient prophets forged their vision—bold, stark, declaring that *now* was the time.

I walk past the trail map, step around some un-trimmed brush, find the lightly worn path, and enter a piece of heaven. Still: the clock is ticking. I have only the morning for this.

Trees—I'm immersed in them now—motionless, silent, rooted for a lifetime to the place of their birth, some since my grandparents' grandparents were alive. They're easy to dismiss as lacking drama, but trees are alive. They speak, listen, adapt; they warn their neighbors of predators. They need each other; a kind of love connects them in a motionless, voiceless conversation. Social beings, trees are. They take water, nutrients, and sunlight, give the forest shade, fruit, places for shelter and safety. They are patient, and at peace with themselves. They endure abuse, and still focus on their purpose: making more trees while feeding the forest around them.

In our ignorance we may not be impressed by something so common. But trees are woven into the Bible so often they're among my faith's most amazing preachers, teachers, prophets, companions, friends, feasts. We wouldn't be here without them.

The trail curves and drops down to a stream washing the rock base underneath. Born in fire and fury when this land was new, rocks overpowered everything in their path. But then they cooled, and here they lay, enduring the relentless assault of wind, water, ice—and trees, who exploit any flaw in the stone as seeds and roots find seams, and begin to grow.

The rock remains, a testimony to toughness. But the cracks are growing; shards of rock lay at the base, pushed away by ice and roots, water and wind. Yes, rocks are impressive. But in the end, seedlings win.

I have mid-afternoon appointments starting at one thirty sharp. It's now seven in the morning.

Along the stream, debris is entangled three feet above the water, signs of the flow I'd have witnessed after a hard rain or snowmelt on a warm spring day. Today, it's a trickle. But unlike mud-laden spring runoff, this water is clear, clean, inviting.

I sit, walk a little further and sit again. Then, hearing traffic in the distance, I realize that it's now ten in the morning. If I don't head back now, I'll be late. But something holds me here. Without cell service, I can't call the office to reschedule. But I must stay awhile.

Looking at the barely flowing water, I hear a kind of voice. *Noel—that is you.* But how? I ask.

Like that stream, the flow of your life as you have known it is diminished.

I know, I acknowledge. I am restless, troubled, unsure. My confidence has been shaken.

But new life is being birthed in you, Noel. Trust that new life. Trust Me. Trust yourself. Remember the resilience of the trees. You are not breaking. Like a seed, you are breaking open.

I turn around, retracing my steps. *You are breaking open* accompanies me on the drive back. But I carry with me another seed. This interlude, this respite, this renewal I find away from concrete and steel, the peace I find when the noise of urban life is muted, calls me to this. Do not the urban poor, the unhoused, also need the restoration I find here? Maybe they need this even more than I do? Could this not save someone's life? This *is* my calling, my burden, and perhaps even my joy.

CHAPTER FORTY-ONE
THE REQUEST

i was raised in a house where the men were absent
stolen by death and divorce
leaving only a lonely fedora hanging on old coat rack
and their last names as reminders of where they'd been
i was raised by women who were trained to survive
who couldn't take the time it took to lick their wounds
who must be modern Hagars, pack child and past on their back
and travel roads far from home

—— Amena Brown, "House Full of Women"

S unday morning. Old First is at about forty percent capacity on most summer Sundays, but since it's Labor Day weekend, about that many of us are on pontoon boats somewhere north of here, enjoying the great outdoors and last holiday in the always-too-short summer.

The upside to low attendance is that it's easier to spot visitors or infrequent attendees. I scan the crowd while the musicians do their part preparing the congregation for worship. I make a few mental notes about folk I should call or who are now out of the hospital; there's a couple whose marriage is struggling and who have another counseling appointment tomorrow. I see someone I'd asked to serve on the Pastor-Parish Relations Committee. They promised to get back to me but haven't. I see Lisa and Cherry—

Lisa and Cherry Grant? What are they doing here? Lisa smiles when she sees me looking at her; I return the smile. Cherry doesn't look up. And as Cherry turns and slides into a row of seats, I try not to look shocked. Why on earth is this sixteen-year-old *pregnant?*

It haunts me all through the service, and as people leave afterward and I stand at the back, I'm scanning the exiting crowd, praying they won't disappear. Usually, I've got Trish standing next to me. All I'd need is to whisper in her ear, and she'd be off on a recon mission looking for them. But this week Trish is in the nursery, where she insists on taking a turn "like every other parishioner should, including the minister, dear husband," she would say. I'm on my own today, desperately wanting to connect with our former houseguests.

When most of the holiday-thinned crowd has left, they head my way.

"Lisa and Cherry! I've been worried about you."

Lisa speaks first. "You even remember our names?"

"How could I forget? Listen—Trish is here somewhere; so is Melissa, and they'll be glad to see you."

Lisa responds. "We'd like that."

I've got an idea. "Trish, Melissa, and I go out for dinner a lot after church. Would you be our guests?"

At a crowded franchise restaurant, we catch up. Much has happened, yet in some ways, very little. The months were not kind to the Grant's. The way they rush through the narrative of that time, I sense they're not telling us how unkind it actually was. They've lived in whatever housing they could scrounge in Chicago. But they're now living in a women's shelter in Rockford that they'll soon vacate. Lisa's found work, and Cherry is enrolled in a special high school program for unwed pregnant kids this fall, and they will soon settle into an apartment of their own. All very interesting, but what is more interesting to me is how Cherry is becoming increasingly pensive. Something's on her mind.

We also confirm Trish's instinct. Lisa is a veteran after all. Married, gave birth to Cherry, a normal life until being called up. Some of her story is as she said in our first encounter: after serving her country she came home to an unfaithful husband dealing drugs and neglecting their daughter. He leaves, is arrested, implicates Lisa. She's innocent but loses her job, then the house, and very nearly her daughter. Another hoped-for relationship ends when his undocumented status leads to deportation. But, she says, unconvincingly, it's no big deal now because they are making a new start.

Dinner's over, the restaurant is starting to thin out, so I suggest dessert largely to give Lisa and Cherry time for whatever they may wish to say. I realize that if there's something personal on their minds, this is not the ideal setting. Trish and Melissa's presence may complicate any need for confidentiality. But for now, there's no hint of a crisis—except for a pregnant young woman.

While we wait for the sweets to arrive, I'm trying to think of some non-threatening way to ask. Trish does it for me. "So, Cherry, is there something we can do for you?"

Lisa begins to reply, but Cherry will have none of it. "Mom, let me explain this, OK? Reverend Garraty, Mrs. Garraty, I'm going to have a baby in December. Mom and I have talked a lot about it, and I'm giving it up for adoption. I'm working with an agency that lets me pick the family that adopts my baby."

Lisa jumps into the conversation. "You see, Pastor Garraty, the father has no interest in the baby, and we don't want anything to do with him either. We've had enough of drugs in our lives. He still uses and sells."

This is Cherry's conversation from this point on. "We—well, especially me—we'd love to keep my baby." She stops; it takes a moment to compose herself. Lisa would probably finish the thought for her daughter, but her emotions are equally fragile. Cherry looks down, swallows, and gathers her composure. "But we can't afford to raise one. We don't have health insurance; we can't even afford to pay for the birth."

When Cherry looks up, there's strength in her voice. "But the family that adopts the baby covers all the expenses." Lisa adds, "I'm supporting Cherry's decision all the way."

Trish is mesmerized. And wisely directs her words to the girl, an unspoken way to honor the teen's resolve. "That's wonderful, Cherry. You've found a family for your child?"

"I think so. I haven't told the social service people, but it's down to two couples, and I think I know which one I want it to be."

I lean forward, looking toward Cherry. "So how can we help?"

"Reverend Garraty, if you can't do this, I'll understand." Cherry shifts in her chair. She's trying to be casual, but whatever she wants, it's huge to her. "But I was wondering if . . . Mom?"

Lisa reaches for her daughter's shaking hand and looks toward me. "When Mr. Jackson told us how hard you tried to find us, we wanted you to know we were OK. But we also wanted to see if—Pastor, adoption is usually a lot of legal stuff. And most of the time, handing over the baby happens in a lawyer's office. But Cherry had a different idea, didn't you, honey?"

This gives the mother-to-be the courage she needs. "I don't want my baby to just get handed over like it's just some legal thing. I want God to be part of my baby's future . . ." For a moment, she's back on the edge, but she recovers. "I know things were rough when we stayed with you. But I saw how all of you really love each other. And Melissa told me that you all love God and Jesus, and—"

Melissa, neither trained nor ordained and who technically shouldn't be in this conversation, boldly breaks pastoral protocol and jumps in. "Cherry? I didn't think you heard a thing I said." Cherry blushes; this isn't her normal topic of conversation. "Like God loves me no matter what? That God's on my side? Yeah, I did. I even started writing my prayers so I don't get distracted."

Lisa, in the voice of a mother who loves her daughter (and is intrigued by this new dimension in Cherry's life), interjects. "She told me she ends each prayer with 'I love you, Jesus.' Is that OK?"

Melissa must have something in her eye. And I have something stuck in my throat. Cherry looks back at me. "Could we have a little service or something? I mean, could Mom and me, my baby, the new parents, maybe even the lawyer, come to the front of the church, and you could say a prayer and maybe read something from the Bible and, you know, ask Jesus or God or the Lord to bless the adoption or something?"

I lean back in my chair. I must look dumbstruck. I've never heard of such a thing. Cherry's theology may be a bit unrefined, but her faith is unmistakable, and her imagination is beyond her years. An adoption *service?* Certainly not in my worship how-to books. They have services for dedicating a new parking lot and blessing pets, but not for entrusting the fruit of your own womb, a living human being, to a new family.

But then, why not? If people can have their houses, their boats, and their pets blessed, why not bless a living, breathing child of God? Why not ask God to bless the beginning of a new family, where a precious child is deliberately welcomed in love? And why not bless a young and vulnerable, courageous teenager as she makes a life-affirming sacrifice out of love? I look at Trish to see if she has an opinion. She's already smiling, though she also seems to have something in her eye. That tells me what I need to know. I decide. Absolutely. I'll do it. In fact, I'd be honored.

"Absolutely. I'll do it. In fact, I'd be honored, Cherry." Though at the moment, I have no idea what this will look like. Nor do I know if when the time comes, I'll have a church in which this can take place.

CHAPTER FORTY-TWO
PREACHERS, PROPHETS, AND FOOLS

Sometimes in conflict, one is free to step away from the battle. I feel free this October day to speak transparently, not my opinions as much as my heart. That includes my love for these good people, and for those who may never see this room but who have also found a place in my heart this year. I do not need to win any more.

Strangely, now—especially now—preaching is a joy. I believe in this band of talented, can-do people who know how to turn an idea into success. They like living on the edge. They climb Himalayan peaks; they challenge the world's most dangerous rivers in kayaks. They will pour a million of their own dollars into an untried idea. That was my professional style once, and I want to tap those skills to do something for God's vulnerable ones. I want to draw my church into sharing my burden. I want us to be spiritual entrepreneurs, putting a roof over someone's head.

But things are truly delicate. Everyone is apprehensive. Some are angry and hurt. Most are confused, finding the place they come for respite tainted by harsh words and rumor. Some are desperate for a word of hope from the minister at the center of the storm, while others can hardly bear to listen to someone who, they believe with some justification, started the whole thing.

I cannot impose this vision on this band of believers. Nor do I need to. If this dream of mine is Spirit-blessed, it's not really mine. It's a collaborative project, in which I play a particular role and no more. Perhaps I was the first to speak it out loud. Perhaps. But I stand in a long line of seekers, thinkers, prophets, and dreamers. I'm also surrounded by critics, doubters, skeptics, thoughtful and faithful voices of resistance. All of these unknowingly conspiring, often unaware of each other's role in refining and clarifying what will become in God's time and way the dream that becomes the reality. All playing a part in what a very confident, patient, stubborn God who gets things done chooses to accomplish, working through and in spite of fools like me.

It has been good to have Brad on board during this time. My actions complicated his transition into this now-conflicted church. But he has taught me invaluable lessons. He has that rare wisdom to know where the landmines are and the courage to speak the Gospel anyway. Brad's been a trustworthy ally, a co-conspirator in shaking the foundations of a self-confident and sometimes proud church. And its minister.

Some say that the least effective way to persuade is monologue: standing and talking. Even the Apostle Paul labeled preaching "foolishness," and at times I feel like the fool, trying to make Christ's seemingly unrealistic, utopian vision—counter to every settled value of my culture—credible to my hearers. But I love this task, which at its best is an exercise in speaking truth bathed in love. It can be joyful, creative, as lyrical as poetry and as terrifying as skydiving.

There are times to be "prophetic" in the pulpit—to preach the hard truth. Play the role of Jeremiah. In conflict, it's tempting to frame your side as Jeremiah's. Tempting, and almost always disastrous. Today, my objective is modest. As best I can (and this is not familiar ground for me, as you've probably noticed), I will use words, the tools of my trade, to simply love a room filled with wounded souls, planting as many seeds of hope as possible. I will let others label me a "prophet." Or not.

Today's crisp and clear, as autumn should be. Worship will be followed by a special meeting of the congregation. A vote will be taken. It will determine my future at Old First. And I am at peace.

CHAPTER FORTY-THREE
POINT OF ORDER

T he meeting will be a vote of confidence on the senior pastor, although that's not how it is billed in the announcements. On bulletin boards, in newsletters and on the website, it is a "Congregational meeting to consider two motions, including one tabled at our annual meeting." One is Andrea's attempt to tie the pastor's pay to measurable benchmarks. The other is Mr. Curillo's new resolution. In reality, both are votes of confidence.

The service ended fifteen minutes ago. A table for the secretary and extra microphones have been set in place. John calls the meeting to order and asks me for an opening prayer. A brief review of the resolutions has been distributed. John is fair and thorough as he explains them, though his gut is churning.

"We will deal with each in order," he says. He reminds people that the first item defers my compensation increase until the church's income has increased, and ties my pay to the net increase. He struggles to describe the second item, and chooses to be indirect: "A second resolution regarding our pastor will also be presented."

Even though Mike's vote-of-confidence resolution is more personal, either will be in my mind decisive. In the meantime, here's a summary of what's happening, and you may need to take notes:

An amendment to Andrea's proposal is moved, instructing the personnel committee to take "all factors" into account in determining salary. Wow. Great idea. Gets the matter out of its binding character. John is thrilled to recognize a second and calls for discussion.

Someone wants to soften the tone of the amendment in question. In his mind, it doesn't matter what you do in a church business meeting, as long as it appears "nice." So he proposes another amendment, deleting the language tying compensation to the meeting of goals. His amendment is seconded.

"Point of order!" shouts the endowment chair. "We cannot consider two amendments at once." The maker of amendment number two apologizes for his parliamentary sin and asks if he can instead amend not Andrea's original motion, but the proposed amendment.

Are you following any of this? I warned you to take notes.

We're considering an amendment to an amendment. Meanwhile, we aren't talking about Andrea's motion itself, though it's still lurking somewhere in the background.

Someone doesn't want to face it quite yet. They suggest we tweak things just a bit more, by amending the most recent amendment. Never mind what it was about because once again, we hear, "Point of order!"

John hates someone asking questions about Robert's Rules, since he's not confident that he can navigate the shoals of parliamentary law. He asks Mr. Curillo what concerns him, Mike obliges. "According to Robert's Rules of Order, you cannot amend an amendment to an amendment."

The room falls silent as we ponder the depths of parliamentary mystery. Meanwhile, our beleaguered Parliamentarian checks—sure enough. "Robert's Rules" did indeed see unspeakable evil in amending an amendment to the amending of the main motion, and since Roberts is the fourth person of the Trinity, John reluctantly rules it out of order. So now we're back to the amendment to the amendment.

Once this is cleared up, guess what? "Point of order!" This time, it's Andrea, who probably reads her well-worn copy of "Robert's Rules" for comfort and inspiration. She feels that both amendments change her proposal substantially, and therefore constitute substitute motions, not amendments. She asks the chair to rule on whether or not this is so.

Andrea knows that John is out of his depth in this procedural quagmire, and embarrassing John equals diminishing one of my already-weakened allies. Even ruling against her—which he does—leaves her with options. Andrea "appeals from the decision of the chair." And no, I've never heard this phrase before either. Neither has John, who stares at her blankly.

Turns out, according to Robert's Rules, anyone can ask the whole group to vote on the chair's ruling. So, in another obscure Robert's phrase, she asks for "a division of the house." We vote. The moderator's decision is upheld, 55 percent to 45 percent. But Andrea got her "division" of the house, all right. This is agonizing, a death in slow motion.

Once again, my family endures. Someone else is suffering too. I glance at James, and he is confused and in tears. He faithfully stands, a fistful of ballots ready to distribute, one of his favorite tasks. But when the church he loves is saying unkind, angry, and simply confusing things, he is terrified. Lord, have mercy. Really.

We vote on the amendment to the amendment, which passes, 65 percent to 35 percent. Next, the now-amended amendment is debated. The naive might think that the debate is swinging my way, but I know better. People like my ministry but not, I sense, as enthusiastically as they did when the year began. Seeds of doubt were planted when this proposal first emerged, and they are bearing fruit in the growing dis-ease of the congregation. Another written ballot decides the matter. Sixty percent reject the amendment; a similar percentage quickly and wearily rejects Andrea's long-delayed motion.

Not exactly a ringing endorsement. In fact, Andrea, Mike, and their allies have, in losing, won. They've turned an almost unanimously supportive congregation into one in which 40 percent have their doubts about their minister. What's also troubling is that only 75 percent of the body actually votes. One out of four are either confused or emotionally unable to vote against a guy who works for God but can't vote *for* this particular clergyman either.

Mike's resolution is placed before the church. I am permitted to stand before my congregation and explain in the best way I could how I had tried to lead them in the months past. I don't take questions from the floor. They would be endless, and often tinged with rage. The risk of getting sucked into a war of words is great enough that I cannot bear the thought of that. I love these people. I have said what I have to say. This is now up to them.

I'd love to tell you how the rest of the meeting is going, but I'm not there. Trish, Melissa, and I proceed to my study, where we await the decision, about twenty minutes after two on a beautiful Sunday afternoon that we have sacrificed in order to discern the future of the church and the fate of its minister.

Finally, the chair comes into my study, beaming, a piece of paper in his hand that I've spent an hour waiting for. Actually, for several very long months. The process leading up to this moment has tried my faith and tested my strength. Trish and Melissa sustained me throughout this trial, but I have learned through these weeks the price a minister's family pays.

A minister is a very public figure, and when they're under fire, their families agonize like few others. When churches fight, friendships evaporate. Families divide. And a minister's family, bearing no responsibility for the

179

battle, feels every sling and arrow. I can handle rejection. If they don't like the direction in which I'm leading, fine. Take it up with the God who's leading me.

But I can't watch the dearest people in my life shredded by anger, condemnation, even ridicule, which should be directed at me. I'm the one who made so many people angry. I'm the one whose vision is being judged. They are not at fault.

John walks toward me with eyes filled with hope. "You won!"

"Oh?"

"The vote came in stronger than I expected. A landslide, frankly. I am thrilled, Pastor." Perhaps because he's supportive of my ministry. Perhaps because he thinks he's escaping the dreary task of forming a search committee.

"Let me see the numbers." He hands me the tally for the second resolution: out of 412 present, 354 people rejected Mike's resolution; 68 approved it. My translation: 354 people like me more or less; 68 would like me better if I were unemployed. An 86 percent winning percentage. Not bad.

But not good enough.

John doesn't know where I'd set the bar in my mind. A president can survive an approval rating of 51 percent; a minister's in trouble with anything short of near unanimity. To a politician, 60 percent is a landslide. To a clergyperson, 86 percent can be a kiss of death. Not all votes are created equal. Some within that 14 percent are passionate, powerful, and determined. I had already decided that anything less than 95 percent was inadequate—and even at that, I was likely to discern that this is a wound on my work here that may not heal.

When people lose, even in a church, the matter is settled only in the numbers, but rarely in the heart. When people believe theirs is a moral crusade, they won't be discouraged by losing a vote. After all, truth, or maybe God, is on their side.

And the people who vote *for* you? They may be supportive, but still harbor reservations. When someone draws a line in the sand, they're often suddenly not available. They come to church for peace and comfort, and fighting even a good fight isn't part of the bargain.

I won't rain on John's parade tonight; I thank him and tell him we'll talk tomorrow. I clearly need to talk to Trish about this, long and hard. And I need to pray, one more night. But barring a message written in the sky, I know which way I'm leaning.

In the meantime, it occurs to me that it's hard to pray for one's adversaries. Whether it's Andrea, or Mike, or anyone else—how can we honestly pray *for* them when we carry negative baggage *about* them?

Perhaps we pray *with* them. Meaning, we are like our "enemies" in one inescapable respect: We are flawed, broken people in need of grace and forgiveness. Putting it another way, isn't there something rather self-righteous in praying that God change someone else?

CHAPTER FORTY-FOUR
A DREAM LARGER THAN ME

The day after the meeting, I almost have my office tell him I'm not in. That would have been disastrous. Jesse Ryan, true to form, just shows up. I guess he assumes I'm always there. But where pastors should spend their time isn't something I feel like talking about right now. I am persuaded that after last night, my ministry here is ending, and I'm writing a resignation letter. I will email it to the council, followed by a congregational mailing that on such and such a date First Community Church of River Glen will not have a senior pastor, and I'll not have a job. When that letter is mailed, all the relevant zip codes will receive it the day after. No doubt the grapevine will spread the news faster than the mailing.

Back to Jesse. He won't get the letter because he's not a member of Old First. In fact, I doubt he'll ever want to join something as conventional as a church. But somehow, he knows what has happened; this reclusive man has a grapevine to Old First of his own, including a connection unknown to me. Now he's telling me of a decision he's made.

"I like your idea, Reverend. I mean your idea for my farm. Poor people." He shakes his head. I think he just said he feels compassion for people at risk, but following the trail of his thinking takes tracking skills most mortals lack.

"I appreciate that, Jesse. I wish we could put your farm to work for them."

"The price was too high, right?"

"Some people felt that way. I didn't object to your price, actually. It was fair for the land you own."

"Too bad your church folk didn't have the faith they should have. Like you said, nothing's too hard for God. Guess they didn't listen."

I'm nodding, silently, eyes on my desk. Truth be told, if I start talking right now, I might start crying. In front of Jesse Ryan? No way. So I just nod.

Jesse's voice changes from reflective to determined. "Well, Pastor, I've made a decision. Promise me they'll do with the property exactly what you said you'd do, and you can have it for whatever price they can pay."

Jesse gets up, walks toward the door. He stops, and without turning around, says, "One more condition: I want to keep living in the house 'til I'm dead. When you've decided, let the real estate agent know. He'll tell me." Jesse the farmer then walks out, closing the door behind him, leaving me speechless. Jesse has that effect on me.

The door re-opens. Jesse doesn't look at me directly, just off to the left, where my office window overlooks the parking lot. For the first time in our encounters, I see almost a smile.

"I like my life as it is, but if you take my farm, I'll have some really interesting neighbors." The door closes, and my head is spinning.

Jesse Ryan has handed me a path to a dream I've cherished through much of this year. A gift. A gold-plated gift that right now scrambles everything I planned to do today.

Does this change my thinking? Maybe. Or maybe, just not now.

Brad knocks on my door. I file my unfinished letter under a legal pad and invite him in. Hypotheticals can wait—Brad is a living, breathing, immediate subject. He bypasses the morning pleasantries.

"Pastor, are you OK with last night's outcome?"

"No."

"And . . ."

"More on that in a minute." Outside of my family, Brad will be the first to know of any resignation—I owe him that. But Jesse Ryan has scrambled that calculus, and it's best I not burden Brad with it yet.

"I've mentioned Jesse Ryan to you, haven't I?"

"Yeah. Is that who just walked out the door?"

"Yes. Brad, he just out of the blue offered his farm to us at a price *we* determine."

Brad sits down. It takes him a moment to absorb what I'm still struggling to believe. "Is that project even still viable, with or without his land? Will this change enough hearts to resurrect it?"

I hesitate. I'm thinking that if I resign, the farm project is dead. If I stay, I may be able to nurture it into reality. But how long would that take? And even if it's viable, will my presence distract a fractured body away from the critical mass to make it happen? In other words, *is it too late?*

"That's an open question."

Perhaps Brad senses my momentary paralysis. "Pastor, I know how tough last night must have been for you. If you wanted to just walk away, I wouldn't blame you. Having said that, I don't believe that Mr. Ryan's visit was just his idea. I would respectfully encourage you to think about this vision in which you've invested so much of yourself as still alive, breathing, and worth the risk of pressing ahead. I don't know why, but I think this is a God thing."

Yeah, I believe that God still speaks, although Brad's spiritual roots are much more comfortable navigating supernatural interventions. Still, for at least three months, I assumed that I was being led into this . . . mission? Vision? Last night, at least up until right now, had convinced me to surrender. Lick my wounds. Look for a fresh start. Now I'm not so sure.

"Brad, I really want this to happen. I can't imagine walking away when it's sitting there, on our doorstep, begging us to pick it up." And I think my heart just spoke more than I was thinking. Maybe it was the Spirit, or both, but in either case, perhaps they just overruled my analytical mind. My colleague and Christian brother shares none of my caution.

"I know I'm new here, and don't fully grasp how this church thinks and operates. I may be naive about it, but I think—my faith demands, actually—that this *must* happen. And because it must, it *can*, and it *will*. I don't have much political capital yet, but what I have is at your service. I'm all in."

I still think my ministry may not survive long-term. One point for resigning and not pressing this project. Sensible, actually. Write the letter.

But even if that's true, why not invest what credibility I have in nursing this dream? What have I got to lose? They could fire me; I'd survive. And in the meantime, I could still press the case for claiming Jesse's farm as holy ground. I will need to be patient. Build a coalition of the willing. Jesus said something about being as shrewd as snakes and as innocent as doves. Yeah. This dream is still breathing.

But it would be easier to build that coalition if two critical facts are in place. One: Jesse's land is in fact within reach. Two: I can concentrate on nurturing this dream without also defending my job.

In my mind, that is unlikely. Furthermore, I am not the issue here. Both the church, and the dream, are larger than me, larger than my presence, my preference, my ego. I conclude that to resign is not to surrender; it is to release the vision and the church into the capable hands of our common Lord.

I finish the letter of resignation.

I schedule a meeting tomorrow with John Barrett. I email the letter to him so he knows what's on my mind. Then I print a copy and walk to Brad's office. He's standing near his desk, and I hand him the letter. He reads it while I wait. There are tears in his eyes as he puts the letter down, and says, "I understand."

Fifteen minutes later, my office manager walks out of my office, knowing that by the time she reaches her desk, the letter will be in her inbox. Mary has my instructions for how the letter will reach the faithful, and when.

Then back to Brad's office. No more hypothetical conversations—this is real now, and he needs to prepare himself for all the *what now* conversations that will put him under a microscope. Brad has earned the right to know my intentions and has my support for whatever role he chooses to assume from this time forward.

He welcomes me in, knowing that every conversation from now on will be important.

"Brad, earlier I was playing it safe with my maybe-this-maybe-that musings, but here's where things really stand. My ministry here ends effective at the end of the year. The letter you saw will go out as soon as Mary can put it together."

Brad takes a deep breath. "OK."

"'OK?'" Brad relaxes, smiling. "I'm still processing your decision—I'm curious about how you decided."

"I had reasons to stay, most of all stability for my family. This could hurt them if I can't put food on the table for a while. Plus, all three of us have deep relationships at Old First and in River Glen. We love this town. I love this church, in spite of what's happened.

"But what's happened has cost me too much credibility, and any bold moves would be met with skepticism. My influence bank account has been drawn down."

"I think you have more credibility than you think, Pastor."

"Thank you. I hope so. I at least hope that I can still bring the Word to receptive ears this fall, if I'm not actively pushing an agenda."

"Is that it? The credibility question?" Brad's smart. He knows that credibility is too subjective a base for a life-changing decision. But it isn't my only reason.

"Credibility's a piece of it. But I also think that by leaving, I'm giving the people who *are* Old First a gift of peace. Some of the trouble —some of it—evaporates when I leave. There won't be a constant reminder of painful times standing in the pulpit. To some degree, I'm setting them free to find God's future for them.

"And I'll tell you another reason that's very personal. You won't like it; nobody who is close to me will either. But I am partly responsible for the pain this church has endured. It was my presumptuousness, my arrogance, that said some really stupid things, starting with Mike Curillo. Actions have consequences, and some of mine had serious ones. I have to own that."

"Pastor Noel, *brother* Noel—I'll be honest. Hearing you say that bothers me. You're certainly within your rights to make that call, but . . . I gotta think about that. I feared you were going to resign—though *that* reason never entered my mind. When you told me about Mr. Ryan's offer, I wondered if I could push back against writing that resignation letter. I wondered if your ministry could recover its momentum. I'm still not sure I'd make the call you're making. But . . . OK. I will support you."

"Thank you. And Brad, I don't think my leaving kills the prospects of using the Ryan land. It may actually be easier with me out of the way."

"But now I wonder about *my* role. Do I still fit in the picture here?"

I lean forward. "Brad, I'm pushing all kinds of boundaries here—I shouldn't try to influence what happens after I leave. But here's my hope: that you'll stay on. In fact, that you'd be open to serving as a kind of 'bridge' for the first few weeks, maybe a couple of months. Not *too* long though. Old First needs a good interim pastor, and—But if the church finds that interim, it leaves you free to shepherd the Ryan land project as part of your portfolio. Plus I was never able to get that racial justice working group off the ground. You'll have more success recruiting the best minds for it."

Brad looks away. He's thinking. I give him a moment. Then—

"Brad, someone's going to ask you if you want to be that interim pastor, or maybe even the next pastor. That's highly inappropriate, but you'll be asked anyway. You're just getting started, and the risks for you are huge. Let someone else do the interim work. After conflict, there will be aftershocks. This was more than 'conflict.' This was—is—collective and personal trauma. That should be part of the interim's portfolio. Let them do that. You do *your* job.

"Oh—one more thing. That 'Noel' thing? I could get used to it."

CHAPTER FORTY-FIVE
WELCOME TO THE FAMILY

Lori O'Brien is on a steep learning curve as the new in-law-to-be. My brother Nathan's fiancé is soaking up as much "Garraty" as she can. Along with Dad, they spent the weekend in River Glen (an education in itself, just a week after my resignation). Now it's Sunday evening, we're in the kitchen, and she's probing her brother-in-law-to-be.

"Did you always feel called to the ministry, Noel?"

"I first felt called to follow in my dad's footsteps during high school."

"Then why did you to go into business if you felt called to this?"

Looking toward my father, I say, "Dad, we've talked about this before—I saw how hard Mom and Dad worked, and how little tangible reward they got, how they were sometimes treated, and I wanted no part of that. I convinced myself that I could do something else, and I was right—I could. And did. Which sometimes happens. We convince ourselves that we'd brilliantly turned the wrong choice into the right one."

"But why leave a successful career at the top of your game? Nate tells me that if you'd stayed a broker, any children we have would've had an honest-to-goodness rich uncle!" Lori catches herself. "I'm sorry, Noel—You don't have to answer my meddling questions."

I wave her apology off. "It's OK. You might as well know how unhinged your relatives are. Someday, I'll apologize to your kids for not being able to send them to Harvard."

I ask her question myself, *What could our lives have been like, if.* . . . So it's easy to ask it again, this time aloud. "What persuaded me to do this after all?" I look dad's way and smile. "Again, he did."

Lori looks puzzled. "I don't know if I get it."

"I saw lives transformed because Dad was there. He still gets calls from people he baptized, married, counseled, or taught thirty years ago who want him to perform a wedding for their kids, or a baptism or a funeral. Clergy can't always do that, but still, what an affirmation. A perk of the job, really. There are people who call themselves believers now, or who have a restored relationship with a spouse, or are in a career serving people in need, all because my dad was there when they needed him. What I did was worthwhile, but no one will track me down in retirement and ask me about their mutual funds. I'm not them; I'm not him. But my father's the most influential source of wisdom and perspective in my life, and a lifelong example."

Nathan's been quiet tonight. As I answer Lori's questions, he holds his tongue. Lori seems content now and thanks me. Nathan speaks, and he's deadly serious.

"Noel, I'm sorry if this isn't a fair question. But I remember when Dad and Mom went through holy hell back in the day, and now I'm watching it happen to my brother—I am . . . *angry.*"

Trish responds before I do. "Thank you, Nate." I sense that in saying that she was speaking volumes to her husband as well: *What has happened is an outrage.*

Nate isn't done. "Trish, I know this happened to you too, and to Melissa. But I need to know from my brother. What happened to you, Noel—what happened to your family—was it worth it?"

Fair question. I look toward Trish, whose eyes seem to say, *I'm not sure it was.*

"Honestly, Nate, I'm not sure yet."

"Why not? I mean, was this all a waste? You pour your soul into this place, but now you just surrender and walk away?" Nathan is livid.

"I pushed the envelope. I thought I knew the risks. I made mistakes that helped land us here. Frankly, I can't predict where all this leads. I guess it's God's problem now."

"You pushed the envelope. You took risks and now it's God's problem. Fine. But that wasn't the question, Noel."

The room is quiet, and everyone's looking my way. "Here's the only answer I've got. I have no way of knowing what we or the people at the church do with this, other than that I think God gets God's work done, visibly or not. Meanwhile: I did what I could, and if it all comes to a halt, then it won't feel worth it. If all that happens is that Trish and Melissa are scarred by this, it *definitely* wouldn't be worth it. That would devastate me. Right now, that's the question that matters most.

"But I believe this did not and will not break us. We lived as honorably as we could through this, we're still standing, and I'm more proud of these two women than I can say. *That* just might make whatever we went through worth it.

"As far as the church is concerned . . . They have a chance. I did my best to lead, and to un-do any mistakes I need to own. Now I'm passing the baton.

"Sometimes, you strike the match, in faith, hope and love. Sometimes, someone else enjoys the fire. Maybe I could live with that."

CHAPTER FORTY-SIX
ADVENT ONE

The new year begins early for Christians. The rest of the country, fresh from Thanksgiving, now races toward Christmas. When the holiday season has climaxed, an exhausted world awaits one last gasp of revelry as December gives way to January. But for most Christians in the western world, the *Christian* New Year begins just days after Thanksgiving, disguised as the First Sunday of Advent.

This morning we don't inaugurate a "Christmas Season," which for believers has a (barely) less commercial flavor, but the annual re-telling of history's greatest drama. Advent is the first of a series of "seasons," followed by the actual twelve-day Christmas season, then Epiphany, Lent, and Easter. Pentecost comes last, carrying us until the next Advent, and the cycle begins again.

This first Advent Sunday is known in our office simply as "Advent One," and I'm sitting in my usual Sunday perch. I'm recalling what some have told me—that if I climb the spire above this room and look southeast, I can see the tops of the Hancock Building, Willys Tower, and assorted structures in Chicago's Loop where fully half of my neighbors work. The spire soars seventy feet, so I'll take their word for it. Closer to the ground and around me this morning, some of the furniture is covered in purple. In fact, I've got purple draped over my shoulders.

To my right is an elegant and over-priced brass candle stand, purchased decades ago in memory of someone few remember. It's designed to hold exactly five candles, four of which will remain un-lit this morning. The room is comfortably full, which means there are about five hundred souls waiting for me to kick things off.

I feel electricity in this room. I feel the power of the story we begin retelling today: God's saving act in the Christ Child and God's vision yet to come. I feel joy mixed with grief, knowing that I will see Christmas in this space, but none of the seasons to follow.

Brad Davis sits to my left, with added stature as the one who will lead them through their first days when my office is vacant. He successfully negotiated a role as a bridge pastor for the first two months.

The people before me still deserve their minister's undivided attention to their concerns, large and small, as they seek connection with the One who inhabits eternity. I will do my best to honor those expectations. I'm still their minister for a while longer.

The music stops. Right on cue, a family of five steps up to the Advent candles. While Mom reads the meaning of the first candle, the oldest child lights it. They take their seats. We sing an Advent hymn. Brad reads from Jeremiah 33, where the ancient prophet announces that "'The days are surely coming,' says the Lord, 'when I will fulfill the promise . . .'"

Brad doesn't just read, he *proclaims* the Word in those words, with passion in his voice that rivets the listeners and fills the room. He reads, "In those days and in that time I will cause a righteous Branch to spring up for David, and He shall execute justice and righteousness in the land."

Brad measures every word, as if reading the verdict in a courtroom, or the news that a revolution is under way. The Word he has declared reverberates in the room and in the soul, even in the silence as he concludes and turns toward his seat. The choir sings "Let All Mortal Flesh Keep Silence," and it is haunting. This day begins our new year, a new epoch. History turns on Advent One.

And then it's my turn. The pulpit awaits. So if you would please excuse me, I have to go to work.

"When I preached my first sermon as your pastor, I described my calling as 'comforting the afflicted, and afflicting the comfortable.' Then we all chuckled, uncomfortably—maybe we were uncomfortable with the truth behind the joke.

"Sometime as we approach Christmas, we may sing these words: 'God rest ye merry gentlemen, let nothing you dismay.' Besides the fact that 'gentlemen' begs to be retired for a word that includes all of us, my other problem is the chorus. It's short: 'O, tidings of comfort and joy, comfort and joy.' Comfort's here when we need it. But sometimes, comfort can be a trap for us. Comfort prefers simple things—either-or, the predictable, the familiar. But comfort is fragile, and discomfort is inevitable for someone who's serious about following the Way of the Savior born as a peasant. That Way is disruptive, and not necessarily serene for us who are already comfortable.

"Today we begin again a new year, a new journey. We know at least some of the challenges we face. We will soon say farewell. And if we're honest, that makes us uncomfortable. At least, it makes me *very* uncomfortable. Sad, really. I will miss you.

"But joy, my beloved church, is often found in *dis*comfort. If we find it hard to have both comfort *and* joy, perhaps that's as it should be. The cry for justice has not yet been answered. God's will is not yet done on earth, and it must be. Holy restlessness, holy dis-ease, holy grief at shattered illusions—they may lead to the joy we seek and the comfort that the Gospel promises in the One who, even in infancy, is our long-awaited Savior.

"Making the comfortable uncomfortable is an inescapable part of the Christian message. Consider Jesus' words: 'The last shall be first,' or 'Love your enemies.' Or when Jesus said, 'Sell all you have, give it to the poor.' Or simply: 'Take up your cross and follow me.'

"So it is my joy this morning to invite you, once again, into the joyful discomfort of this season of yearning, looking ahead, leaning forward, hungry for more than all we have and know and are. Yearning for Jesus, Word of God in human flesh, Himself poor and marginalized, lover of children, lover of us."

CHAPTER FORTY-SEVEN
SEVEN FIGURES TO THE LEFT

I remember this room, but not with pleasure. The last time I was here, I sat in the same corner facing the same person. It was an ugly moment, and things went downhill from there. Mike Curillo called yesterday and asked to meet me for lunch. He was just as tense as the last time we talked, but there was something different in his voice. Tense, but not hostile.

On this mid-December day, despite my task list at the church I still serve for two weeks more, I arrive right on time. The room is full. It seems every mover and shaker in Illinois is spending their year-end bonus on expensive lunches for each other. Mike's already seated. He sees me, waves me over. His face shows no enthusiasm, but no hostility either. He greets me with not quite a smile. I shake his hand and sit across from him. No pleasantries. I wait for him to begin. He picks up his water glass but doesn't drink. Instead, he slowly swirls the ice in a lazy circle, studying it like it's the most important thing in the world. Without looking up, Mike speaks. "We've got at the most fifteen minutes, then someone else joins us. But I wanted a few minutes just with you."

"OK . . ."

"First of all, thanks for coming. It wouldn't have surprised me if you'd never want to talk to me again. I've made your life difficult this year."

I'm tempted to comment on that being an understatement, but I keep quiet, fiddle with my napkin, and wait. Mike sets the glass down, folds his hands on the table, and speaks. "I've had a lot of time to think since the vote at church. In fact, it's all I've done since then. I thought that, once that was behind us, I could move on to other things, but I've just been stuck on that whole . . ."

He looks up, briefly at me, then off into space beyond my left shoulder. "This is really hard for me."

"I'm listening." Now *that's* an understatement. Every nerve in my body is primed, my senses on high alert. I'm not sure I want to know what he's going to say, but he has my full attention. He looks directly at me. His eyes are moist. He speaks barely above a whisper.

"I'm sorry."

I say nothing. This is his to finish. I will not disrupt this moment, which becomes a very long moment before he speaks again. When he does, he's the straight-ahead, strong, decisive Mike Curillo I've found so hard to love.

"I don't agree with a lot of what you've done or said. Professionally, I think what you said to me last winter in front of the finance committee was irresponsible."

I try to respond, but just as I open my mouth, he holds up his hand to silence me. I comply.

"I'm not finished, and if I don't get through this now, I might not ever say it. Frankly Reverend Garraty, I don't even like you."

He pauses, and when he speaks again, the edge on his voice is gone. He's calm; I even detect a hint of warmth. "But I respect you. You're an honorable man, even when I think you're wrong. What I've done to you, however, hasn't been honorable. I wanted to embarrass you because you embarrassed me. I never thought that it would go as far as it did, but it began to snowball out of control, and here we are. *I* should be leaving First Church, not you. And because of that, I need to say, I'm sorry."

"Mike, we need more than fifteen minutes to talk about this."

"I planned it this way because I knew if I had to say more, I'd lose it—and that's something I will *not* do in front of this crowd. Besides, I've said most of what I want to say."

I start to ask what else he may have on his mind, but he's seeing someone and waves them over to us. I assume it's a waiter, and I desperately need my own glass of water. Instead, it's Sherman Jackson.

He looks at me; I look at him. He shakes Mike's hand, then mine, and then sits between us. He's at least wearing a coat and tie, a long way from cover material for GQ, but it's a decent attempt for someone usually in a T-shirt and jeans.

My soon-to-be-former parishioner speaks first, since he is apparently the only one at the table who knows what's going on. "Thanks for coming, Mr. Jackson. I know we don't know each other, but I'd like to change that."

"I'd like that too, Mr. Curillo. May I ask what you have in mind?"

Wow. For Sherm, whose in-your-face contempt for the rich and smug is virtually all I've ever seen, his response is downright elegant.

"I asked Rev. Garraty to be here because," he looks my way, and he's actually grinning at me, "this is largely his fault."

I stare at Mike, and then look to Jackson. "Sherm, I have no idea what this is about." Our host looks back at Sherm.

"I have some money I'd like to give to the causes of homelessness, domestic abuse, and addiction. Based on what I've heard from my pastor here about you and how much he respects you, I'd like to give this money to you. There are conditions, but not, I think, unreasonable ones."

"Such as . . ." My friend from the inner city gives absolutely no indication of delight, gratitude, or even much interest. He's cool and steady. It takes a lot to impress him.

"One: that you form an appropriate oversight body to administer these funds. Two: that Rev. Garraty be invited to serve on that body. Three: that you *spend* it. I don't want to fund a self-perpetuating bureaucracy. Spend it as fast and as wisely as you can. Four: that my identity as the source stays at this table. Five: that you distribute it among each of these areas of need so as to make a difference. I mean no disrespect, but I think it's too much too fast for one small non-profit agency to manage well. I *do* want it used to lift those who are unhoused or home-insecure—men, women, families—and your shelter certainly can benefit from a portion of this money. Six: that what it pays for be explicitly Christ-driven in every respect: meeting needs in body, relationships, and soul. Seven: that you spend at least half of it out here, away from the city, in a safe, peaceful setting where people can find long-term help. I think Rev. Garraty here has some ideas along those lines."

I'm shocked. Disoriented. I feel like I just won . . . what? The lottery?

I speak next, because I'm thinking that he's putting a lot of restrictions on what's probably at best a five- or maybe, just maybe, a six-figure gift. Not only that—I'm feeling some anger, thinking that Mike's underestimating the capabilities of one of the savviest people I know. Sherm sees me start to speak, and gives me a look that says, *Shut up, Garraty.* Instead, he calmly asks, "Mr. Curillo, how much are we talking about?"

Mike pulls a check out of his coat pocket, and hands it to me first. It takes me a while to absorb what I'm seeing. I count seven figures to the left of the decimal point.

"Remember you said I should give it all away? Well, after Uncle Sam got done with it, that's what's left. Oh—actually, not quite. I bought my wife a rather nice dinner, so it's about $175 short, with the tip."

I hand the check to Sherm without comment. And for the first time I can remember in this remarkable year, the unflappable Mr. Jackson actually shows a reaction. He responds with visible disbelief—just like the director of a chronically underfunded shelter would to an unexpected windfall. "Are you serious, Mr. Curillo? I mean, is this for real?" When a street-savvy curmudgeon like Sherman Jackson asks a stupid question like that, while holding the cashier's check for $5.3 million in his hand, you know he's in shock.

"Yes. I'm quite serious. Do you accept the money under my terms?"

"Are you kidding?" He looks like he's ready to kiss Curillo on the spot. But he catches his breath, and the old Sherman Jackson momentarily reappears. "I accept conditionally, only in that I need to talk to my board and our attorney. But if they're cool with it, and they'd better be, yes, I accept. And, Mr. Curillo, thank you. Beyond that, I don't know what to say."

Neither do I, frankly.

Last winter, Mike Curillo turned a tithe of his windfall into a Hollywood production. Today, he turns over five times that amount, not into a moment of personal vanity, but an emphatic expression of a new heart. Less than a year ago this may have never crossed his ambitious mind. Today, it is natural and genuine. I doubt Mike knows how dramatically his life has changed. More precisely, is changing. This is chapter one in the script now being written by the Spirit of Christ.

The look on Mike's face is one I've never seen before. Because as far as I know, it's never *been* there before. Old things—those of which I know, and no doubt many, many more—are passing away. All things are becoming new. Mike Curillo is at peace with God, with himself, with his world, and with me. Lord, grant me that same peace.

CHAPTER FORTY-EIGHT
HOLY MOMENT

I will give you a new heart and put a new spirit in you;
I will remove from you your heart of stone
and give you a heart of flesh.

—Ezekiel 36:26 (NIV)

When we leave, Sherm heads back to the shelter, check and all. I pull Curillo aside in the coatroom. "Why? And how did you persuade your wife to go along with this?" He thinks for a moment and invites me to share a cup of coffee in the lounge.

"About Linda: actually, I bribed her with that dinner." We both chuckle. He leans forward, his face becoming serious. "I knew I had to do this. You were more right last winter than you knew. I've seen what lottery winnings can do to people—especially when they're not used to money on that scale. I thought—in fact, I was confident—that I was money-savvy enough to handle it. I was wrong. The money poisoned me. Poisoned *us*. Poisoned my spiritual life, and eventually poisoned my church. It was a noose around my neck; it made me arrogant. It closed me to others. When you challenged me, you scored a direct hit on my soul, and I didn't see it until now. But I've come to see that even ten million dollars—it isn't enough. Money's never enough.

"I didn't know how Linda would respond. But over that dinner that the Lottery Commission paid for, I just laid it all out, kind of opened my heart to her, and said that I didn't like how the money was changing us before we'd spent a dime of it. I told her I wanted it out of our lives before it killed us, and I wanted no trace of it hanging around; not even a receipt for something we'd bought. When I told her what I wanted to do with it, I expected her to suggest we spend some of it on a psychiatrist for me, and then some more for a divorce attorney."

"What did she say?"

"She looked at me for the longest thirty seconds of my life. Then she got up, walked around to my side of the table, and told me to stand up. And right there in the middle of the most expensive restaurant in the suburbs, she put her arms around me, kissed me, and with everyone within five tables in every direction staring at us, told them all that she was married to the finest man in Illinois." He grinned. "Of course, I already knew that."

I grinned back. "Seems you missed my sermon on humility."

He laughed quietly, and then playfully scowled at me. "No, I heard it. And, my dear Reverend, it made me furious. How dare you preach to me like that?"

I hold up my hands in mock surrender. Then, for just a moment, we look at each other wordlessly, before he spoke again. "And by the way, I heard some others too. Like the one from Isaiah on justice. You were right—there's no wiggle room there. Isaiah was saying precisely what God meant.

"I need to say one more thing. I suspect I know the answer, and I understand. But I'll ask anyway. Reverend Garraty, we're very different people. And in some ways, very much alike. We both have a driven side; we both are competitive; we've both tasted the good life. And don't tell me you don't miss the things you had when you were in my business."

I won't lie to him. "Guilty as charged—especially the BMW."

Mike shrugs. "I'd love to buy you one, Pastor, but you made me give away all my money.

"In any case, I personally haven't liked you very much, and I know it's been mutual, so don't lie to me about that either. Having said that, I trust you and I respect your skills. I could use someone like you in my firm, and I'd let you write your own job description. I want my business to be shaped by my faith, not the other way around. I wouldn't trust anyone I know except you to keep me and my values on track. Think about it." He gets up, pats me on the shoulder, and walks away.

For a minute I sit there, trying to give a coherent prayer of thanks for a most amazing lunch, all the while still trying to comprehend what has happened. For Sherman Jackson, a lot of needs are about to be met. But for Mike Curillo and me, the check was a symbol of something else. Whatever it is, it's good, and saturated with grace. Even his offer of a job—an answer to my uncertain future? A new kind of ministry—ministering between Sundays, to ambitious and driven men and women on their turf, alongside them in the midst of the "world" I warn my congregation about? Tantalizing. I'd be good at it. Very good, possibly. But would its temptations suck me back in?

Yes, Mike, I could return to finance. It's attractive. I've been able to function without that rush for years. Like an addict, I've been clean, and I'm tempted to think that just one taste wouldn't hurt. But would I be able to resist the excesses that thrilled me? Perhaps the industry is better served by those who can keep their heads amidst the pressures and pulls, not people motivated by wealth and power. And furthermore, I'm called to preach, and despite what's happened, even though it's fraught with risks and pain, it's still safer for my soul.

When it's clear I won't sort it out over half a mug of cold coffee, I stand and turn toward the door. There, not five paces from me, is Mike Curillo. I stop. He walks slowly but deliberately right toward me, eyes fixed on mine. When he gets a comfortable distance away, he keeps on coming, until he throws his arms around my shoulders and crushes me, in front of the entire professional class of our city. Without a word, he releases me, squeezes my upper arms until they hurt, and with tears streaming down his face (OK, I admit it—mine too), turns and walks away. And I'm keenly aware that the room is deathly silent.

Hope you enjoyed the show, ladies and gentlemen. You just saw a holy moment.

CHAPTER FORTY-NINE
BITTERSWEET

On Christmas Day in River Glen, the Garraty family has gathered—in two different places. My brother and his fiancé were tugged toward Lori's family in upstate New York. That will be true again in Christmases to come, and sadly Nathan's absent as we gather for one last time in this home. But Dad is here, and his presence is his greatest gift to me.

The day includes one intrusion. I made a promise to Gerald, one of Old First's oldest members. He's ninety-eight (he won't tell me his age and I pretend to not know, though his baptismal record betrays him). He's also one of our poorest. Which is one reason why I want to visit this parishioner on this very holy day.

I drive into the trailer park west of town, struck by the way the least desirable housing in River Glen, religiously avoided by its more fortunate residents, displays more Christmas decorations per acre than anywhere else in the city. At Gerald's modest unit, lights adorn the full length and width of his trailer, around doors, windows, and the wooden railing that lines the steps to his home-made plywood entry vestibule. Walking toward those steps, I'm met by a cocktail of dreary and bright, depressing and defiant, enhanced when I reach the door and hear Handel's "Messiah" booming loudly from inside. Gerald's hard of hearing. But he's also celebrating this day, and I know he's embracing the choir's message: "*Wonderful! Counselor! The mighty God! The everlasting Father! The Prince of Peace!*"

Gerald was widowed just before I came to River Glen. His was my first pastoral visit, on the second day in my new office. His family is gone. He lost his only child, a daughter, when she was in her twenties, lost his bride of sixty years a decade ago, and outlived his three siblings. Yet he bears his life with hope and even a delightful sense of humor. Gerald walks with the steadiness of a man who will not surrender his dignity.

Coffee awaits. Store-bought cookies and Danish *Kringle* already grace the small round table. A brightly decorated tree—a balsam, in defiance of the artificial-trees-only regulation in the park—is in front of the one large window that frames the front of his home. We chat. We reminisce. I share Communion with him. All of my elderly members appreciate gathering at the Lord's table when I come, and none more intensely than Gerald. He insists that Communion's simplicity is part of its depth, and in this home, it's still called a "feast." He will provide the home-baked bread as well as the wine (he favors Merlot) for our simple service. It's already prepared and waiting on what remains of their once extensive silver service. I recall from memory the words of the simple liturgy I share at times like this: "This is Christ's body, broken for you and me . . . this is the cup of blessing, poured out for you and me."

I make it a practice to visit my older members, especially those who are confined or alone, but Gerald is special. He worked hard all his life—a skilled craftsman whose talents were meagerly rewarded at best. And what little he had was severely drained by his late wife's uninsured care. With their comfortable home long gone, this battered trailer is all that shelters someone worthy of much more. Then again, in this place which endures contempt and ridicule from most residents of River Glen—Gerald's neighbors also deserve so much more.

It matters to me that Gerald, my first pastoral call, would be the one with whom I share the bread and cup near the end of my time as his pastor, made more meaningful on Christmas Day. He speaks of Harriet, who taught him well, he claims, to be a good host. I assure him that he is a gracious host indeed.

We chat briefly, I receive just one more slice of *Kringle*, and then apologize—though he says I don't need to—for leaving to rejoin my family. I invited him to join us last year, but he brushed the invitation aside, and I won't insult him by asking again. "I hope, Gerald, that you won't be alone all day today." He assures me that he'll be all right. Though I know that while some neighbors will soon drift in for the rest of the coffee and treats, Gerald likely will be alone again when tomorrow's sun appears. He will not let you believe that it bothers him. He waves my concern aside.

"I'm never alone—especially today, Pastor. My Lord is born. A promise made, a promise kept."

Christmas music plays in the background, the gifts have been opened, and we've parted the red (and blue, green, and gold) sea of wrapping paper, revealing that there's still hardwood under it all. The fire's in the fireplace. The love is palpable. A day in which the rest of the world is set aside, and we bask in the warmth of those we love. We laugh, we exchange gifts, and we graze at a buffet abundant enough to fatten the county. It is bittersweet, knowing that this will be the last Christmas in this wonderful old house.

Yesterday I shared in four services. There was, of course, Sunday morning—just a simple sermon to mark the occasion. Then the early Christmas Eve service, and finally at eleven p.m. the Candlelight Service. They were hard to conduct as emotions all too often bubbled to the surface.

Perhaps the hardest service was not at Old First. It took place last evening at the now-familiar shelter in Chicago. Sherm asked me to share his Christmas Eve service for a room full of people who had outwardly nothing to cheer about, and I was honored to serve in this sacred place. I read the scripture and prayed, but the honor was simply to be there, among God's favorite people. I am learning to love them, every nameless, unwashed, unkempt face, each radiating the visage of my Savior, and I know that when I am with them, I stand on holy ground.

I feel as if I'm already done at Old First. This is a week of tying up loose ends and saying a long good-bye to this place and the people who *are* First Community Church. Sunday, New Year's Eve, will be marked by a simple reflection, and a liturgy of parting.

It's hard to think about leaving those I would call friends, those I could not trust, those whose thoughts remain a mystery. Still, they became family to me—my siblings, every one of them. The Body of Christ.

It's not unlike a death. I see that picture on the bookcase of a confirmation class and their water-balloon-soaked minister. Or the desk calendar with its messy, hand-written witness to all that happened. I *love* what I do. I hate knowing that I won't face Sundays with that complicated, oh-so-real gathering of people, engaged or distant, pro and con, children of God, stumbling toward wholeness.

Did I fail? One could argue that. Conflict not yet resolved, goals and dreams unrealized, relationships wounded; a church and its pastor suffered, and no one yet knows what the future will reveal.

Old First will chart a different path away from whatever "normal" was. They have been humbled; so have I. But neither they nor I need be discouraged. Philippians 1:6 applies to us all—God, who began a good work in them and their soon-former pastor will carry that work toward whatever conclusion God has in mind. They can find their way as I find mine, and into that future I release them.

In the meantime, unfinished business awaits. My bitterest adversary reached out to me, and even offered me a job, a good one at that. But the One I serve warned long ago that we can't serve God and money, and Sherman was right too. Money is never enough. But there's more than a job offer between Mike and me. In that offer he reached out in forgiving grace. I have not yet responded in kind, but I will. I watched a true conversion, and $5.3 million is only the tip of the iceberg.

It is said that the wise learn more from their enemies than fools learn from their friends. I'm still learning. It's complicated, forgiveness; it hurts, and in time it heals, and my enemy becomes my friend.

I'll have a year-end-thank-you lunch with my staff. There may be tears; there have already been. They're good people, and when I leave I will miss them. The new pastor, whoever that person is, will probably build their own staff, so these fine people would be wise to consider their options.

The remaining task I am most conscious of is on New Year's Eve in the chapel. My last pastoral act will be to conduct a small, simple, intimate service, and I have no idea how I'll get through it.

CHAPTER FIFTY
WATERMARK

When dessert completes our New Year's Eve dinner, Trish, Melissa, and I head in silence to the church. I drive toward this one last task estranged from the holiday, as I suspect my unhoused friends feel: on the outside looking in, another celebration taking place without them.

I unlock the door and turn on the lights inside First Community Church. We pass my empty office, leaving it dark. I illuminate the foyer and walk past the sanctuary. I look toward the pulpit, silhouetted against the back-lit, stained-glass picture of Christ. I slowly close the door, as if not to disturb anyone. It is, after all, a sanctuary. The building is empty except for Melissa, Trish, and me. It is strangely quiet. Since we left the house, we've not said a word. The hush is holy, and we brought it with us.

We enter the chapel and turn on the lights that illuminate the altar. That's all that will be needed. We stand before it in silence.

A car door. Then another. Melissa steps into the hallway and meets those for whom this service will take place. Trish, knowing that we've got perhaps thirty seconds of privacy, puts her arms around me, pulls me close to herself, and rests her head on my shoulder. "I love you" is all she says.

We hear feet being scraped across the track mat at the entrance, and when those feet begin walking toward the chapel, Trish steps back, straightens my tie, and smiles.

My congregation will consist of nine souls. I knew four of them before this night: Trish, Melissa, Lisa, and Cherry. As Melissa escorts the Grant's into the chapel, I meet Amanda Grace, in the arms of her mother. She is beautiful—truly so. And while Amanda Grace may be unaware of how this night will shape her destiny, I for one can hardly bear how awe-filled and supremely holy is this night.

In a while, I will meet the remaining three who will attend this service of worship. They know what will first take place without them, and at Cherry's request graciously agreed to a later arrival. But first, we gather to present Amanda Grace for Christian baptism.

To those who have not witnessed it, baptism is strange—yet it's the near-universal rite of entry into the Christian church, and has been since Day One. In the service, parents, witnesses, and God promise to surround this child with love, prayer, and example, to live in the Way of Jesus, to show love and justice. Some churches use hardly enough water to wet the forehead, some pour water over the one being baptized, and in some traditions the person is entirely immersed. Every group has its way of embracing a new member, and for twenty centuries in rivers, lakes, pools, oceans, or holes cut in winter ice, in forests, prisons, homes, storefronts, or cathedrals, we welcome one another with baptism.

Tonight the amount of water will be negligible, but for this preacher unforgettable. Baptism best takes place amidst the congregation, a living greenhouse in which faith can flourish. But Amanda Grace will likely not see Old First again. So the five of us will speak promises that we must trust others to keep, believing that the God who created and loves Amanda Grace will be sufficient, even when we cannot be.

We don't have much time. After a prayer, I compose myself enough to speak.

"When you buy really good paper and hold it up to the light, you can see an image shining through, where the maker's mark has been pressed into place. We call that signature the watermark. It's how that sheet of paper is permanently identified as the product of the one who made it.

"In baptism, I do not magically fix Amanda Grace's spiritual destiny by pressing water on her forehead. God it is who creates, who guides, and who provides for her. So our task is to make what promises we can on her behalf, and then, using water—so simple a sign of something so amazing—we add the Maker's 'watermark' to one of God's most precious creations.

"We are responding to the covenant love God has already shown in the Good News that in Christ, God meets us in our need, forgives and accepts us by simple faith, and makes us God's children. Tonight we will pray that Amanda Grace will see that covenant love lived out through God's people, wherever she meets them. And we will pray that in some way, God's Spirit will draw her persistently, patiently, to her Savior, and then release her gifts in service to a needy world."

I turn the page and speak familiar words, but from my heart. "Obeying the Word of our Lord Jesus Christ and assured of His presence with us, we baptize those whom He has called to become His own."

I turn to Cherry and ask her the first of two sets of questions this night. We talked our way through these promises before, and she knows that in some ways she will not be able to keep them. She will not raise her daughter. But she wants this to be as genuine and true as possible, even if at some points, she speaks only to her prayers and hopes, if not her actions.

"Cherry, do you desire to have Amanda Grace baptized into the faith and family of Jesus Christ?"

"I do."

"Will you encourage her to renounce the powers of evil and to receive the freedom of new life in Christ?"

"I will, with the help of God."

"And do you promise, by the grace of God, to be Christ's disciple, to follow in the way of our Savior, to resist oppression and evil, to show love and justice, and to witness before Amanda Grace to the work and Word of Jesus Christ as best you are able?"

"I do, with the help of God."

"Do you promise, according to the grace given you, to grow with Amanda Grace in the Christian faith?"

This takes her a while. I wonder if these time-honored questions are too much for a mid-teen girl, with so much riding on her shoulders tonight. But she's determined to complete the task.

"I do, with the help of God."

I fill a shell-shaped vessel with water. It's not very pretty, as sterling silver should be perhaps, but it bears the patina of nearly a century of use for this purpose. I lift it over Amanda Grace's head, and slowly pour, saying words that Jesus spoke in the last paragraph of Matthew's Gospel:

"Amanda Grace: I baptize you in the name of the Father, and of the Son, and of the Holy Spirit.

"Scripture tells us that God will feed us like a shepherd feeds his flock. God will gather the lambs in loving embrace and carry them. The Holy Spirit be upon you, Amanda Grace—child of God, follower of Christ. Amen."

A car has pulled into the lot. Its doors open and close.

Jim and Carol arrive with Brittany, their attorney, who understands that despite this being a holiday in the Christmas Season—no, precisely because it *is* the Christmas Season, it is the perfect time for what would otherwise happen in her office. When Jim and Carol leave tonight they will take Amanda Grace, their adopted daughter, to her new home.

"We are here," I begin, "because of Cherry's choice, one that she is confident is the right one for her daughter. In the scriptures, we find this statement: 'Now abide faith, hope, and love, and the greatest of these is love.' Tonight is an expression of faith and hope. Cherry is putting her faith and hope in God, who through Christ comes into our lives, especially at difficult times, with healing grace, joy, and strength.

"And she is putting faith and hope in you, Carol and Jim, confident that she has chosen the best possible home for her daughter. You were hand-picked. You reflect Cherry's hopes and dreams for her child. She is thankful for all the ways you've already helped her.

"And this is an expression of love. After all, 'the greatest of these is love.' What Cherry does tonight is love in its highest form: making the best choice for Amanda Grace, even when it is also the hardest. Cherry, you are a courageous young woman. And you truly know how to love.

"Lisa, we know how difficult this is for you as well. But you have found a way to love, encourage, and support your daughter in a challenging and difficult time, and we are in awe of you."

Then I turn toward Amanda Grace's mother. "Cherry, with faith, hope, and love, will you now release Amanda Grace into the loving care of Jim and Carol, to be their adopted daughter?"

"Yes." It is all she can say.

"Jim and Carol, with faith, hope, and love, will you now receive Amanda Grace into your hearts and your home, and will you honor Cherry's love with your own toward this precious child?"

They look toward Cherry. "Yes, we will."

"Will all of you gathered here entrust Amanda Grace into the care of Jim and Carol, and into the care of the God who created her, loves her, and whose hand will rest upon her all of her days?"

Trish, Melissa, Brittany, Lisa and I say "Yes."

I then motion to Cherry; she knows what I mean. She looks down at Amanda Grace, kisses her forehead, hugs her . . . and then turns to Jim and Carol. She smiles. She actually smiles at them; her face filled with a radiance that overshadows the pain we all know she feels. Carol opens her arms to receive Amanda Grace. Cherry hesitates for the briefest of moments, and then gives her daughter to the couple who will now raise her.

Jim and Carol are crying. Lisa is sobbing, her head on Trish's shoulder. Trish is crying, so is Melissa. I'm barely under control, tears flowing freely down my face.

I look to the third row; the lawyer is crying.

The only person who isn't is Cherry. She will, many times. She already has. But in this moment, she exhibits the strength and grace of a person who knows what it is to love supremely, and who, I believe, draws added strength from the One in the room that we cannot see, except in Cherry's face, and in the face of her child.

I pronounce a benediction. "May God embrace each one of us, as God blesses this moment of releasing and enfolding Amanda Grace, this child we love so deeply. May God bind us together for her sake, so that as her life unfolds, she will always know that in our hearts and homes, she is and always will be loved and precious, a child of God.

"Go in peace, little one. Amen."

CHAPTER FIFTY-ONE
TO WALK AGAIN ON JESSE'S LAND

If there is anywhere on earth a lover of God who is always
kept safe, I know nothing of it, for it was not shown to
me. But this was shown: that in falling and rising again
we are always kept in that same precious love.

—Julian of Norwich

There are the briefest of formalities: a signature here, initials there, then handshakes, hugs, and goodbyes. Jim, Carol, Brittany, and Amanda Grace depart. Lisa, Cherry, Trish, and I remain until we hear them drive away. Then we walk red-eyed out of the chapel. I'm unable to speak as I turn out the lights and look one last time at this place that had defined much of my life for five years. We walk slowly toward the door I'm about to leave for the last time. Cherry breaks the silence.

"Thank you."

I smile. I stop, turn, and face these four women—but not forgetting the precious and beautiful infant on her way to a new home. She too is co-conspirator with God—*five* women who overwhelmed me and changed my life.

"I need to say this. Last winter, I was so distracted that I treated you, Lisa, and Cherry like a problem to be solved so I could get back to what I thought was my work. I didn't realize that you and the others who came for help with nowhere else to go—*are* my work. God made promises to you and expected me to keep them, and I didn't want to. I am so sorry. If I'd refused, I would have missed the greatest joys of my life. I need to thank *you*."

Lisa's expression changes. Looking directly at me, she tilts her head, as if to get a different perspective. "You're different," she says. "I always felt that church people were above me, judging me. At first I felt that way about you. After all the turn-downs we got I kind of expected it. But your wife and daughter truly welcomed us. And when you said you'd help Cherry in what we did tonight, it was like we were meeting you for the first time—a different you. I felt welcome—respected even. Did something change you?"

"You did. You opened my eyes. And your amazing daughter. And, a few other folk I met this year."

We walk through the door, and I stop until it slowly closes. I hear the lock engage.

Standing at the living room window, I see an occasional streak above the neighbor's home, then a brief starburst, followed by another. It's not quite midnight on New Year's Eve, but someone can't wait. Fireworks are not legal in these parts, but I for one hope the authorities let it pass.

Trish enters the room. She sees me at the window, and I hear her walking toward me. She stands next to me, silently at first, and then simply says, "What a year."

"Yeah. One year ago tonight I had no idea that the next day, I would miss the end of a football game and accompany Margaret Kaskey as she stepped into widowhood." Trish glances my way, then back to the window which frames the view of our snow-dusted street, lit only by streetlights and the occasional burst of a five-dollar rocket. "What a way to start the year. It certainly wasn't boring."

She's right. Fifty-three weeks ago, surrounded by love and abundance in this generous home, I celebrated the birth of history's most homeless Man, while a mother, her daughter, and a dying man spent the holiday on cold city streets.

And just now, I remember something that in the turbulence of these past months, I have forgotten. Something I must not forget. It was Christmas Eve. But not the Christmas Eve a week ago—rather, *fifty-three* weeks ago. And those children . . .

The early service was held at four thirty. Early enough for families, late enough so that when we sing "Silent Night" in a space lit only by candlelight, the sun has set. It's our best-attended service, better than the eleven-p.m. service, which happens to be my favorite. In its quieter tone, my soul opens to the holy tension of God entering humanity among the poor, in that most fragile of human conditions—an infant. People seem more relaxed during that last hour of the day. No doubt some Christmas Eve dinner wine helps to mellow the faithful. And when we sing "Joy to the World" on our way out the door—it's truly Christmas. But I digress.

It was one p.m., fifty-three weeks ago. The staff and I were gathered by the door, sharing last-minute greetings as Frank pushed a cart bristling with paper products and every cleaning tool imaginable into its closet. The clock told me that before 3:45, I needed to grab a late lunch, make a hospital call, and hopefully find a few minutes to unwind. We almost escaped. The door buzzer announced an unscheduled family outside. Two adults—a mom and dad I surmise, plus two kids. One's maybe three or four, the other in a stroller.

Quitting time or not, Mary invites them in. Nice people. Friendly, polite. I won't try to guess their nationality. They look and sound tired. They are also hungry. He'd lost his job; she's a domestic worker who wouldn't be working again until after New Year's. They apologized for being pests, especially on Christmas Eve, but if we have a little something for a meal. By now you know what my feelings are (or *were*) about "unscheduled guests." But Mary seems to forget. "Of course. Let me see what we have, OK?" Must be her Christmas spirit. Frank's already digging into his jacket and pulling out a bill or two.

The three-year-old decides to hug my leg. The baby is both cute and sound asleep. Dad is grateful. Says he thinks he has just enough cash for gas to drive to her brother's for Christmas. Brother lives in Minneapolis, 400-ish miles away. But he hasn't got enough for gas *and* food. Mary doesn't blink. "I'm just leaving. Follow me—I'll get you a meal. McDonald's OK?" They're very thankful. She leads them to Mac's. I'm uneasy with that, so I follow, park, and walk with them inside. I'm thinking they'll order, I'll offer to pay, and they'll be on their way.

Can I trust them? Don't know. Mary does. She adds a Coke to the order, and says she'll sit with them. I feel I should follow suit, and the two of us sit down with this family of four. We talk (mostly, I listen). I don't remember much of what we talked about, but what I remember is that on Christmas Eve fifty-three weeks ago, with a three-year-old hugging my leg, I bought a family on their way to Minnesota a cheap meal.

Once the food is eaten, Mary insists on filling their gas tank. I give them what cash I have—thirty-seven bucks. Mary gives the cutest three-year-old in the world the quarters in her purse. Mom thanks us, choked up, and asks if she can hug us. I say OK. She hugs, then Dad does. Little Boy just squeezes my leg. I get home, eat, make a hospital visit, get to church a bit frazzled at 4:15, but the service goes just fine. And I promptly forget about the family who needed food, gas, and love.

Could that have been just a random—No. Not the way this year has turned out. I'm haunted by something a dear, faraway friend once told us. On our last night in a memorable English town, our friend David took us to a "proper British pub" to wish us farewell. As we lamented the end of our visit and the friends we'd made, he said, "Friends come into our lives for a reason, for a season, for a lifetime." It took me awhile to tease out what he meant, but it means at least this: our encounters change us. People are powerful, in ways irresistible and often unforgettable.

Einstein said that time is relative. He was right. Whether fifty-two or fifty-three weeks ago, I was not the person I am still becoming.

For me, for all of us after this year of confusion, death, and turmoil, there is trauma—genuine, deep trauma that inflicted lasting harm collectively and acutely among some of us, and it must be addressed; I pray that it will be. And may I have the courage to face mine.

There is satisfaction. I played a role in that congregation's life in wonderful, terrifying ways, as we all struggle to be reborn. I shared its births and deaths, marriages and divorces, estrangements and reconciliations, baptisms, confirmations, graduations—all the joys, sorrows, and passages of life. I played a stumbling role in turning an old farm into new hope for dozens of the world's throw-aways.

Where was God? Fair question. Did I see God anywhere? In Margaret Kaskey, Mary, Frank, Sherman, Melissa, Trish and dozens like them. In Amanda Grace, her mother and grandmother. In Brad Davis, and even in Mike Curillo. I saw God, vividly, in Carl. His life seems such a failure to the world, but his life and death tore open my heart, a hole so big that light flooded in.

Moses heard God speak, as did Abraham, Samuel, Peter, Paul—and Elijah, who after fire, earthquake, and wind, heard God's "still, small voice." People like that image. A still, small voice fits a comfort-favoring pop religion. But I rarely if ever heard a reassuring "still, small" voice, certainly not in the year just ended. I still believe in God's comfort, but we don't need to be soothed as often as we think. God faithfully and often speaks to people like me, at ease in well-manicured lives of privilege, through shouts of discomforting, love-soaked truth.

God spoke in furious love this year, as God did through prophets like Amos, whose uncompromising call to repentance angered as it shattered pious mythologies. Or John the Baptist—perhaps better, John the Bulldozer—who came filling valleys, leveling mountains, demolishing pretenses, preparing a way for the Lord. I heard *that* voice in Trish's and my father's challenges to face what I sought to deflect.

Most of the world's great religions call for social justice, but to see in my own sacred texts a God whose passion for the overlooked and oppressed burns white hot, it grips me still. If God's voice were audible, it would have sounded like Sherman Jackson, the most abrasive, frightening, truth-telling prophet I have ever known.

If I claim to see or hear God at work in holy disruptions and up-endings, I also claim to see redemption as well. One more time, I confess to seeing the fingerprints of God in unexpected places. In Jesse Ryan, a closed soul opening like spring flowers, without any help on my part. In Mike Curillo, against all odds. In Brad Davis, who held me and my church accountable to do the hard and long work of justice. And in myself, a work in progress, far from complete.

Will First Community Church survive? Yes. Old First will be just fine. Will it thrive? That depends. Old First will need to become New First, and for that there is hope. Things will never be the same; the world is wilder, more fluid, and its institutions must not retreat into nostalgia. Believe it or not: in my mid-forties, I'm almost too old to keep up.

I knew I couldn't stay, but I saw them through some tender, formative months toward a new vision of love. I can feel it; I can taste it; I can almost see it. The insurrection broke through a wall, and fresh air began flowing. A revolution is coming to First Community Church of River Glen, Illinois, and it is already driving mountains into the sea.

I hear a car horn, then another, then several more, announcing the passing of one year into the next. What became last year seconds ago is not one I want to repeat. But I wouldn't have missed it for the world. Maybe I will yet see the completion of what began in me, during fifty-three holy weeks. And I may yet walk again on Jesse's land, with others who dream of what was unthinkable.

The phone in the kitchen rings. Trish is there, fixing late-evening snacks. I hear her walk toward the phone and pick it up. It's probably Dad, or my brother—who else would call at midnight on New Year's Eve? I'm half listening: "Happy New Year! . . . well, ah, hello—how, ah . . . how can I help you?" Interesting. There's surprise in her voice.

"Why certainly. I'll tell him. And happy new year to you and Linda too, Mike."

There's only one Mike I know who would have the audacity to call on New Year's Eve.

Happy New Year, Mike Curillo, my beloved no-longer-estranged brother—Happy New Year.

ACKNOWLEDGEMENTS

F*ifty-Three Weeks* bears the stamp of more than the author. I am indebted to trusted friends who saw this work unfold, including early versions in dire need of honest, constructive feedback. More times that I want to admit, they humbled me, but without them, this book could not exist. Among them: Ilene, Kitty, Marina, Tim, Don, Rod, and Taylor, my indispensable and patient editor-in-chief. Thank you, dear ones. Any remaining errors or omissions are on me.

Thank you to Clyde, whose innovative work with the addicted inspired a key part of this story. And to David, an English friend who taught us that we come into each other's lives for a reason, a season, and a lifetime. I am grateful to others who watched me wrestle with my dream of being a novelist and cheered me on. You kept the dream alive over the years.

Speaking of cheerleaders: thank you, dear family: Beth, our children and grandchildren, brother and sisters, and a host of others too numerous to mention without forgetting someone—you know who you are—you too lovingly pestered me to just get on with it. Thanks. I needed you.

I honor six precious congregations who called me their pastor. Yes, pieces of my life with you inspired moments in *Fifty Three Weeks*, but the story in this book is an imagined world, not a remembered one, and not patterned after any particular church or person I served. Through hard and joyous times, I learned from you, and I have nothing but gratitude for your patience and welcome. You inspired the best in me. You also were the springboard for many of my person-to-person encounters with the people whose lives are the heart of this book: those without homes, the poor and marginalized.

Because statistics about race and homelessness are sprinkled throughout this book, I sought to be as accurate as possible. But the numbers are fluid, and vary wildly at times. My sources included newspaper and magazine accounts, academic papers, and relevant books—examples of the latter include *Whose Problem is it?* by Ted Gottfried, *Down and Out in America: The Origins of Homelessness* by Peter H. Rossi, and more recently: *Evicted* by Matthew Desmond and *Shelter Theology: The Religious Lives of People without Homes* by Susan J. Dunlap.

One source deserves special mention. In the April 2004 edition of *Christianity Today*, Dean Alford's essay ("A Bridge Over Troubled People") described a church for the unchurched and unwelcome, meeting under a bridge carrying Interstate 35 through Waco, Texas.

"For Waco's homeless and hard-living people," Alford reported, "there may be no safer place than this bridge on Sunday morning—as safe from street crime as from the glares of worshipers in other churches." They don't want a building; a freeway overpass is sufficient. Their mission? To reach "the unchurched of all socioeconomic levels and races . . . They may have robbed a store the night before, [but] our role as the church is to love them as Jesus loved them."

Imagine: a church without a church, being truly The Church.